SAY YOUR P[...]

Rumpole and the Man of God by John Mortimer
Can Rumpole, barrister *extraordinaire*, exonerate an alleged kleptomaniac in cleric's clothing? And what about the mysterious past of a fellow lawyer's lady friend?

The Price of Light by Ellis Peters
When the old, nearly blind monk claims that the monastery's new silver candlesticks have been taken by the Blessed Lady, herself, it is up to Brother Cadfael to catch a thief of a more corporeal nature.

The Dutiful Son by Ralph McInerny
The dying woman's last wish was to have her dead child exhumed and buried in hallowed ground. But Father Dowling goes digging for clues when he unearths a most unholy crime.

And seven other tales of suspenseful sacrilege

THOU SHALT NOT KILL

THOU SHALT NOT KILL

Father Brown, Father Dowling and
Other Ecclesiastical Sleuths

John Mortimer, G. K. Chesterton,
Ralph McInerny, Ellis Peters, and
Six Other Modern Masters of Mystery

Edited by Cynthia Manson

A SIGNET BOOK

SIGNET
Published by the Penguin Group
Penguin Books USA Inc., 375 Hudson Street,
New York, New York 10014, U.S.A.
Penguin Books Ltd, 27 Wrights Lane,
London W8 5TZ, England
Penguin Books Australia Ltd, Ringwood,
Victoria, Australia
Penguin Books Canada Ltd, 10 Alcorn Avenue,
Toronto, Ontario, Canada M4V 3B2
Penguin Books (N.Z.) Ltd, 182–190 Wairau Road,
Auckland 10, New Zealand

Penguin Books Ltd, Registered Offices:
Harmondsworth, Middlesex, England

First published by Signet, an imprint of New American Library, a division
of Penguin Books USA Inc.

First Printing, July, 1992
10 9 8 7 6 5 4 3 2 1

Grateful acknowledgment is made to the following for permission to re-
print their copyrighted material:

"Straight Down the Middle" by Thomas Adcock, copyright © 1990 by
Davis Publications, Inc., reprinted by permission of the author; "A
Face to Remember" by Mary Amlaw, copyright © 1987 by Davis Publications, Inc., reprinted by permission of the author; "The Dutiful Son"
by Ralph McInerny, copyright © 1988 by Ralph McInerny, reprinted by
permission of the Ellen Levine Literary Agency; "Death of an Alum-
nus" by Janet O'Daniel, copyright © 1988 by Davis Publications, Inc.,
reprinted by permission of the author; all stories previously appeared
in *Alfred Hitchcock's Mystery Magazine,* published by Davis Publications,
Inc.

"The Second Commandment" by Charlotte Armstrong, copyright © 1967
by Davis Publications, Inc., reprinted by permission of the Brandt &
Brandt Literary Agency; "Justina" by Dorothy Salisbury Davis, copyright
© 1989 by Davis Publications, Inc., reprinted by permission of McIntosh &
Otis, Inc.; "Rumpole and the Man of God" by John Mortimer, copyright
© 1979 by Advanpress, reprinted by permission of Sterling Lord Li-
teristic; "The Price of Light" by Ellis Peters, copyright © 1983 by Ellis
Peters, reprinted by permission of Warner Books and Headline Book Publish-
ing; "In the Confessional" by Alice Scanlan Reach, copyright © 1962 by
Alice Scanlan Reach, reprinted by permission of the Ann Elmo
Agency, Inc.; all stories previously appeared in *Ellery Queen's Mystery
Magazine,* published by Davis Publications, Inc.

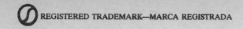

ACKNOWLEDGMENTS

I would like to thank the following people who made a significant contribution to this book: Cathleen Jordan, Eleanor Sullivan, and Charles Ardai.

CONTENTS

INTRODUCTION

"Thou Shalt Not Kill" is the sixth commandment in the Bible, and it seemed an appropriate title for this collection of ecclesiastical mystery stories. In this unique volume the protagonist in each story is a person of the cloth, be it clergy or nun, who becomes involved in an intriguing mystery. In most cases, the amateur sleuth searches out clues with little or no assistance from a professional detective *or* intervention from the Holy Spirit.

In each story the fact that it is clergy or nun facing a moral dilemma during the process of resolving the mystery adds to the complexity of the plot. The darker side of humankind seems all the more sinister when probed by the devout followers of the church.

In this anthology we meet a number of familiar sleuths such as Ralph McInerny's Father Dowling, Ellis Peters' Brother Cadfael, G. K. Chesterton's Father Brown, and Alice Scanlan Reach's Father Crumlish.

This collection of wonderful stories should provide you with an entertaining array of mysteries all of which have two things in common: they are ecclesiastical in theme and were written by masters of suspense who may have had some inspiration from above.

                                        Cynthia Manson

THE DUTIFUL SON

Ralph McInerny

When Roger Dowling came out of the church after saying the noon Mass, he stopped to inhale the odor of lilacs that filled the air. The sun on his face, that wonderful smell, and the prospect of the lunch Mrs. Murkin would have ready for him added an animal content to his spiritual peace.

"Father Dowling?"

He opened his eyes and in the sunlight had only the impression of a person, a silhouette. He stepped back out of the sunlight.

"I didn't mean to startle you, Father. Could I talk with you?"

It was tempting to tell the man to come back in an hour. He did not like the prospect of being cheated of a peaceful lunch. But that was temptation.

"Have you eaten lunch?"

"I attended your Mass."

"Come along. We can talk while we eat."

His name was Francis Stendall, he had come from Oakland, California, specifically to talk with Father Dowling about a most important matter. A matter, as it turned out, not wholly apt as a luncheon topic.

"I had no idea I was known in Oakland."

Stendall did not smile. Perhaps he thought Roger

13

Dowling was serious. It seemed best not to assume a sense of humor in this short, stocky, bald-headed man.

"I came to see whoever was the pastor of St. Hilary's."

Marie Murkin, reconciled to this stranger's consuming half the lunch she had prepared for the pastor, began to apportion it between them.

"My parents lived in this parish many years ago."

"Stendall?" Marie said, giving it some thought. The guest looked surprised that the housekeeper should enter into the conversation.

"How long ago was that?" Roger Dowling asked.

"It was during the Depression. Nineteen thirty-one, perhaps 1932."

"That was before your time, wasn't it, Marie?"

She glared at him and huffed off to the kitchen with a serving bowl.

"I have the address. Before coming to you, I found the house."

"I see."

"I want an exhumation."

"An exhumation?" This seemed an abrupt change of subject. Father Dowling had thought they were talking of the house in which Stendall's parents had lived.

It turned out that the two topics were one. Francis had the story from his mother, who told it to him in great detail during her final days. "She died of cancer two months ago. She exacted a promise from me and I am here to keep it." Francis Stendall had the look of a man who did not make promises easily but kept the ones he made. Roger Dowling was forming the somewhat grotesque idea that Stendall's mother had made her son promise to exhume her body, ship it from California, and bury it in the yard of the house in which they had lived all those years ago. Not wholly off the mark, as it turned out.

"My mother gave birth to a baby while they lived in that house. The baby died almost immediately. The doctor, who was a Catholic, baptized the baby and helped my father bury the body in the back yard." He waited for a shocked reaction from Roger Dowling and when he did not get one went on. "I, of course, was shocked by this. My first thought was that it was illegal. But that was the least of my mother's concerns. Everyone was poor then, as she told it, and burial expenses for a dead infant would have been a luxury. They buried the baby in the yard to save money."

"Is that what bothered your mother?"

"Oh no. Not at all. It was the thought of her child lying in unconsecrated ground, perhaps liable to be dug up accidentally. It weighed on her mind that new construction would have taken place, that perhaps a high-rise building had been put up over that gravesite. What would then have happened to the remains? She could not be at peace until she knew her child would be exhumed and reburied in consecrated ground. I assured her it would be done."

"Well."

"I have come to you for two reasons. I would like you to be there when the digging is done. And you will know how to go about doing this."

"Well, I know who to call, anyway."

He called Phil Keegan, captain of detectives on the Fox River police force, an old friend, and after a number of other calls, suggested by Phil, got in touch with McDivitt the undertaker as well. All problems but one were swiftly solved.

"Have you talked with the present owner?" Father Dowling asked.

"My hope is that it will be a parishioner of yours."

Roger Dowling had the feeling that he was the one keeping Stendall's promise to his mother. Well, why not?

"What is the address?"

"It's a house on Macon. Thirty-three-oh-six."

While Roger Dowling tried to visualize the neighborhood a voice was heard from the kitchen.

"Whelans," Marie Murkin said. "The Whelans live there. Have for years. I don't envy you asking Jennings Whelan if you can drop by and dig a hole in his yard."

Francis Stendall cocked an ear as Marie spoke, then said to Roger Dowling, "I'm sorry. I didn't hear all that. My hearing is going, just as my father's did."

"Mrs. Murkin thinks I had better contact the present owner right away."

"Is he a parishioner?"

Fortunately Stendall did not hear the laugh from the kitchen.

Jennings Whelan had been on the books of the parish for years, but two years ago he'd informed Roger Dowling that he no longer recognized in the Catholic church the faith of his fathers.

"Mr. Whelan, I assure you that nothing that takes place at St. Hilary's . . ."

"St. Hilary's has nothing to do with it. It's been my parish, yes. But as part of a diocese, part of a global church. I used to know where the Church stood. Now every paper I read seems to have some crazy nun or priest denying the creed. I give up."

It had been the start of a long and eventually unsuccessful argument. Roger Dowling had been unable to convince Whelan that whatever he might hear in the news there was more clarity about Catholic teaching now than there had ever been. Every time he had made headway, some other outrage would make Whelan's anger return, more virulent each time.

"This isn't personal, Father Dowling, I have nothing against you."

"Come to Mass, Jennings. Say your prayers. Don't let things upset you so."

"I'll say my prayers. Don't worry about that. But I'll support the Church again when it gets its act together."

What would Jennings Whelan make of the request Father Dowling must convey to him on Stendall's behalf?

"I'll come with you," Stendall said.

"I think I'd better go alone."

"Whatever you say." He seemed relieved. "I am staying at the Holiday Inn just outside Elgin. I'll call you tonight."

He had rented a car and went away in it. Marie Murkin cleaned up with a little smile on her face.

"You should have taken him with you."

He decided not to give her a chance to repeat her condemnation of Jennings Whelan. The man's decision to stop coming to Mass had prompted a good old fashioned anathema from the housekeeper.

"What if everyone did that?" she wanted to know.

"I couldn't afford to keep you on."

"Hmph. No Jennings Whelan is driving me out of here."

Now he said how admirable it was of Francis Stendall to fulfill his mother's dying wish.

"I don't wonder it bothered her. Burying a baby in the back yard. What did Captain Keegan think of that?"

"You mean rather than the front yard?"

"You know what I mean."

"They won't prosecute."

Suddenly there was a glint in her eye. "Maybe they can prosecute Jennings Whelan."

Roger Dowling decided to stop by Whelan's without telephoning first. This did not seem like a good idea when he stood at the Whelan door, pressing the doorbell for the fourth time.

Still no answer. Roger Dowling walked around the house and there was Whelan in a lawn chair. He wore swimming trunks and a sunhat, but his large body, white as the belly of a beached fish, was exposed to the sun.

"Mr. Whelan?"

He came sputtering awake, looked up and tried to get to his feet. He lost his balance and began to trip across the lawn until Roger Dowling caught his arm and steadied him. His hat askew on his head, Whelan regarded the priest.

"You have me at a disadvantage, Father Dowling."

"I am truly sorry. I rang the bell several times and then took the chance of coming round to the back yard."

"I was catching some of this sun."

Roger Dowling looked out over the quarter acre of grass that made up a yard surrounded by a high hedge that provided Whelan with privacy for his sunbathing. The edges of the lawn were lined with flower beds and there was another bed set halfway to the back, a circular plot alive with spring blossoms.

"I see you are quite a gardener."

"I am not. That is Imelda."

Mrs. Whelan. "She does a splendid job." Imelda Whelan slipped away to Mass without her husband's knowing it.

"She wouldn't have heard the bell," Whelan explained. "She is taking a nap. As I was."

"You must forgive me."

"I hope you don't think you can change my mind about you know what."

"I never lose that hope. But that is not why I'm here."

"I watched a talk show last night, local, some woman on it claimed she was a nun. She looked like a weight-lifter. All about how terrible her life was, everyone telling her what to do just because she took the vow of obedience."

"A man whose parents once lived in this house came to see me today."

Whelan looked confused.

"His parents lived here in the early thirties."

"I bought it in '42," Whelan said.

"He has a most unusual request to make."

Whelan smiled indulgently. "Not unusual at all. I know just how he feels. Drove into south Chicago a few years ago and stopped at the house where I grew up. Asked if I could take a look at the inside again. Nostalgia. They let me. A colored family."

"This is more than nostalgia. In fact it isn't nostalgia at all. I don't think this man ever lived here."

"Who is he?"

"He lives in California. His mother died recently and he promised to exhume the body of an infant and have it reburied in consecrated ground."

Whelan looked at Father Dowling as he must have looked at talk shows. "I don't follow you."

"His mother had a baby in this house. It died almost immediately."

"Yes."

"They buried the baby in the yard."

"In the yard? Good God!"

"The idea is to rebury the child."

"You want to dig up the yard?"

"I'm afraid that's the idea."

"You say they buried a baby here." Whelan looked out over the carefully kept lawn, at the flower beds that ringed it. He had the air of a man whose home has just become an unfamiliar place. "You'll have to talk to Imelda about that, Father."

Imelda had even more difficulty grasping the nature of the request than her husband had. Jennings had put on clothes and sat listening to Father Dowling explain it to Imelda. This might have been one more proof that the world was coming unglued.

"Dig up the yard? But where will they dig?"

"His mother gave him very explicit instructions which he will pass on to McDivitt."

"McDivitt?"

"The undertaker."

He kept at it, not losing his patience. After all, this was not an ordinary request. Imelda Whelan did not like the thought of her yard being dug up, but that was not the worst of it.

"You mean all these years there has been a body buried out there?"

"We've been living in a cemetery," Jennings said with mordant satisfaction. He was not a lot of help.

Eventually Imelda and then Jennings Whelan gave

their permission. He had assured them that the legal
aspects had been looked into and that McDivitt knew
his business. Neither Whelan looked happy to be reminded of McDivitt's trade; they were all too likely
to provide business for him in the near future. But
perhaps what swung it was that they wanted any
corpses in the back yard removed. Jennings said he
didn't think he could sunbathe out there until the matter had been taken care of.

It was a somewhat weary but satisfied Roger Dowling who returned to his rectory. He said his office,
read a few cantos of the *Purgatorio*—Dante was one
of his two favorite authors, St. Thomas Aquinas being
the other—smoked a pipe, drank coffee, and was well
disposed when Phil Keegan called to suggest they
watch the Cubs that night. He meant at the rectory,
of course, and he was inviting himself for dinner as
well. There was never an objection from Marie when
Phil Keegan joined him at the table.

"Good," Marie said. "I want to ask him about this
business of burying people in your back yard."

"I wouldn't advise it, Marie. This was during the
Depression, and unusual things were permitted then."

"They asked permission?"

"Oh, I doubt that."

It was a sad scene, a man whose infant had not
survived out in his back yard with the doctor, con-
signing it to the ground. How that must have haunted
the parents over the years.

Francis Stendall called while Phil was there and
Roger Dowling told him that everything was set for
the following day.

"So soon?"

"There's no point in delay."

"I hadn't expected it would be tomorrow. Father,
I'm not sure I can be there."

"Well, that isn't necessary, of course. The reburial
won't be tomorrow in any case. There are legal
delays."

"Could I call you at this time tomorrow?"

"Of course."

He and Phil talked a bit about the strange case, but the conversation wandered, both because the Cubs made an unexpected rally in the late innings and because Phil was inclined to want to pursue Jennings Whelan's grievances.

"He's right, Roger. Look at the church now and when we were kids."

"Look at us."

"The church is supposed to stay the same."

"It is supposed to last until the end of time. That's not the same as not changing."

He was glad to get off the subject when the fortunes of the game changed and the Cubs snatched defeat from the jaws of victory.

After Phil had gone, he sat up in the study, having a final pipeful, thinking again of that long ago scene, a father and the doctor, digging a grave in the back yard of a home in Fox River to bury a newborn infant who had not survived. Despite the mother's fear, the infant had lain undiscovered all these years. Maybe it would have been best to let well enough alone.

McDivitt, with the instructions he had been given by Stendall, made short work of it. Unfortunately, the digging had to be done where it disturbed the round flower bed in the middle of the lawn, and Imelda had to be persuaded again.

"Thank God you're here, Father," McDivitt whispered. Pink complexion, hair like cotton, McDivitt did not look like a man who had made a living burying the dead.

The body was found ten minutes later. But it was the body of an adult, not of a child. Also found was a valise containing stocks and bonds. McDivitt stopped the operation at once.

"The police must be called," he announced. He obviously thought he had been deceived and he did not like it. But his surprise was as nothing compared with Father Dowling's.

"I'll call them," he said.

The Whelans were in the house, preferring not to witness what was happening in their back yard.

"Are they done?"

"The police are going to have to be called."

"Doesn't McDivitt have a license?"

"The body that has been found is that of an adult, not a child."

Imelda Whelan had not understood and her husband repeated it to her. Her mouth fell open as if she were going to cry out, but no sound came.

"Some money has been found, too," Roger Dowling said as he dialed Phil Keegan's number.

"I'd better go out there," Jennings Whelan said.

Phil arrived and he brought Cy Horvath and Agnes Lamb with him, as well as a mobile lab unit. The Whelans looked more and more like guests in their own home.

"Get hold of this guy Stendall," Phil told Horvath.

"He's staying at the Holiday Inn in Elgin," Roger Dowling said. "I'll call him."

"Wait," Phil said, "I want to think a minute." But in less than a minute, he said, "Call him but don't tell him what happened."

"Are they going to keep digging until they find the baby?" Jennings Whelan asked.

"If there is a baby," Keegan growled.

There was no Francis Stendall registered at the Holiday Inn in Elgin. Nor had there been in recent days. It was a confused Roger Dowling who put down the phone and thought about his conversations with Francis Stendall.

"I checked the plat book," Whelan said. "If they lived here, they were renters. No Stengels ever owned this house."

"Stendalls."

"No one with a name anything like that."

Roger Dowling went out into the back yard where the mobile lab unit had put the body on a large rubbery sheet and were peeling back the burlap in which it was rolled. It was like seeing a mummy unwrapped.

The crew, after some preliminary examination, put the corpse in a body bag and sent it downtown. The valise went into another car. Two experts remained to examine the burial site.

"I feel like a fool," Roger Dowling said to Phil Keegan.

"He must have made up the story just to get that body dug up."

"And the stocks?"

"I'll bet he didn't know about that."

"Whoever he is."

"Don't worry, Roger. We'll find him."

Roger Dowling walked back to the rectory, wishing he could share Phil's confidence. From half a block away he saw the car parked in front of the house. His step quickened. He was certain that was the car Francis Stendall had been driving the day before.

Caution overcame him as he neared the house, and he cut through the playground of the school so he could approach the rectory from the church. This brought him to the kitchen door.

He went up the three steps to the back porch, then stopped, frozen in place. Voices. From the kitchen. Marie Murkin's and Francis Stendall's.

The voices went back and forth, antiphon and response, seemingly just an ordinary conversation, a passing back and forth of words to make the time go. After what had happened in the Whelans' back yard, Father Dowling felt no compunction at all about eavesdropping. Marie seemed to be reassuring the man.

"It's perfectly understandable," she said.

"No, it is cowardly. It's not as if it were a brother I had known."

"Were you born in Fox River?"

"No. My parents moved west before I was born."

Roger Dowling tried to detect duplicity in the man's voice and he could not. What a consummate actor he was. The priest backed silently off the porch to make another, audible approach to the door, and nearly bumped into an old man. Erickson. If Erickson had not put out a hand to stop him, Roger Dowling would have toppled the ancient parishioner.

"Mr. Erickson, I'm sorry."

The old man looked warily at the pastor. Erickson had reached an age where everyone treated him like a child, an idiot child. Confused by the way Roger Dowling had come off the porch, he seemed on the verge of thinking that his mind really had gone.

"Oh, it's you," Marie said from the doorway. She meant Roger Dowling. "Hello, Mr. Erickson." Her voice changed as she addressed the old man.

"Thanks," Roger Dowling said to Erickson, in a normal voice. "I might have fallen."

"When I was a kid we used to do that, walk backward." Erickson's face, though lined, had a peaches and cream look about it; little wisps of white hair stood up on his head. He looked newborn.

"How did everything go?" Stendall said, coming out on the porch.

He seemed the same as he had the day before. There was no apprehension in his voice or manner, no indication that he knew what had been dug up in that yard.

"Not quite as expected."

"How do you mean?"

"Let's go inside." He turned. "Goodbye, Mr. Erickson. Thanks again. Are you going back to the school?"

A little delay and then Erickson nodded. Roger Dowling waited until he started back to the school, which had been turned into a center for senior parishioners.

"How about lemon meringue pie?" Marie said brightly. There were two plates on the kitchen table. When in doubt, serve food was Marie's motto.

"We better talk in the study," Roger Dowling said

to Stendall, avoiding Marie's look of disappointment. Clearly she wanted all the gory details.

Roger Dowling shut the door of the study after Stendall was seated and then went around the desk and got settled.

"I tried to call you from the Whelans' house."

"I was probably already here."

"The Holiday Inn in Elgin said you weren't staying there."

"Did I say Holiday Inn? I'm at the Howard Johnson's."

Roger Dowling opened the telephone directory to the yellow pages, found the number and dialed it. Stendall looked puzzled. A voice said, "Howard Johnson's."

"Mr. Stendall's room, please."

"One moment."

Roger Dowling listened to the phone ring, looking across his desk at Francis Stendall.

"Why are you doing that?" Francis Stendall said, genuinely puzzled. Roger Dowling put down the phone.

"It was not an infant who was buried in that yard. It was an adult."

Francis Stendall watched him as if waiting for a clue that the priest did not mean what he was saying. "An adult?"

"The body was wrapped in burlap sacks. A man, apparently. The remains were taken away."

"My God." Francis Stendall sat back in his chair as if he had been pushed.

"Is there anything you want to change in what you have told me thus far, Mr. Stendall?"

But Stendall was staring at a bookshelf, not seeing it.

"Did your parents own that house?"

He looked at Roger Dowling, there and not there. "No. No, they rented. They were poor."

"Do you have any idea who that man is?"

"No. Of course not."

"Your mother gave you instructions about where to dig."

"Yes, yes."

"Then she must have known what was buried there."

"She told me it was a child, her child." He looked at Roger Dowling. "Was she lying?"

That was not a question about which Roger Dowling could be of any help to the man. He lit his pipe while his visitor was clearly reviewing those moving scenes he had described the day before, his mother's deathbed, the anguished tale of the infant, extracting the promise that he would have her child exhumed and buried in consecrated ground.

"Was your mother prepared to die?"

"She knew for months it was inevitable. I used to think that would be an advantage. Now I don't know."

"In what way an advantage?"

He looked at the priest as if he should not have to explain. "You could prepare."

"Did your mother see a priest?"

He nodded slowly, as if not quite trusting his memory.

"Before or after she told you this story?"

"Both. She saw him frequently. Father, I still can't believe that she lied."

"What we know is that where she told you an infant was buried the body of an adult was found." He still did not want to mention the valise.

"I wonder whose body it is?" Francis Stendall said.

"I should tell you that when the body was found, the police asked me to contact you. I called the Holiday Inn and you were not there. They—I—assumed your story about the infant was merely a device to have the adult body found."

"But I didn't know!"

Roger Dowling believed him now. "They will want to talk with you, I'm afraid."

"Of course." He rubbed his forehead as if it ached.

"There's something else."

"What?" He seemed ready for a further blow.

"A valise was found with the body. It contained stocks and bonds."

He actually sighed. "My parents were poor."

He almost cheered up. Whatever dark speculation had been going through his mind was eradicated by the news of the stock certificates. He pushed back his chair. "I'll go see the police now."

"Why don't we have them come here? Captain Keegan often comes to my Mass at noon. We can all have lunch together."

"I'll go to Mass, too."

The body was of a male adult of perhaps thirty years of age. It had been lying in the yard for nearly half a century. It was going to be very difficult to make an identification.

"It's more a research problem than anything," Phil said, tying into Marie's lasagna. "Checking old newspapers."

"How did the man die?" Francis Stendall asked.

"Oh, there's no difficulty there. He was shot." Phil wiped his mouth with his napkin and called to the kitchen, "Marie, this is marvelous!"

"Would you like more?"

"As long as you're up."

Francis Stendall had reached a numbed point where further information simply registered without reaction on his part.

"What about the money?"

"That should be easier."

"How much is there?" Roger Dowling asked.

"It's difficult to say. Some of the companies may be defunct, or they may have been absorbed by others. But it will amount to a large sum."

"Who does it belong to?"

Keegan shrugged. "All I know is that Whelan said he was going to talk to his lawyer. He thinks if it was found in his yard it ought to be his."

"Does he want the corpse, too?"

Phil was watching Marie refill his plate. He smiled at Roger Dowling. "I'll ask him."

"More lasagna, Francis?" Marie asked their other guest.

"No. No, thanks. It's good."

"You should eat."

This nostrum held little appeal for him, and Roger Dowling felt sorry for the man. He had come on a pious mission, keeping a promise to his mother, and was caught up in a mystifying business.

Over the next several days, some things became clear. Or rather, things became more obscure when the conclusion became unavoidable that the man who had been dug up in the Whelans' back yard was Stendall's father. Roger Dowling had asked Stendall if he would like to stay in a guest room at the rectory while this baffling matter was being investigated, and he accepted with relief.

"I'll turn in my rented car, too. It's costing me a fortune." As a teacher, Stendall did not have money to throw around and Roger Dowling was happy to help him cut down on his expenses. When Phil called the rectory to reveal the startling turn of events, Stendall was upstairs reading.

"The damnedest thing, Roger. The dental records match those of a man who served in the First World War whose name was Philip Stendall."

"And he was about thirty when he died?"

"Do me a favor, Roger. Ask him what his father's name was."

"Philip," Francis Stendall answered. "Why?"

"What kind of man was he?"

"We didn't have many photographs of him and my mother was reluctant to talk about him. I do have a diary he kept in France."

"France?"

"He was in the AEF in World War I. He was gassed and sickly, and I guess that's why he died so young. He was a delayed casualty of war."

"Did he die in California?"

Stendall nodded. "Why all the questions?"

"Francis, there is a possibility that the buried body is that of your father."

There was no way to cushion the blow, so he didn't try. Poor Stendall had been absorbing so much psychic punishment that this added horror brought no visible reaction. His cigarette had hesitated as he brought it to his lips, but he dragged on it and then let smoke slip from his mouth.

"My father."

"Is it possible he never went to California?"

"I have only my mother's word." He smiled sadly. "I asked her where he was buried and she said a military cemetery. That was one of the things I always wanted to do, find out where he was buried, visit his grave. The tomb of the unknown father."

He fell silent. Neither of them said anything about the fact that the body of a dead stranger was now Stendall's father. The big question remained: Who had killed him?

Stendall excused himself, saying he wanted some air, some time to think about all this. From the window Roger Dowling watched the man pace back and forth on the triangular walkway that ran between rectory and school and church. He disappeared into the church for a time and then emerged. Roger Dowling had gone back to his desk, and when he looked out again he saw Stendall talking with Erickson. Stendall tried to get away, but Erickson stayed with him. Finally they parted and Stendall came inside.

"I see you met Erickson, the old fellow."

"He didn't say what his name was. That's a good idea, using the school for old people."

"It's a place for them to come."

"Are they all parishioners?"

"Mostly. We don't turn anyone away. Erickson has lived in the parish forever, I guess."

"He wanted to know if I did. I said no and he asked my name. I really must look woebegone."

"Why?"

"I had the impression he was trying to cheer me up." He sighed. "I guess there's no escaping the fact that my mother killed my father."

Roger Dowling said nothing.

"It's the only way it makes sense. The guilt she felt was real enough, but she couldn't tell me the source of it, not even when she was dying. I guess I'm not surprised. But she had made up her mind she wanted me to know what she had done."

"Why?"

"The stocks? I don't know. Where did they come from?"

That was the other clarification that did not clarify. No report of missing stocks had shown up. No robbery, no misappropriation of funds. Stendall had thought his father was an invalid, that he had received a pension until he died. But there was no record of his having been gassed or wounded in any way. He had not received a pension.

The Stendalls had had a phone, a forty call number as it was classified, a special low rate unless the number of their calls exceeded forty a month.

Cy Horvath paused and looked across the desk at Father Dowling. "That's the kind of thing they've filled computers with."

"Where did Stendall work?"

"He was a bank guard."

Roger Dowling's brows lifted. "Is that where the money came from?"

Horvath shook his head. "There is still no indication on that. We've got people inheriting money, that sort of thing, but no big theft. Twenty-five dollars would have counted as a major haul in the early thirties."

Who would get it? Jennings Whelan called to ask Father Dowling to stop by. An urgent matter. Dowling went over, wondering if the odd events of recent days had prompted a change of heart in Whelan, but the urgent matter did not concern the recalcitrant parishioner's soul.

"Imelda is mad as blazes because I say that money is ours. Can you imagine that?"

"Mr. Whelan, right now I can imagine almost anything."

"Would you talk with her?"

"To what purpose?"

"Talk some sense into her."

"You mean, persuade her you should initiate lengthy, costly legal proceedings of dubious outcome?"

Whelan threw back his shoulders. "You've been talking with Amos Cadbury."

"Is he your lawyer?"

"Not on this matter! He doesn't think the court would go my way, necessarily. Do you know why?"

Roger Dowling shook his head. "I haven't discussed it with Amos."

"I'll tell you why. Because I'm not an heir or consign of the poor devil they dug up. Does he think they're going to find a relative when they don't know who he is?"

"They've identified him, Mr. Whelan. And he does have an heir."

Whelan's face went blank and he sat down. "You're not just saying that?"

Imelda Whelan, who must have been listening from another room, came and put her arm about her husband.

"Who was he, Father?"

"A man named Stendall."

"No. I meant the corpse."

"That's what I mean. It appears that the body is that of the father of the man who asked that it be dug up."

"Telling us it was a baby!" Whelan shook his head at the baseness of mankind. "He knew it was his father and he knew there was money."

"How did he die?" Imelda asked.

"He was shot."

"Killed himself and tried to take it with him?" But even Whelan saw the silliness of that remark. He said, "I have been assuming they wouldn't be able to identify him."

Imelda patted her husband's shoulder. The remark was equivalent to a statement of a complete change of heart. He was going to reject his dreams of avarice.

Amos Cadbury was more than willing to represent Francis Stendall in any claim he wished to make for the money. "If it isn't stolen and it was found with him and the man is his son, I should think the decision would go in his favor. Of course there will be taxes. And my fee. Both exorbitant, needless to say." Amos paused. The silence indicated he had made a joke. "That will still leave a considerable sum."

"I will suggest that he contact you."

But Francis Stendall shook his head. "No, Father. I don't want it. I don't know where it came from or how it got into the grave with him, but it doesn't interest me."

"You might want to think about it before you decide."

"I won't change my mind. It would be ghoulish. Do you know what I thought of when you first mentioned the money? *Treasure Island*. I would bet there is some story of greed and treachery that explains the money. Dear God, I wish my mother were still alive so I could ask her some questions. Why did she want to put me through this?"

"When you first talked to me it was with the intention of reburying an infant in consecrated ground."

He nodded. "Of course. Could we do that for my father?"

"Certainly."

"A funeral mass, too?" He shook his head. "After all these years I'll be able to attend my father's funeral. And only weeks after attending my mother's."

"Maybe that is what she really wanted, not to put you through an agonizing experience."

"She should have told me."

"It is not easy for us to admit to having done something so wrong."

"Murder?"

"We don't know that."

"That is what is hard. Not knowing."

Agnes Lamb continued the routine search, trying to locate anyone who had been neighbors of the Stendalls all those years ago. And she came up with two people, a man and a woman, unrelated, who had lived as children in the neighborhood. They were both in their sixties and, somewhat to Agnes's surprise, seemed to consider it perfectly normal to be asked about a neighborhood as it had been well over half a century ago.

"They talk about it as if nothing had changed. The man, Peters, can close his eyes and name every family on the block, both sides of the street. Of course, he still lives there."

"In the same house?"

"When he married he brought his wife home and they stayed there when his parents died. The woman's memory is much more selective."

"How so?" Roger Dowling noticed how Keegan looked on with approval as Agnes showed how good she was. He had come downtown to Phil's office to hear what she had found.

"She remembers her mother talking about the Stendalls. One or the other was being unfaithful, she doesn't remember which, if she ever did know. The move to California was meant to solve that problem."

"Remove one or the other from temptation?"

"That's right. Rose says her mother always thought it was someone who lived right there on the block."

"Well, well."

Phil said, "Tell him your theory, Agnes."

She made a little bow. "I say he was the one fooling around and that mama put him in the cold, cold ground. The California move was meant to cover that.

Or maybe they decided to go and he started acting up again, a last fling."

"Why the money?" Roger Dowling asked.

"That is the flaw in the ointment, Father," Agnes said. "But I don't know any theory that's going to make burying that much money and just leaving it there make much sense."

"Maybe leaving it there wasn't part of the plan."

"Well, then the plan fell through."

Of course it could have been buried by mistake, but such explanations were considered the last refuge of the scoundrel in Phil Keegan's department. He urged his people to live in a completely determined universe; every event had a cause. Just sometimes they weren't able to find it. But that is what they must say, not that something just happened one way as opposed to a million others.

Agnes handed him a printout of her findings. They were counting on him to keep Stendall informed, figuring he had a right to know whatever they learned. But how much more bad news about his parents could the poor fellow take?

On the way back to St. Hilary's Roger Dowling decided that the remarks by the woman Agnes called Rose could be regarded as mere gossip and there was no need to pass it on to Francis Stendall. If something further came to light, maybe, but for the nonce he would not add further to Stendall's load.

The memorial Mass and burial service for Stendall *père* went off with some pomp and circumstance. Marie urged the stalwarts of the parish to be there, and Mrs. Hospers suggested to the oldsters at the school that they might want to attend. Erickson, of all people, volunteered to line them up and march them over.

It was difficult to know whether Erickson knew anything about Stendall's situation, but he at least guessed the younger man had received bad news of some kind and required moral support. More than once Roger

Dowling looked out to see Stendall and Erickson pacing back and forth on the parish sidewalks.

"What does he say?" Roger Dowling asked, curious.

Stendall laughed. "He doesn't get a chance to say much. I have to keep reminding myself to put questions to him. So far I've told him a lot about Mother. There isn't much I want to say about my father just now."

"I hope you haven't decided we know how your father died."

Stendall started to say something, then stopped. "Oh, it doesn't matter. I talk about growing up in California. I guess I'm looking for clues in those years for what is coming to light now. My mother was a good woman, Father. As you say, we don't know how my father died, but the fact remains that she was a good mother to me."

Aside from a few lies and deceptions. Well, Erickson might be an ideal sounding board for a man who was trying to salvage as much of his past as he could.

Mervel of the Fox River *Tribune* got wind of what had been happening and wanted to interview Stendall.

"Why are you calling me?" Roger Dowling said, crossing his fingers.

"Peanuts Pianone says he's been staying with you. Is that right?"

"He has been through a lot, Mervel. I really don't think he should be put through any more. Whatever story there is is over half a century old."

"That's the story!"

"Are things that slow?"

"Father, I understand what you're saying. Reacting just personally, I might feel exactly the way you do. But I have a duty to my readers. And those readers have a right to know."

A right to know what Mervel and others like him decided people should know. "Why don't you talk with Mr. Stendall about it?"

"That's why I'm calling."

"He is out of the house at the moment. Where should he call you?"

"I'll call him," Mervel said, his voice heavy with skepticism. But Stendall had left the house, if only to go over to the school and give Edna Hospers a hand. "It occurred to me that most of them are the age of my parents. The men are the age my father would have been."

It was remembering that remark that led Roger Dowling reluctantly to pick up the phone and call Phil Keegan.

"Phil, did Agnes check on births during those years?"

"Whose?"

"Was Stendall born here or in California?"

"Does it make a difference?"

"I'm just curious."

"What was he told?"

"California."

"He must have a birth certificate."

"Would you ask Agnes and have her call me?"

"What are policemen for? What did he think of the story Agnes dug up about his parents?"

"I didn't tell him. How do we know it's true?"

"Maybe you're right."

Agnes dropped by a Xeroxed copy of the birth announcement and Roger Dowling read that a son had been born to the Stendalls of 3306 Macon Street on April 20th at home. Perhaps being born at home was not all that unusual at the time, but the memory of Stendall's original story when he came to the rectory gave the priest an odd feeling.

He put the Xeroxed page in his desk drawer along with the papers Agnes had given him a few days before.

"Jennings Whelan is with us." Marie Murkin whispered this stagily as she stood in the door of his study.

"Show him in."

"Not here in the rectory." She gave him a look. "At the school. With the other old people. Maybe it's a first step."

And maybe not. Should he drop by the school and accidentally run into Whelan? A tempting idea, but first he wanted to have a talk with his houseguest. Francis Stendall had said the night before that he would be heading back to California soon. He hadn't done what he had come to do, but no doubt he had accomplished what his mother had in mind when she gave him those instructions. He had stood at his father's new grave the previous day, a lonely figure, staring down at the rather sumptuous casket that contained what was left of his father after more than half a century mouldering in the back yard of the house on Macon Street. To think of a man Stendall's age as an orphan was odd, but he had the look of a man who had been abandoned by both his parents. No wonder he wanted to go back to his own life now and escape the haunting presence of his mother and father. But Roger Dowling thought he should stay on at least for a few days more.

"What's the point, Father? I feel like a parasite as it is, camping in your rectory like this."

"Nonsense. Marie appreciates someone with a better appetite than I have."

"I can't understand why you're not overweight. She is a wonderful cook."

And so she was. He had decided early in his tenure as pastor that he would have to hide behind the excuse of an inadequate appetite or he would balloon up like a monsignor.

"They sent over the notice of your birth in the local paper if you'd like to see it?"

He shook his head. "That's one thing I am sure of, that I was born."

Roger Dowling did not push the matter. But it was agreed that Stendall would stay several more days at least.

"It sounds morbid, but if I do stay, I'd like to see that house."

"The Whelans'? I'll see if I can arrange it."

Equipped with an excuse, Roger Dowling sauntered over to the school. He dropped by Mrs. Hospers' office and they talked a bit about the program she had developed. What he liked about it was that it left the old people to figure out many of the activities themselves. How awful it would be to fall into the hands of some breathless enthusiast who would insist you must keep busy, do this and that, whatever your inclinations.

When he went to what had been the gym, there were card games in process, three checker matches, one game of chess, and, of course, shuffleboard. The one game all the old people seemed to like was shuffleboard. And there indeed was Jennings Whelan, playing a game with Erickson. Roger Dowling stopped at a checker game not far from the shuffleboard area, kibitzing a while, giving Whelan a chance to notice him and disappear if he liked. But the game went on and Roger Dowling went over just as Erickson, with a practiced push, managed to remove all Whelan's markers from the target area.

"Damn it!" shouted Whelan and turned to Roger Dowling. "Did you see what that burglar did?"

"It's part of the game," Erickson said, clearly enjoying himself.

"I was counting on beginner's luck," Whelan moaned as they trudged to the other end of the playing area.

It soon became clear to Whelan that he was no match for Erickson and he returned his pole to the rack.

"I'm going to quit while I still have my house."

"Speaking of which," Roger Dowling said, and Whelan's eyebrows went up.

"Oh, no. Not another archaeological dig in my back yard."

"Only metaphorically. Stendall wondered if you'd let him come visit the house."

"Why not? He managed to get the back yard ruined. He never did see the result of that, did he? Sure, send him over."

"When would be a good time?"

"Well, Carl and I are moseying back home now. He can come along, if he wants."

"Carl's going, too?"

"To his own house, of course. He's given up trying to buy mine."

"You're neighbors?"

"For my sins," Whelan said. "For my sins."

"We must talk about those some day."

"You never quit, do you, Father? You're as bad as Imelda."

"Thank God for Imelda."

Whelan puffed out his lips, then nodded vigorously. "I do. I do. The very words that got me into it and I'd do it again tomorrow. I'm not sure she would, though. Being married to a lapsed Catholic is hard on her."

"It's harder on you."

"Where is this young Stendall? We've got to get going. Right, Carl?"

"I think I'll stay," Erickson said. "You have someone to walk with now. You don't need me."

"Were you going just to do me a favor?"

Erickson didn't answer.

After Stendall and Whelan had gone, Roger Dowling sat at the desk in his study, smoking his pipe, looking straight ahead but not seeing anything.

After a few minutes, he opened the drawer of his desk and took out the first papers Agnes Lamb had given him. The list of residents of Macon Street when Stendall's parents had lived there. Was he really surprised to find the name of Carl Erickson on the list? And what did it mean? One thing it explained was Erickson's interest in Francis Stendall. He had known his parents, though apparently he had not admitted this to Agnes Lamb. Might he even have seen Francis

as an infant? Not impossible. But Roger Dowling had
the feeling that there was more.

He called Mrs. Hospers. "Edna, would you ask Carl
Erickson if he would like to join me for lunch? After
the noon Mass. Tell him I would particularly like him
to come."

One of the advantages of saying Mass facing the
people—a change that had followed on Vatican II—
was that he knew who was in church. Carl Erickson
was not there, and he wondered if he would show up
for lunch.

"You have a guest," Marie Murkin said when he
came in the kitchen door. Another answered prayer.
"He's in the study."

"How glad I am you could come," Roger Dowling
said when he joined Erickson.

"I don't have that busy a schedule, Father. Not
anymore."

"Lucky man. Come, let's have our lunch."

Where had he gotten the impression that Carl Erickson was a doddering old imbecile? He was an
enjoyable table companion, with many amusing obser-
vations about growing old, and much praise for what
Mrs. Hospers was doing in the school.

"I was surprised to see Jennings Whelan there this
morning."

"I suggested he come."

"Are you friends?"

"I think of him as one of the new boys on the
block."

"Ah, the block. I want to talk with you about that.
When we go back to the study."

"I noticed you have a complete set of St. Augustine."

"Oh, yes. I've been reading him for years."

"I know only the *Confessions*."

"Have you read it?"

"It has become a favorite. A good book for old
sinners."

When they had adjourned to the study, it was easy

to continue the conversation along those lines. "You seem struck by the story of Francis Stendall."

For the first time, Erickson seemed ill at ease. "It is a fairly incredible happening."

"Did you know his parents?"

There are gestures, looks, remarks that prove to be *open sesames*, and that question sufficed to open Erickson's heart.

"I had wondered if that would become known. The police called and asked about the Stendalls—they knew I had lived on the block in those days—and I am afraid I lied to them. But in many ways I have been living a lie for all these years."

Roger Dowling knew that all he need do was wait, be silent, be receptive, and the story would be told.

And what a story it was. Carl Erickson had been Mrs. Stendall's lover. He used that term, not without irony. "That makes it sound much more romantic than it was. Those were gray days, Father. Impoverished days. A movie was an event. Her husband worked nights as a bank guard, my wife was tending to her sister's children, I asked Rosemary to go to the movies. It was one of those frothy Depression pictures. They plied us with tales of the idle rich at a time when a square meal was rare for many. That is how it started."

It ended with Rosemary getting pregnant. Her husband was upset. "He lived almost like a monk just so she wouldn't have children, not yet, and here she was, pregnant. Both Rosemary and I formed the idea that the child was mine."

"Was it?"

Erickson looked at Roger Dowling in anguish. "I don't know. She didn't know. There was no way of knowing for sure. But she said she was sure. The child was mine. I felt as much terror as joy. I had a wife, Rosemary had a husband. It was an impossible situation. And they quarreled constantly about her pregnancy. He decided they would move to California. Like so many others, he had the notion you could live in California on nothing. There was sun, there was fruit, it sounded like paradise. She thought it a crazy idea. We decided to run away. I had no money, but I had lots of worthless stock as it then was, but stock in which I never lost hope. I put all the certificates in a valise; they would go with us. Other bags were packed and waiting. I was ready to desert my wife." He said this as if even now, after all these years, he could not believe his intended perfidy. "But I had already been unfaithful. I seemed caught up in something that deprived me of my freedom."

And then came an awful night, a weekend when her husband was home, just days before the planned flight. They argued and she told him her child was not his. He became enraged. "She telephoned me and I went over."

He paused. "There are moments in life when everything is settled. They do not announce themselves as so significant, but in the event they are the great hinges on which everything turns.

"When I showed up, not knowing what she had told him, he immediately drew the appropriate inference. He lunged at me. We fought. He was much stronger than I. I thought he would kill me until there was a shot. She had killed him with his own revolver."

The dead body of the husband had purged them both. Any thought of running away together was now repugnant. It was one thing to be joined by a child, but to have a killing link them was too much. And so they had decided to do what they had done. In the still of the night—there was no moon—Erickson dug the grave. Meanwhile, she got gunny sacks from the basement and wrapped him. "She seemed to want to make him warm." And then Erickson carried him out into the back yard and buried him. Before he covered the body, in a fit of disgust, as a symbol that he was rejecting his plan to flee, he pitched the valise into the grave and covered it and the body.

"I could hardly believe afterward what labor I had engaged in. Yet I did it swiftly and effortlessly, carried along by panic. When I was done, we decided she would say her husband had left for California. She would follow after her baby was born. I would let it be known that they had impetuously decided to put his romantic plan into effect."

After she left, there was complete silence. She did not write. He did not know where she was or even if she had actually gone to California.

"The house was sold, then sold again to Jennings Whelan, and from time to time I would dread that the body would somehow be discovered. But I had dug deep, at least six feet, that seemed important, and there was little danger."

"Whelan said you tried to buy the house."

Erickson looked away. "I was motivated by greed rather than fear. Those worthless stocks are far from worthless now. The companies revived, shares split and split again. I do not dare guess what they are worth. I used to dream of ways of digging up that valise but nothing feasible ever occurred to me. And then a year ago I heard from Rosemary."

He held his hands in a praying position and brought the tips of his fingers to his lips.

"She was dying. She was determined to tell her son what had happened."

"She wrote you?"

"Yes, and I telephoned her, many times. Her voice sounded unchanged and it was like talking to the half hysterical woman I had parted from that awful night. I begged her to keep the secret. What difference did it make? Her answer was that her conscience bothered her. Not the murder, she had long since confessed that, but the thought of him lying there wrapped in gunny sacks in unconsecrated ground. I was still trying to dissuade her when she died. You can imagine what it has been like for me during these past days."

Roger Dowling let silence settle, a not uncomfortable silence. It was clear that Erickson was relieved finally to have told what had happened.

Roger Dowling said softly, "I doubt very much that anyone will guess what happened."

"But you must tell the police?"

The priest shook his head. "No. I don't think so. If a crime was committed, it was not by you. Unless the burial was a crime, and that has been rectified now."

After Francis Stendall had left for California, his strange visit over, Father Dowling missed him. Even Marie lamented not having another mouth to feed. Amos Cadbury had convinced Stendall not to disclaim the stocks until he had given it more thought.

"I won't change my mind," Stendall told Roger Dowling.

"You can give it to charity. Think of something you would like to support."

"Thank you for your hospitality, Father."

Erickson drove Stendall to the airport with who knew what emotions. Was he saying farewell to a son or not? Phil Keegan had problems of his own.

"I hate a crime where there is no criminal to indict," Phil said. It was received opinion that the wife had killed the husband.

"Well! no one profited from the crime, anyway."

"I would like to know why that valise was buried with the body. There must be a perfectly logical explanation of that."

"Remorse?"

Phil laughed. It seemed to cheer him up. Marie, drawn by the laughter, brought Phil a beer, and they settled down to watch the Cubs. Perhaps there was a logical explanation for that, too, but Roger Dowling did not know it.

THE SECOND COMMANDMENT

Charlotte Armstrong

Halley was sure glad the damn fog had rolled up and was billowing off over the mountains. Hey, if you looked southwest, you could even see a couple of stars. Lucky. They might have to hang around, maybe till morning.

And it was a little too quiet out here. Not much traffic on California Route 1; on a night like this there had better not be. The sea kept booming; it always did. The men shouted once in a while at their work, but they knew their business. They'd have her up on the road, and pretty quick.

Hey, here's my chance, thought Halley, to get all the stuff down, like they keep telling me. So the young Sheriff's Deputy opened the back door of his official car and leaned over to let the dome light fall on his paper work. The husband was sitting inside, and quiet.

"May I please have your name again, sir?" Halley used the polite official drone.

"Hugh Macroy." The other's voice, even in exhaustion, had a timbre and a promise of richness. A singer, maybe? Young Halley's ear had caught this possibility when he had first answered the call. He never had seen the man—at least, not too well. Now the lighting was weird—red lights flashing on the equipment, for instance.

"Address?" Halley asked, after he had checked the spelling.

"382 Scott—no, I'm sorry. 1501 South Columbo."

"That's in Santa Carla, sir? Right out of L.A.?"

"Yes." The man was holding his head at the temples, between thumb and two middle fingers. Poor old guy, he didn't hardly remember where he lived. But Halley, who knew better than to indulge in emotions of his own over one of these routine tragedies, figured himself lucky the fellow wasn't cracking up.

"Your age, sir?"

"Forty-five."

(Check. Kind of an old-looking guy.) "Occupation?"

"I am the Pastor at St. Andrew's."

Halley became a little more respectful, if possible, because—well, hell, you were supposed to be. "Just you and your wife in the car, right, sir? En route from Carmel, didn't you say, sir? To Santa Carla?"

"We had expected to stay the night in San Luis Obispo."

"I see, sir. Your wife's name, please?"

"Sarah. Sarah Bright."

Halley wrote down *Sara*. "*Her* age, please?"

"Fifty-five."

(Huh!) "Housewife, sir, would you say?"

"I suppose so." The man was very calm—too beat, probably, thought Halley, to be anything else. Although Halley had heard some who carried on and cried and sometimes words kept coming out of them like a damn broken faucet.

"And how long you been married?" the Deputy Sheriff continued politely.

"I think it has been two days, if today is Wednesday." Now, in the syllables, the voice keened softly.

"Any chil—" (Oh, oh!) "Excuse me, sir."

"There is Sarah's daughter, in San Luis Obispo. Mrs. Geoffrey Minter. She should be told about this, as soon as may be. She will have been worrying."

"Yes, sir," said Halley, reacting a little crisply not only to the tone but to the grammar. "If you've got her address or phone, I can get her notified, right now."

The man dictated an address and a phone number as if he were reading them from a list he could see. Halley could tell that his attention had gone away from what he was saying. He was awfully quiet.

Halley thanked him and called in from the front seat. "Okay. They'll call her, sir. We probably won't be here too long now," he told the silent figure and drew himself away and shut the car doors gently.

He strolled on strong legs to the brink. He could hear the heavy water slamming into rock forty feet below. (Always did.) The night sky was clearing all the way overhead now. There was even a pale moon.

Some honeymoon, thought Halley. But he wasn't going to say anything. It had occurred to him that this one might not be routine, not exactly, and that Halley had better watch his step, and be, at all times, absolutely correct.

"How's it going?" he inquired cheerfully of the toilers.

They had a strong light playing on her as she came up in the basket. She was dead, all right.

Macroy got out of the car and looked down at her and maybe he prayed or something. Halley didn't wait too long before he touched the clergyman's arm.

"They'll take her now, sir. If you'll just come with me?"

The man turned obediently. Halley put him into the back seat of the official car and got in to drive.

As the Deputy steered skillfully onto the pavement Macroy said, "You are very kind. I don't think I could drive—not just now." His voice sounded shaky and coming over shaky teeth, but it was still singsongy.

"That's all right, sir," said Halley. But he thought, Don't he know his car's got to stay put and get checked out, for gossakes? That kind of voice—Halley didn't exactly trust it. Sounded old-timey to him. Or some kind of phony.

On the highway, that narrow stretch along the curving cliffs, Halley scooted along steadily and safely toward the place where this man must go. By the book. And that was how Halley was going, you bet—by the book. It might not be a routine case at all.

So forget the sight of Sarah Bright Macroy, aged fifty-five, in her final stillness. And how she'd looked as if she had about four chins, where the crepey skin fell off her jawbone. And thick in the waist, but with those puny legs some old biddies get, sticking out like sticks, with knots in them, and her shoes gone so that the feet turned outward like a couple of fins, all gnarled and bunioned. Um boy, some honeymoon! Halley couldn't figure it.

So swiftly, decisively, youthfully, Halley drove the official car, watching the guy from the back of his head, in case he got excited or anything. But he didn't. He just sat there, quiet, stunned.

Sheriff's Captain Horace Burns was a sharp-nosed man of forty-seven and there was a universal opinion (which included his own) that you had to get up early in the morning to fool him. His office had seen about as much wear as he had, but Burns kept it in stern order, and it was a place where people behaved themselves.

Burns had felt satisfied with Halley, who sat up straight on the hard chair by the door, with his young face poker-smooth. His report had been clear and concise. His mien was proper. The Captain's attention was on this preacher. He saw a good-looking man, about his own age, lean and well set up, his face aquiline but rugged enough not to be "pretty." He also saw the pallor on the skin, the glaze of shock in the dark eyes—which, of course, were to be expected.

Macroy, as invited, was telling the story in his own words, and the Captain, listening, didn't fiddle with anything. His hands were at rest. He listened like a cat.

"So we left Carmel early this afternoon," Macroy was saying. "We had driven up on 101. We thought we'd come down along the ocean, having no idea that the fog was going to roll in the way it did."

Behind him a clerk was taking it down. Macroy didn't seem to be aware of that.

"But it did," said that voice, and woe was in it. "As thick a fog as I have ever experienced. We had passed Big Sur. You can't, you know, get through the mountains and change routes."

"You're stuck with it," the Captain said agreeably.

"Yes. Well, it was very slow going and very tiring. We were so much delayed that the sun went down, although you could hardly tell."

"You stopped," Burns prodded, thinking that the voice sounded like a preacher's, all right. "About what time?"

"I don't know. There was a sudden rift and I was able to see the wide place to our right. On the ocean side. A scenic point, I imagine." The Captain nodded. "Well, it looked possible to take the car off the highway there, so I—so I did. I had been so tense for such a long time that I was very glad to stop driving. Then, Sarah wished to get out of the car, and I—"

"Why?"

"Beg pardon?"

"Why did she wish to get out of the car?" The Captain used the official drone. When the minister didn't answer, Burns said, "It has to be included in your statement."

"Yes," said Macroy. He glanced at the clerk. "She needed to—"

When he got stuck, Halley's face was careful not to ripple.

"Answer a call of nature," droned the Captain. "Has to be on record. That's right, Reverend?"

Macroy said with sober sadness, "Yes. I took the flashlight and got out to make sure there was enough

margin between us and the edge." He stared over
the Captain's head, seeing visions. "The light didn't
accomplish much," he went on, "except to create a
kind of blank white wall, about three feet before
me. But I could check the ground. So I helped her
out. I gave her the light and cautioned her. She promised not to go too far. I, of course, got back into my
seat—"

He hesitated.

The Captain said, "Car lights on, were they?"

"Yes."

"She went around behind the car?"

"Yes."

"Go on. Full details, please. You're doing fine."

"I was comforting my right shoulder with a little
massage," said the minister with a touch of bitterness,
"when I thought I heard her cry out."

"Motor off, was it?" The Captain's calm insistence
held him.

"Yes. It was very quiet. Except for the surf. When
I heard, or thought I heard . . . I listened, but there
was no other cry. In a short while I called to her.
There was no answer. I couldn't . . . couldn't, of
course, see anything. I called again. And again. Finally, I got out."

"And what did you do?" said the Captain, and
again his droning voice held the man.

"The flashlight," he said, "was there."

"On, was it? The light on, I mean?"

"Yes." Macroy seemed to wait for and rely on these
questions. "It was lying on the ground, pointing to
sea. I picked it up. I began to call and range the
whole—the whole—well, it is a sort of platform, you
might say, a sort of triangular plateau. I shuffled over
all of it—between the pavement and the brink—and
she wasn't . . ."

"Take your time," said the Captain.

But the minister lifted his head and spoke more
rapidly. "At last, and I don't know when, a car came
along. Mercifully it stopped. The driver offered me a

ride. But I couldn't leave her." The anguished music was back in the voice. "How could I leave her?"

"He didn't get out? The driver of the car?" said Burns, again coming to the rescue.

"No. No. I begged him to send some help. Then I just kept on ranging and calling and—hoping and waiting, until help came." Macroy sank back.

"He called in, all right," Burns said in his flat tone. "Hung up without giving his name. But he can be found, I think, any time we need him."

Macroy was staring at the Captain with total incomprehension. He said, "I would like to thank him—yes, I would like to some day." Not now, wept his voice. Not yet.

"Can be arranged." Burns leaned back. "Just a couple of questions, Mr. Macroy. Was it your wife's suggestion that you stop the car?"

"I beg your pardon?"

"Did she ask you to stop? Or was it your idea?"

"Oh, I'm sorry. I wasn't following. No, it was my—well, you see, I knew she was in distress. But it was I who saw the opportunity."

"I see," said the Captain. "And you got back in the car for reasons of—er—privacy?"

"Values," said Macroy with sudden hollowness. "How ridiculous! In that dangerous spot. I knew how dangerous it was. I shouldn't have let her. I shouldn't."

The Captain, had he been a cat, would have had his ears up, and his tail, curled, would have stirred lazily.

"I will always—" Macroy was as good as weeping now. "Always regret." His eyes closed.

"You were only a few miles from low ground," said the Captain calmly. "You didn't know that?"

Macroy had his face in his hands and he rocked his whole body in the negative.

The Captain, when his continued listening was obviously proving unprofitable, said for the record, "You didn't know. Well, sir, I guess that's about all, for now."

"Where have they brought her?" Macroy dropped his hands.

"I—er—wouldn't go over to the funeral parlor. No point. You realize there's got to be an autopsy?" Macroy said nothing. "Now, we aren't holding you, but you're a lot of miles from home. So I think what you'd better do, Reverend, is go over to the motel and rest there for the night. We'll need your signature on your statement, for one thing. In the morning will do." The Captain stood up.

"Thank you," said Macroy. "Yes. I couldn't leave."

"Did you push your wife?" said the Captain conversationally.

Macroy's face could be no paler. "No," he said with wondering restraint. "I told you."

"The motel," said the Captain in exactly the same conversational manner, "is almost straight across the highway, a little to your left."

Macroy ducked his head in farewell, said nothing, and walked to the door. Halley jumped up and politely opened it for him.

"Halley." Burns was mild but Halley turned quickly and let the door close itself behind the minister.

"Yes, sir."

"This one is going to splash," said Burns glumly. "So watch yourself."

"Yes, sir. Did he do it, sir?" My Master will know, of course, Halley's face said.

"Whether he did or not, we're going to be able to say we went looking for every damn crumb of evidence there ain't going to be." This was, however crossly said, a palsy-walsy kind of thing for Burns to be saying.

"You saw the woman, sir?" The Captain stared sourly but Halley went on. It bubbled out of him. "I can't help thinking—some honeymoon! I mean—"

The Captain grunted. "Yah, and *he's* a pretty good-looking Joe." (Halley thought he concealed his astonishment.) "Well, kiss the cow," said Burns with a warning glare. (Halley hadn't fooled him.) "And keep your little old baby face *shut*."

"Yes, *sir*."

"Thing of it is," said the Captain, less belligerently, "there was this opportunity. But if he did it, he don't *know* why. And he can't believe it, so he don't really know it at all. Don't think that can't happen."

Halley marveled respectfully.

"You get on over to the funeral parlor and when the daughter shows, bring her by."

Burns turned to instruct the clerk. Damn vultures, he thought. The damn press was out there. Well, *they* didn't have to go by the book; but they'd get precious little out of him.

Saul Zeigler, aged twenty-two, was standing with Carstairs in the hallway of the low building. Zeigler was a local, just out of college, working for peanuts, and green as grass. He deferred to the older man, who was semiretired these days, but still picked up occasional plums for the big L.A. paper. Carstairs, with his connections, had already been on the phone to Santa Carla. Zeigler was impressed.

When they saw a man come out of the Captain's office alone, Carstairs moved in before Zeigler could get his own wits going. The hall was a barren length, with institutional green walls, a worn linoleum floor, and three naked light bulbs strung in a line overhead. The tall thin man looked ghastly.

"Reverend Macroy?" Carstairs was saying. "Excuse me. Terrible tragedy. Could we talk a minute?" Carstairs did not wait for permission. "Your bride was Sarah Bright? That's right, isn't it, sir?"

"Yes."

"My name is Carstairs," said Carstairs, forcing the manly handshake. "I'm that necessary evil, the newspaperman. But it's always best to get the facts from the ones who were there. Better all around."

Smooth, thought Zeigler, as Carstairs kept boring in.

"Sarah Bright was the widow of Herman Bright? Bright Electronics?"

"Yes."

"A very successful enterprise, I understand."

"Yes, I—Yes."

"I understand you'd moved into her mansion on South Columbo?" Carstairs was chatty-sounding.

"Her house," said Macroy wearily.

"About how long had you two been courting, Reverend?" Carstairs became the old buddy.

Zeigler thought the drawn face winced, but the man said quietly, "We met about six months ago."

"She was an older woman?"

"Older than I," said Macroy. "If you would excuse me, please, I am not feeling up to an interview. I would like to get over to the motel now and be alone."

Carstairs brushed this off as if it had never been spoken. "Bright died four years ago, wasn't it? And your first wife died when?"

The minister put out one hand and braced himself on the wall. "Nine years ago," he said patiently.

"You and Sarah Bright got married Monday?"

"Yes. In the morning."

"And took off for a honeymoon trip?" Carstairs had shouldered around to face Macroy, who seemed driven closer to the wall.

"Yes. Yes. May I please—" Macroy pleaded.

"I'm very sorry," said Carstairs, "I know this is a very bad time." But his feet in their battered alligator shoes didn't move. "If you could just run over what happened, just briefly? I certainly want to get it absolutely straight, absolutely correct."

"We left Carmel early this afternoon." The minister put his free palm over one eye. "I took the scenic route because I thought she would enjoy—"

"Bum choice this time of year, wasn't it?" said Carstairs in a genial way.

The minister took his hand down and moved until his shoulders touched the wall. He was blinking, as if there was something going on that he could not understand. His silence was thunderous.

Zeigler found himself pushing in to say respectfully, "I understand, sir, that the whole coastline was closed in tight. Worst fog in years. Pretty bad, was it, sir?"

"Yes," said Macroy, but he was looking at the older man and a hostility had sprung up, as invisible but as unmistakable as a gust of wind. The dazed look was beginning to lift from the dark eyes, like mist being blown away.

Carstairs said blandly, "Now, you stopped, sir? Why was that?"

Macroy didn't answer.

"I'm trying to find out how this terrible thing could have happened," said Carstairs, all innocent patience. "Why you stopped, for instance? What I mean, there couldn't have been a whole lot of scenery to see, not in that fog and after dark." Now his innocence was cruel, and he was defensively hostile. Zeigler could feel it on his own skin.

Macroy said, "No." His voice had gone flat.

"Why did you get out of the car? Or, I should say, why did the lady get out? By herself, did she? Didn't have a little lover's spat, I'm sure. Then why did she get out?"

Carstairs was bullying now, and young Zeigler discovered that *he* couldn't take it. So he tugged at the bigger man. "She hadda go, for gosh sake," he said deep in his skinny young throat, "and you know it, so why badger the poor guy? Lay off!"

"So okay," said Carstairs, in the same strangled manner, "but you tell me how in hell she could have *fallen* off that damn cliff?"

"Maybe you don't understand women," said Zeigler fiercely.

Carstairs laughed. Then Zeigler saw the minister's face. He stood there, leaning against the wall, having made no move to escape. On his face there was such a look—of loathing and sorrow and bewilderment.

"People are always interested," said Carstairs cheerily, turning back on his prey. "Do you happen to know what Mrs. Bright—excuse me, Mrs. Macroy—was worth?"

Macroy shook his head slightly. His lips were drawn back. He looked like a death's-head. Abruptly he thrust himself from the wall. "Let me pass."

"Why, certainly. Certainly." Carstairs played surprise that his courtesy could possibly be questioned. "Thank you very much, sir," he called after Macroy, who walked away from them. Then he said to Zeigler, "And how do you like them velvet tonsils? I'll *bet* he knows. The merry widow was worth millions, kiddo. So maybe she hadda go. Right?"

Zeigler didn't dare open his mouth.

Then, at the far end of the hall, the street doors burst open and a woman and two men entered. The woman came first, weeping violently, her head down, a handkerchief over her mouth.

Macroy saw her and said, "Eunice. I'm so sorry, my dear. So sorry." The music was back in his voice.

But the woman dropped the handkerchief and lifted red-rimmed furious eyes. She was about thirty, already thickening at the middle, no beauty at best, and now ugly in hysteria. "I don't want to talk to you," she shrieked, recoiling. "I never want to see you again. Ever!"

A dapper man with dark-rimmed eyeglasses put his arm around her. "Come now, Eunice. Hush up, sweetheart."

"All *I* know," the woman screamed, "is that my darling mother was just fine until she had to marry *him*, and now she's all smashed up and dead and broken." She wailed and hit out at the air.

Captain Burns was there as if he had flown in. He didn't care for scenes. He and Halley took hold of the woman between them. But she cried out to her husband, "You tell him. He's *not* going to live in my mother's house and have all my mother's lovely things."

Burns said, "You'll come with me, now, Mrs. Minter."
And she went.

But Geoffrey Minter lingered to say to Macroy in
a high, cold, uninflected voice, "You'd better not
try to talk to Eunice, not just now. She's very
upset."

(The understatement of the year, thought Zeigler.)
Macroy said, "Geoffrey, believe me—"

But Geoffrey said, "By the way, Eunice wants *me*
to take charge of the funeral. And I certainly hope
you aren't going to raise any objections."

"No," said Macroy, staggering. "No. None at all."
He walked away, curving erratically to brace himself
against the wall at every few strides.

Zeigler said, "He's never going to make it across
the damn road."

"So be his guide," said Carstairs. "You and your
bleeding heart. But what you get you bring back to
Papa. I'll cover the loved ones."

Young Zeigler went sailing after the minister. Carstairs was waylaying the son-in-law. Zeigler heard
Minter's high voice saying, "I don't know the legal
position. No new will has been drawn, not since the
marriage. We'll find out." He, too, seemed furious,
in his own tight way.

Zeigler took the Reverend Macroy's arm and began
to lead him.

The arm he held was tense and deeply trembling
and it accepted his hand only by default; but Zeigler
got them safely across the highway and into the
motel office. Zeigler explained to the woman there—
"tragic accident"—"no luggage"—"Sheriff's Captain
suggested."

The woman was awed and a little frightened. It was
Zeigler who took the key. He knew the place. He
guided Macroy into the inner court, found the num-
bered door, unlocked it, switched on a light, glanced
around at the lifeless luxury.

He didn't know whether he was now alone with a

heartbroken bridegroom—or with a murderer. It was
his job to find out, if he could. He said, "Looks all
right, sir. Now, how about I call up and have somebody bring some hot coffee? Maybe a sandwich? Probably you ought to eat."

A funny thing was happening to Zeigler's voice.
It was getting musical. Damn it, whichever this man
was, he was suffering, or Zeigler was a monkey's
uncle.

But the minister rejected music. "No, thank you.
Nothing." He remained motionless, outside the room.
There were hooded lights close to the ground along
the flowered borders of this courtyard, and they sent
shadows upward to patch that stony face with black.
Zeigler looked where the man was looking—at three
high scraggly palm tops, grotesque against the clearing
sky; between them and the stars some wispy remem-
brances of that deadly fog still scudded.

"Come in," coaxed Zeigler. "I'll be glad to stick
around a little bit, if you'd like—"

"I'd rather be alone."

It was the time for Zeigler to insist solicitously.
But he heard himself saying, "Okay. I don't blame
you." As he turned away, Zeigler said to himself in
disgust, and almost audibly, "But I'm one hell of a
newspaperman."

Macroy said, "And I'm one hell of a clergyman."

He didn't seem to know that he had spoken. He
was standing perfectly still, with his face turned up.
His hands were clenched at his sides. Up there the
palm fronds against that ambiguous sky were like a
witch's hands, bent at the knuckles, with too many
taloned fingers dripping down.

The moment had an eerie importance, as if this
were some kind of rite. To placate the evil mist, now
departing? Or a rite of passage?

A goose walked over Zeigler's grave.

Then the Reverend Macroy went into the room and
closed the door.

*   *   *

Carstairs pounced. "What? What?"

"Nah. Not a word," said Zeigler, lying instinctively. "Shocked stupid. Poor guy."

"How stupid can you get, for more than a million bucks?" said Carstairs. "Especially if you're untouchable."

"What? What?" said Zeigler immediately.

"I just got off the phone with his Bishop." Carstairs looked disgusted. "Whad'ya know? Your buddy is a Lamb of God or something and pure as the driven snow."

"What did he ever do to you?" asked Zeigler curiously.

"What did I do to him, for God's sake?" Carstairs' eyes looked hot. "So I don't live in the dark ages! I got to get back on the phone."

Zeigler wondered who was guilty of what. He honestly didn't know.

The Bishop, whose name was Roger Everard, came as soon as he could, which was at about ten o'clock the following morning. "I don't think it's wise, Hugh," he said soothingly, as he pulled up his trouser legs to sit down and gaze compassionately at this unshaven face, so drawn with suffering. "I don't think you should make any such decision, and certainly not so precipitously. It is not wise at this time."

"But I *cannot*—" said Macroy.

"Surely you understand," said Everard, who often had a brisk executive way of speaking, "that these people are only doing what is their obligation, according to law. Nobody seriously imagines, my dear fellow, that this was anything but an accident. And you must not feel abandoned, either. After all, you should realize that the members of your congregation can scarcely rally around when they don't even know where you are. Now, now." The Bishop didn't pat him on the head, but he might as well have. "There are certain things that must be done and I am here to do them."

"I am not—" said Macroy in triple gasps, "good enough—for the job."

"You have had a terrible shock," said the Bishop didactically, "a grievous loss, and a very bad night. I beg you to be guided by me. Will you be guided by me?"

The Bishop had already tried praying aloud, but when he had seen from a corner of his eye that the praying was only increasing Macroy's distress, he had cut it short.

"You know," he continued, leaving God temporarily unmentioned, "that I am perfectly sure of your complete innocence, that I entirely understand, that I mourn your dear wife with you, and that I want only to be helpful and do what is best? You know that, do you not?"

"I know," groaned Macroy.

"Well, now. Here is what I advise. First, you must make yourself presentable. I believe that your suitcase is now available. Then, since you are not to be in charge—and after all, Hugh, Sarah *isn't here*—you must come home."

"Where is home?" Macroy said. "I gave up the apartment. And I cannot go to Sarah's house."

"Home with me, of course," said the Bishop triumphantly. "Now, I have brought along young Price. His father used to do my legal work and the son has more or less inherited. Freddy may not be the churchman his father was, but he is trained and intelligent and surely he can be helpful in this unfamiliar thicket. There must be an inquest, you see. I want you to talk to him, and then you must talk to the Sheriff's man, but I should imagine only briefly. And, Hugh, I want you to brace yourself to your tasks. I shall drive you by your church and you will go to your office long enough to cancel or rearrange your appointments and delegate your responsibilities. You must be strong and you must not be afraid, for remember—" and the Bishop went into scripture.

When he had finished, the face was looking somewhat less strained; so the Bishop did pat Macroy, although only on a shoulder, and then he trotted back across the road to see whether there was any other way in which he could be helpful. A very busy man himself, the Bishop had had to cancel several appointments; but he did not begrudge his time and effort in this emergency. Obviously, poor Macroy was devastated, and the Bishop must and would take over.

Frederick Price, a busy young man in his middle thirties, ready and willing to be useful, came swinging into the court of the motel, carrying the Reverend Macroy's suitcase, which had been taken from Macroy's car. The car was now parked behind the Sheriff's office, still subject to examinations of some technical kind.

Price knocked on the proper door and went in, introduced himself, and offered the minister his own possessions. He saw the strain and the fatigue, of course, and was not surprised. He didn't believe this man was guilty of any crime. He guessed him to be a sensitive type and thought the whole thing, especially the damned red tape, was a rotten shame under the circumstances. But Price was well acquainted with red tape.

As Macroy opened the suitcase and took out his shaving kit and a clean shirt, Price said, "I've been talking to Burns and the others. The inquest is set for Friday morning. I don't think we'll have any trouble at all, sir. I'll be with you. You'll be all right, sir, so don't worry. It's only a formality. As a matter of fact, there is no evidence of *any* kind."

"Evidence?" said Macroy vaguely. He went into the bathroom to shave, leaving the door open.

"Oh, by the way," sang out Price, loudly enough to be heard over the buzz of the little electric machine, "they found that motorist. The one who came by?"

Price was practising lay psychology. He'd better not pour it on too thick or too soon—not all that he had found out. Chat a little. Engage the mind. Distract the sorrow. Un-numb the man, if he could.

"Captain Burns was pretty clever," he continued. "As soon as that call came in last night, he guessed from where. So right away he calls a man—Robbins is his name—the man who runs the first all-night gas station you hit once you're off the cliffs. He asked this Robbins to take a look and see if anyone had just been using the phone booth, and if possible to get the license number on his car. But the gas-station man did even better, because the fellow had used his credit card."

Price got up and ambled toward the bathroom, not sure he was being heard. Macroy seemed to be avoiding the sight of himself in the mirror while he shaved.

"Name was Mitchell Simmons."

"I beg your pardon?"

"The man who stopped, out there. On California One." Price understood Macroy's fragmented attention.

"He was very kind," murmured Macroy.

"What he was," said Price, "was very drunk. Oh, he corroborates what you say, of course. He's a salesman. Admits he was in high spirits, to coin a pun, and in the mood to pick up waifs and strays. Which is a risk, you know."

"It is?"

"Matter of fact," said Price cheerily, "it was one of his strays who phoned the Sheriff's office. Your kind friend was in no condition to dial, I guess."

The minister turned his clean-shaven face and it was full of pain.

Price said quietly, "I'm sorry. Didn't mean to say he wasn't kind. Look, I've got some further details. I suppose you'll want to know—er—just how she died. Burns will tell you. Or I can, if you like."

"Thank you," said Macroy. He came back into the

bedroom and started to unbutton his rumpled shirt. "Yes?"

"She broke her neck on the rocks," said Price. "So it was instantaneous, if that's any comfort. No pain at all."

Macroy's face was still.

"She—well, you see—" Price was remembering uncomfortably that it may have taken very little time to fall forty feet, but it had taken some. "She was washed to and fro until she was—" Price didn't have the heart to say how battered. "Well, soaking wet, for one thing. The Coroner says that her bladder was empty, but that has *no* meaning. With death—"

Macroy sat down abruptly and put his hands over his face. "Go on," he said.

"That—er—part of it," said Price. "It's a little unfortunate that it has to be brought out. But I think I can assure you that it will all be handled in good taste. I think, by the way," Price changed the subject gladly, "that Minter was cooled off considerably. He certainly made a few poorly chosen remarks last night—about her estate, I mean. But he's thought twice about it and he'll be more circumspect in the future."

Macroy was shaking his head. "I don't want her money. I won't have anything to do with Sarah's money. That wasn't what she was worth."

Price was unable to keep from sighing his relief. "That's fine," he said innocently. "Now, please don't worry about Friday's inquest, sir. I'll be there, right by your side all the time. The thing is to give your testimony as quietly as possible and try to—I could coach you a little, perhaps. I've been through this before, you know."

"Thank you. Have they—finished with her?" Macroy took his hands down and seemed stiffly controlled. He didn't look at Freddy Price.

"The body will be released in time to be flown to Santa Carla for services on Saturday. Mrs. Minter wants the services there—because of her mother's friends. I'm sure—" Price stuck. The fact was, he couldn't be sure that Macroy was going to be welcome at his wife's funeral.

Macroy stood up and reached for his clean shirt.

"As for this inquest, that has to be, you know," said the young man. "It *will* be an ordeal. Why should I lie to you?"

Macroy looked at him curiously.

"But there's nothing to worry about, really," said Price heartily. "The important thing is to get you completely in the clear."

"Is it?" said Macroy monotonously.

In the car later on, the Bishop excused himself and began to work on some papers. Price was riding next to the Bishop's driver. Macroy sat silent in a rear corner.

When they pulled up before St. Andrew's, the Bishop noticed that Macroy was looking at it as if he had never seen it before. "Come," said Everard briskly, "run in. Your secretary will be there, I assume. Just make your arrangements as quickly as possible."

Price looked around. "You clergymen sound as if you're in the old rat-race, just like everybody else."

"Too true," sighed the Bishop, "too true."

Macroy got out and walked through the arch and across the flagstones and then into his office. Miss Maria Pinero, aged forty, leaped up and cried out, "Oh, Mr. Macroy! Oh, Mr. Macroy!" She had heard all about it on the air.

In the car Price said to the Bishop, "It's still a little hard to figure how she could have fallen. They didn't find a thing, sir. They can't even be sure just where she went over. Too many people messed around out there, while they were getting her up the cliff. But there's nothing for *him* to worry about, that's for sure."

"I see," said the Bishop, looking sternly over the tops of his spectacles. "Guide him, Freddy, will you? He's in a sad state, I'm afraid."

"Do you think, sir," said Freddy Price, "I could possibly ask him to tone down his voice? It might sound—well, just a bit theatrical."

The Bishop's brows moved. "Bring it to his attention. That is, if you can get his attention." The Bishop sighed deeply. "No relatives. Nobody who can reach him on that needed human level. Well . . ."

"I'll take care of everything," Miss Pinero was saying. "Of course, I will. I understand just how you feel. It seems so cruel. To get out, just to stretch her legs after a long, long drive—" She began to weep.

Miss Pinero was not an unhandsome woman, but something about her did not appeal to men. As a matter of fact, Miss Pinero did not like men, either. But the Reverend Macroy was different. So kind, so clean and gentle—and so distant. She would do almost anything for him. She had been so happy that he wouldn't be lonely anymore.

"But God knows, doesn't He," she wept, "and we must believe that it is, somehow, for the best?" Carried away by her own noble piety—for it was her loss, too—she snatched up his right hand. Macroy snatched it away.

She looked up at him with tear-dimmed vision. She had never so much as touched him before, but surely he must know that taking his hand would have been like kissing the hem of his garment.

"I must leave now." He sounded strange.

"I'll be here," she cried, "and whatever you ask—"

"Forgive me," he said hoarsely.

He walked away. She knew that he staggered as he turned a corner, and her heart skipped. He sounded as if he couldn't bear to think of what she had almost done. Neither could she. Miss Pinero trembled. She wished it hadn't happened. She wished that Sarah Bright was still alive. Maria had felt so deliciously safe, and free to go on worshipping him.

The newspapers gave the story considerable space. After all, it had everything. They cautiously asked no questions, but they inevitably raised them. How could the elderly bride have fallen? There were some blithe spirits in the city who took to collecting the assorted circumlocutions having to do with the poor woman's reason for going off alone into the foggy dark. There was one columnist, based in the east, who—supposing that, of course, there was no such thing in Southern California as a religious group that was *not* led by some crackpot—was open to a suit at law. The Bishop considered it wiser to ignore him.

Macroy did not read the newspapers.

On Friday the inquest came rather crisply to the verdict of "Death from Accidental Causes."

Halley, telling how he had been the first to see a body, down below, was a model of professional objectivity. The medical part was couched in decently euphemistic language. Eunice Minter had not attended at all. Geoffrey Minter said that, as far as he knew, Mrs. Sarah Bright Macroy had been a happy bride. He exuded honorable fairness. Freddy Price was pleased on the whole with Macroy's behavior.

The minister, however, looked beaten and crushed. His voice was low and sad and tired. Everything droned along properly. When the Coroner, who was a straightforward country type, said bluntly, "You got back into the car for reasons of leaving her alone to do what she had to do?" Macroy answered, his voice dead against the dead silence of the room, "I thought, at the time, that it was the courteous thing to do."

A soft sigh ran across the ranks of those present.

"So you have no idea how she came to fall?" pressed the Coroner.

"No, sir."

And the Coroner thought to himself, "Well, the truth is, me neither."

But when Price spoke finally, to inform the world in a quiet and matter-of-fact manner that the Reverend Macroy firmly and irrevocably refused to have any part of the Bright money—that did it.

Price got the minister through the swarming cameras and away, with an air of "Aw, come on, boys, knock it off," jaunty enough to arouse nobody's aggressions.

But afterward, as they drove back to the Bishop's house, young Price for the life of him could think of nothing to chatter about. Freddy would have enjoyed hashing it all over; he'd done his job. But this man was a type he didn't understand. So Freddy made do with the car radio.

The Bishop's spacious residence was well staffed; Macroy had every creature comfort. But the Bishop was simply too busy to spend many hours or even an adequate number of minutes with his haunted guest, who from time to time renewed his plea for a release from his vocation.

The Bishop, refusing to consider this, continued to advise patience, pending a future clarity. But, he said, obviously someone else would have to take over the Sunday services at St. Andrew's. The Bishop had resolved to do it himself.

But he did think that if Macroy, with the help of God, could find the fortitude, he also ought to be there.

This martyred innocence, thought the Bishop (who *had* read the papers), had its rights, but also its duties. A man, he mused, must stand up to adversity.

On Saturday, at two o'clock, the funeral of Sarah Bright Macroy was well attended. The Minters and their two teen-age children sat invisibly in a veiled alcove. But those of Macroy's congregation who had had the temerity to come spotted him and nudged each other, when he arrived a trifle late and sat down quietly at the very back of the chapel.

He did not join the family at any time, even afterward. Nor did he speak to any of his own people. When it was over, he vanished.

He had looked like a ghost. It was a little—well, odd.

On Sunday the Bishop, at the last minute, found himself unable to conduct the nine-thirty service, which had to be cancelled. (Although the organist played.) In consequence, at eleven o'clock, St. Andrew's had all its folding chairs in its aisles.

Macroy, in his robe, was up there, inconspicuously, at the congregation's right or contra-pulpit side where, when he was sitting down, he was actually invisible to most. When they all stood, it was noticed that he did not sing the hymns; but he did repeat with them the Lord's Prayer, although his voice, which they were accustomed to hear leading, so richly and musically, the recitation of the ancient words, seemed much subdued.

Then the Bishop, who had never, himself, dwelt on some of the circumstances, and did not, for one instant, suppose that anyone *here* could do less than understand their essential pathos, made an unfortunate choice of words in the pastoral prayer.

"Oh, God," he prayed in his slight rasp, "Who, even in fog and darkness, seest all, be Thou his comfort; station him upon the rocks of his faith and Thy loving kindness, that he may stand up—"

The ripple ran, gasping from some of the listeners, yet not so much sound as movement, swinging the whole congregation like grass, before it ceased and all sat stiffly in a silence like plush.

The Bishop sat down, a bit pinkly. He could not see Macroy very well. Macroy did not seem to have taken any notice. In fact, Macroy had been moving, looking, acting like an automaton. The Bishop was very much worried about him, and he now bemoaned his own innocence, which had tripped him up, on occasion, before. When it was time, he preached an old sermon that was sound, although perhaps a little less than electrifying.

Then there they were, standing together in the Narthex, as was the custom at St. Andrew's, Macroy a tall black pole beside the little black-robed beetle-bodied Bishop.

Now the people split into two groups, sheep from goats. Half of them simply went scurrying away, the women contriving to look harassed, as if they were concerned for a child or had something on the stove at home, the men just getting out of here. The other half lined up, to speak first to the Bishop and gush over the honor of his appearance in their pulpit.

Then they each turned righteously to Macroy and said phrases like "So sorry to hear" and "Deepest sympathy" or a hearty "Anything I can do."

About twenty of them had gone by, like a series of coded Western Union messages, when Macroy put both hands over his face and burst into loud and anguished sobs.

The Bishop rallied around immediately and some of the older men shouldered through to his assistance. They took—almost carried—Macroy to his own office where, Macroy having been put down in his chair, the Bishop firmly shut the door on everybody else. He sat down himself, and used his handkerchief, struggling to conquer his disapproval of a public exhibition of this sort. By the time the Bishop had recovered his normal attitude of compassionate understanding, Macroy had stopped making those distressing and unmanly noises.

"Well, I was wrong," the Bishop announced good-naturedly. "I ought not to have urged you to come here and I am sorry for that. You are still in shock. But I want you to remember that *they* are also in shock, in a way."

The Bishop was thinking of the reaction to his boner. He was not going to quote what he had inadvertently said, since if Macroy had missed it, the Bishop would accept this mercy. Still, he felt that he ought to be somewhat blunt; it might be helpful.

"I'll tell you something, Macroy," he said. "You have got a fat-cat suburban bunch in this church, with economic status and—may the Lord help them all— middle-class notions of propriety. My dear fellow, they can't help it if they don't know *what* to say to you, when it has probably never crossed their minds that the minister or his wife might sometimes have to go to the bathroom."

Then the Bishop sighed. "This is especially difficult for them, but they'll stand by you—you'll see. I'm sure that you can understand them, as well or better than I."

"It's not that I don't understand them," said Macroy. "It's that I can't love them." He had put his head down on his desk, like a child.

"Oh, come now—"

"I cannot," said Macroy. "So I must give it up. Because I cannot do it."

"I think," said the Bishop in a moment, "that you most certainly can't—that is, not yet. You must have time. You must have rest. Now, I shall arrange for substitutes here. Don't worry about it."

"Don't you still understand?" said Macroy drearily.

"Of course I do! Of course I do! It was simply too much for you."

"Yes. Yes, if you say so."

"Then, if the coast is clear, we had better go home." The Bishop thought that this might become a serious breakdown. Poor tortured soul.

That evening the Bishop bustled from his study into his living room, where Macroy was sitting disconsolately idle.

"Now," the Bishop said in his raspy voice, "you know that you are very welcome in this house. There is plenty of room. The cooking is *not* bad. Everything here is yours. However, I am afraid that I shall have to be out of town for a day or two, beginning tomorrow. And I do not like to leave you all alone in your present state. So I am going to ask you to do something for me, Hugh. Will you promise?"

"Yes?" said Macroy listlessly.

"Will you talk to a Dr. Leone tomorrow?"

"A doctor?"

"He is a psychiatrist whom I've known for years. There have been occasions . . . he is excellent in his profession. He can give you a full hour tomorrow, beginning at one o'clock. I have set up the appointment and I think it is wise—very wise—that you keep it. He can help you through this very bad time."

"What?" said Macroy strangely. "Isn't God enough?"

"Ah, ah," said the Bishop, shaking a finger, "you must not despise the scientist. In his own way he is also a seeker after the truth. And God knows that you need some human help. That's why I simply cannot leave you here—don't you see?—alone. Yet I should go, I must. So will you please be guided by me and please do as I suggest?"

"Yes, I will," said Macroy apathetically.

"She died when you were twenty-five?" Doctor Leone said. He had observed the harsh lines on this face relax in memories of childhood, and he began to forgive himself for his own faulty technique. Well, he had to push this one. Otherwise the man would still be sitting silent as an owl by day, and there wasn't time. The doctor already knew that he would never see this man again.

"You were the only child?" he continued. "You must have adored her."

"I didn't pray to her, if that's what you mean," said Macroy with a faint touch of humor. "I loved my mother very much. But she wasn't perfect."

"How not?"

"Oh, she wasn't always—well, she didn't love everyone. She had a sharp tongue sometimes." But the voice was as tender as a smile.

"Didn't always love you, for instance?" the doctor said lightly.

"Of course she loved me. Always. I was her son." This was unimpassioned.

"Tell me about your father."

"He was a machinist, a hardworking man. A reader and a student by night. Very solid and kind and encouraging."

"You were how old when he died?"

"He died when I was twenty-seven—suddenly and afar."

The doctor listened closely to the way the voice caressed a phrase. "He loved you, of course. And you loved him."

"He was my father," the minister said with a faint wonder.

The doctor was beginning to wonder. Is he putting me on? He said with a smile, "Just background—all that we have time for today. Now, tell me about your first wife. Was it a happy marriage?"

"It was, indeed," said Macroy. "Emily was my young love, very dainty and sweet. A cherishable girl." The doctor heard the thin and singing overtone.

"You had no children?"

"No. We were sad about that. Emily, I suppose, was always frail."

"After she died, what did you do?"

"Went on, of course."

The doctor continued to suspend judgment. "Now, this second marriage. What did you feel for Sarah?"

"She was a lovely, lively spirit," said the minister. "We could talk. Oh, how we could talk." He fell silent.

"And you loved her?"

"Not with the same kind of love," said Macroy, faintly chiding, "since we weren't young anymore. We were very—compatible, I believe, is the accepted word."

Putting me on? He must be, thought the doctor. "And her money was no object," he said cheerily.

"The love of money is the root, Doctor."

"All right. I know my questions may sound stupid to you," said Leone. "They sound pretty stupid to me, as a matter of fact." He leaned back. Leone never took notes. He was trained to dictate, in ten minutes, the gist of fifty. "Now, I'm going to become rather inquisitive," he announced, "unless you know that you not only can but should speak frankly to me."

Macroy said gently, "I understand." But he said no more.

Going to make me push, thought the doctor. All right. "Tell me about your honeymoon."

"I see," said Macroy. "You want to know—whether the marriage was consummated? Will that phrase do?"

"It will do."

"No, it was not," said Macroy. "Although it would have been, sooner or later, I think. She was—so warm-hearted and so lovable a presence. But you see, we had understood, quite well . . ."

"You had both understood," said the doctor, more statement than question.

"I told you that we could talk," said Macroy, catching the latent doubt. "And that meant about anything and everything. That was our joy. As for—after all, in my case, Doctor, it had been nine years. I was a Minister of the Gospel," he added in a moment, gently explanatory.

"Did you try with Sarah and fail?" the doctor said easily.

"No."

"There wasn't a disillusion of any kind in the intimacy?"

"No. No. We enjoyed. We enjoyed. I can't be the only man in the world to have known that kind of joy."

Macroy's face contorted and he became silent.

"Which you have lost," the doctor said softly.

"Which I have lost. Yes. Thank you." The man's head bent.

"So the very suggestion that you—yourself—might have thrown all this violently away . . . It must have been very painful to you."

"Yes."

"Knowing that you wouldn't, couldn't, didn't—there's still that sense of guilt, isn't there?"

"Yes."

"Surely you recognize that very common reaction to sudden death, to any death, in fact." The doctor wasn't having any more nonsense. "You have surely seen it, in your field, many times. People who compulsively wish that they had done what they had not done and so on?"

"Oh, yes, of course. But am I not guilty for letting her venture alone on that cliff?"

"It was the natural thing."

"It is the human convention." The voice was dreary and again it ceased.

The Doctor waited, but time flew. So he said, "Every one of us must take his time to mourn his dead. But Bishop Everard tells me that you wish to give up the ministry, *now*. Why, Mr. Macroy?"

Macroy sighed deeply.

"I am thinking about the silly, but seemingly inevitable snickering, because of the circumstances."

The doctor hesitated. "The—er—circumstances do make an anecdote—for thoughtless people," he said. "That must be very hard for you to endure."

"Oh, my poor Sarah."

"Then, is this a factor?"

"I will say," said Macroy, "that I don't altogether understand that snickering. And why is it inevitable? If I may speak frankly to you, Doctor—"

Leone thought that there was a glint of life and challenge in the eyes.

"Surely," said Macroy, "every one of us knows his body's necessities and furthermore, knows that the rest of us have them, too. Yet all of man's necessities are not as funny as all that. Men don't think it funny, for instance, that they *must* eat."

"The whole toilet thing," said the doctor, "is too ancient and deep-rooted to be fully understood. It may be that the unpleasantness is too plain a reminder of our animal status."

"We laugh at what we hate so much to admit?" Macroy said quickly.

"Possibly." The doctor blinked.

"'Tis a pity," Macroy said in mourning.

"Why," said the doctor, who was beginning to feel that *he* had fallen into some trap, "is it that a man like you, who can look with this much detachment at human inconsistencies, cannot transcend an unimportant and temporary embarrassment? Surely, you ought not to be driven out of a life's work just because of—"

"*I* didn't say that those were my reasons."

"I'm sorry. Of course you didn't. What are your reasons?" The doctor was sunny.

"I cannot continue," said Macroy slowly, "because there are too many people I cannot love."

"Could you—er—amplify?"

"I mean that I felt so much anger. Fury. I hated them. I despised them. I wanted to hit them, shake them, scream at them, even hurt them back."

"In particular?"

"It began—" said Macroy. "No, I think that when the police officer asked me whether I had pushed Sarah to her death . . . Oh, it hurt. Of course, it did. But I remembered that he might be compelled, by the nature of *his* duties, to ask me such a thing. But then there was a newspaperman. And when to him . . ." The face was bitter. "Sarah's death meant somewhat less than the death of a dog would have meant to a man who never cared for dogs . . ."

Macroy's voice became cutting-sharp. "That's when I found myself so angry. I hated and I still do hate that man. From then on I have seemed to be hating, hating . . ."

The doctor was lying low, rejoicing in this flow.

"Sarah's own child, for instance," Macroy went on, "who was so cruel in her own pain. Oh, I know she was not herself. But I had better not go near her. I would want to make her suffer. Don't you see? Of all the contemptible . . . I want revenge. Yes, I do. That young lawyer who missed the point. I know he meant no harm, but I just couldn't . . . I even loathe my poor secretary. For making some kind of idol out of me. But I'd known and understood and borne that for years. Even if she is wrong to do that, I should not suddenly *loathe* her for it. Yet I find I do. And I loathe the cowards and the hypocrites and the snickerers—they all disgust me. There seems to be no way that I can bring myself to love them. I simply cannot do it."

"You cannot love?" droned the doctor hypnotically.

"Even the Bishop, who is a good man. When he refuses—oh, in all good heart—to hear the truth I keep trying to tell him, sometimes I must hang on desperately to keep from shouting at him. Isn't that a dreadful thing?"

"That you can't love?" said the doctor. "Of course it is a dreadful thing. When your young love died so many years ago, perhaps—"

"No. *No!*" Macroy groaned. "You don't seem to understand. Listen to me. I was commanded to love. I was committed to love. And I thought I could, I thought I did. But if I *cannot do it*, then I have no business preaching in His Name."

"I beg your pardon?" The doctor's thoughts were jolted.

"In the Name of Jesus Christ."

"Oh, yes. I see."

"No, you don't! You don't even know what I'm talking about."

The doctor got his breath and said gently, "I see this. You have a very deep conviction of having failed."

"Indeed," said Macroy, "and I am failing right now. I would like, for instance, to hit you in the mouth—although I *know* you are only trying to help me."

The minister put both hands over his face and began to cry bitterly.

The doctor waited it out, and then he said that they wouldn't talk about it any more today . . .

*   *   *

When the Bishop returned to town he had a conference with Dr. Leone.

"He's had a traumatic experience," the doctor said, "that has stirred up some very deep guilt feelings, and, in projection, an almost unmanageable hostility that he never knew was there. I doubt he is as sophisticated as he thinks he is—in his understanding of the human psyche, I mean. He does need help, sir. He isn't really aware of the demons we all harbor. It is going to take a lot of digging to get at the root."

"Hm. A lot of digging, you say?"

"And I am not the man," said Leone. "I doubt that he and I can ever establish the necessary rapport. Furthermore, my fees—"

"I know." The Bishop was much distressed. "But what is to be done, I wonder. He isn't fit, you imply, to go on with his tasks?"

"You know he isn't."

"Oh, me." The Bishop sighed. "And he has nobody, nowhere to be taken in. Since I—" the Bishop shook his head sadly—"am not the man, either. You don't think this—this disturbance will simply go away? If he has shelter? And time to himself?"

"May I suggest," said Leone smoothly, "that the State Hospitals are excellent? Very high-class in this state. And even the maximum fee is not too high."

"Well, as to that, there is what amounts to a Disability Fund. I should also suppose that the Minters, who are very rich people—" The Bishop was thinking out loud. "—even if the marriage has to be declared invalid. But wouldn't it be cruel?" The Bishop blinked his eyes, hard. "Am I old-fashioned to think it would be cruel?"

"Yes, you are," said the doctor kindly. "He needs exactly what he can get in such a place—the shelter, the time, the trained attention. As far as time goes, it may be the quickest way to restore him."

"I see. I see." The Bishop sighed again. "How could it be done?"

"He would have to commit himself," said Leone gently.

"He would do so, I think," said the Bishop, "if I were to advise him to. It is a fearful—yet if there is no better alternative—"

"The truth is," said Leone fondly, "you have neither the free time nor the training, sir."

"We shall see," said the Bishop, who intended to wrestle it out in prayer. "We shall see."

Two years later Saul Zeigler approached the entrance with due caution. He had stuck a card reading PRESS in his windshield, anticipating argument since he wasn't expected; but to his surprise there was no gate, no guard, and no questions were asked. He drove slowly into the spacious grounds, found the Administration Building, parked, locked his car, and hunted down a certain Dr. Norman.

"Nope," said the doctor, a sandy-colored man who constantly smoked a pipe, "there is no story. And you won't write any. Absolutely not. Otherwise, how've you been?"

"Fine. Fine," said Zeigler, who was up-and-coming these days and gambling that he could become a highly paid feature writer. He'd had some bylines. "Just insane, eh?"

The doctor grinned cheerfully. "Not my terminology."

"Put it this way: you're not letting him out?"

"Uh-uh."

"Will you ever?"

"We hope so."

"When?"

The doctor shrugged.

"Well, I suppose I can always make do with what I've heard," said Zeigler impudently.

"Saul," said the doctor, "your dad was my old buddy and if I'd been the dandling type, I probably would have dandled you. So you won't do this to me. Skip it. Go see Milly. She'll have a fit, if you don't drop in to say hello."

"So would I," Zeigler said absent-mindedly. "Tell me, *did* he murder his wife?" There was no answer. "What set him off, then?"

"I'm not going to discuss a case with you or any-body else but the staff," said the doctor, "and you know it. So come on, boy, forget it."

"So how come I hear what I hear?" coaxed Zeigler.

"What do you hear?"

"You mean this is an instance of smoke without even one itty-bitty spark of fire? Not even one *semi-* miraculous cure?"

The doctor snorted. "Miraculous! Rubbish! And you're not going to work up any sensational story about him or this hospital. I can't help it if millions of idiots still want to believe in miraculous cures. But they're not coming down on us like a swarm of locusts. So forget it."

"I've met Macroy before, you know," said Zeigler, leaning back.

"Is that so?"

"Yep. On the night it happened."

"And what was your impression?"

"If I tell you," said Zeigler, "will you, just for the hell of it and off the record, tell *me* what goes on here?"

The doctor smoked contemplatively.

"Religion and psychiatry," said Zeigler, letting out his vocabulary and speaking solemnly "have been ap-proaching each other recently, wouldn't you agree, Doctor?—in at least an exploratory manner. Suppos-ing that you had, here, a clue to that growing relation-ship. Is that necessarily a 'sensational' story?"

"Oh, no, you don't," said the doctor. "For one thing, he isn't preaching religion."

"How do you know?"

"I know."

Zeigler said, "You won't even let me talk to him, I take it."

"I didn't say so. If we understand each other—"

"Well, it was a long drive and it shouldn't be a total

loss. Besides, I'm personally dying of curiosity. My impression, you want? Okay. I felt sorry for him, bleeding heart that I am," Zeigler mocked himself. "He was in shock and he sure had been pushed around that night. If he didn't always make plain sense, I wouldn't have made sense, either." Zeigler waited.

"I will admit," said the doctor between puffs, "that there have been some instances of sudden catharsis." He cocked a sandy eyebrow.

"Don't bother to translate," said Zeigler, crossing the trouser legs of his good suit, because Zeigler got around these days, and needed front. "I dig. How many instances?"

"A few."

"Quite a few? But no miracles. Didn't do a bit of good, eh?"

"Sometimes treatment was expedited." The doctor grinned at his own verbiage. "We *are* aware of a running undercurrent. One patient advises another. All right, you can go and talk to him."

"So if he doesn't preach, what does he do?"

"I don't know. They talk their hearts to him."

"Why don't you find out?" said Zeigler in astonishment.

"Tell me this, Saul. On that night was he annoyed with *you* in any way?"

"Might have been." Zeigler frowned. "He sure brushed me off. But he had taken quite a beating. I didn't blame him."

"Why don't you go and see him?" the doctor said. "I'd be interested in the reaction. Afterwards, come by, and we'll make Milly feed us a bite of lunch."

"Where can I find him?" Zeigler was out of the chair.

"How should I know?" said the doctor. "Ask around."

Zeigler went to the door, turned back. "I don't want to hurt him, Doc. How shall I—"

"Just be yourself," the doctor said.

Zeigler came out into the sunshine of the lovely day. He had never been to this place before and it astonished him. He had expected a grim building with barred windows and here he was on what looked like the sleepy campus of some charming little college, set between hills and sprawling fields, with the air freshened by the not too distant sea. There were green lawns and big trees, and some mellow-looking buildings of Spanish design. There was even ivy.

It was very warm in the sun. He unlocked his car, tossed his jacket inside, and snatched the PRESS card away from the windshield. He locked the car again, and began to walk. Ask around, eh? There were lots of people around, ambling on the broad walks, sitting on the grass, going in and out of buildings. Zeigler realized that he couldn't tell the patients from the staff. What a place!

The fourth person he asked was able to direct him.

The Reverend Hugh Macroy was sitting on a bench along the wide mall under one of the huge pepper trees. He was wearing wash trousers and a short-sleeved white shirt without a tie. He seemed at ease—just a handsome, well-tanned, middle-aged gentleman, quietly growing older in the shade.

Zeigler had begun to feel, although he couldn't tell who-was-who around here, that *they* could and were watching him. He approached the man with some nervousness.

"Mr. Macroy?"

"Yes?"

"Do you remember me, sir? Saul Zeigler."

"I don't believe I do, Mr. Zeigler. I'm sorry."

Zeigler remembered the voice well. But the face was not the old mask of agony and strain. The mouth was smiling, the dark eyes were friendly.

Zeigler said smoothly, "I'm not surprised you don't remember. I met you only once, a long time ago, and very briefly. Is it all right if I sit down?"

"Of course." The minister made a token shifting to give him more welcoming room on the bench and

Zeigler sat down. "This place is sure a surprise to me," said Zeigler.

The minister began to chat amiably about the place. He seemed in every way perfectly rational. Zeigler felt as if he were involved in a gentle rambling conversation with a pleasant stranger. But it wasn't getting him anywhere.

He was pondering how to begin again when Macroy said, "But you are not a patient, Mr. Zeigler. Did you come especially to see me?"

"Yes, I did," said Zeigler, becoming bold. "I am a writer. I was going to write a story about you but I am not allowed to. Well, I wanted to see you, anyway."

"A story?"

"A story about all the good you do here."

"The good *I* do?" said the man.

"I've heard rumors about the good you have done some of these—er—patients."

"That isn't any story." Macroy seemed amused.

"So I'm told. And even if it is, I'm not going to be permitted to write it. I've given my word. Honestly, I won't write it."

The minister was looking at him with a pleasant smile. "I believe you," he said.

Zeigler found himself relaxing. "The truth is, I want in the worst way," he admitted, "to know what it is that you do here. Do you—well, preach to them, sir? I know you are a minister."

"No, sir. I am not. Not anymore. And so, of course, I don't preach."

"Then what?"

"Oh, I listen to them. Some of them. Sometimes."

"But that's what the doctors do, isn't it? Do you listen *better*?"

Macroy said, as if to correct him gently, "The doctors here, and all the staff, are just as kind and understanding as they can be."

"Yes. But maybe you listen *differently*?"

Macroy looked thoughtful.

"The point is," pressed Zeigler, "if there is some

kind of valuable insight that *you* have, shouldn't it be told to the world?"

"I'm not saving the world, Mr. Zeigler," said Macroy dryly. "I'm not *that* crazy. Or that good, either." He was smiling.

Zeigler, who had momentarily forgotten that this man was supposed to be insane, said, "Just a mystery, eh? You don't know yourself?"

"It may be," said Macroy melodiously, "because I am one of them. For I understand some of these sheep."

"In what way do you understand them, sir? I'm asking only for myself. Last time I saw you . . . Well, it has bothered me. I've wished *I* could understand." Zeigler really meant this.

Macroy was looking far away at the pleasant hills beyond the grounds. Then, as if he had reached into some pigeonhole and plucked this out, he murmured, "One hell of a newspaperman."

"*Yes*, sir," said Zeigler, suddenly feeling a little scared.

But Macroy didn't seem perturbed. In a moment he went on pleasantly, "Some of them don't speak, you know. Some, if they do, are not coherent. What man can really understand them? But there are others whom I recognize and I know that I love them."

"That's the secret?" Zeigler tried not to sound disappointed. "Love?"

Macroy went on trying to explain. "They've fallen out of mesh, out of pattern, you know. When they have lost too many of their connections and have split off from the world's ways too far, then they can't function in the world at all."

Elementary, my dear Watson, thought Zeigler.

"But it seems to me," Macroy continued, "that quite a few of *them* didn't do what they were pressured to do, didn't depart from the patterns, because they could sense . . . Oh, they couldn't say how, they couldn't express it. Yet they simply knew that somehow the mark was being missed, and what the world

kept pressuring them to do and be just wasn't good
enough. Some, poor seekers, not knowing where there
was *any* clue, have made dreadful mistakes, have done
dreadful things, wicked things. And yet . . ." He
seemed to muse.

Zeigler was scarcely breathing. Wicked things? Like
murdering your wife, for instance?

"In what way," he asked quietly, "are you one of
them, sir?"

"Oh." The minister was smiling. "*I* always wanted
to be good, too. I was born yearning to be good. I
can't remember not listening, beyond and through all
the other voices, for the voice of God to speak to me,
His child."

He smiled at Zeigler, who was feeling stunned. "I
don't mean to preach. I only say that, because I have
it—this yearning, this listening, this *hearing* . . ."

In a moment Zeigler said, rather vehemently, "I
don't want to upset you. I don't want to trouble you
in any way. But I just don't see . . . I can't understand
why you're not back in the pulpit, sir. Of course,
maybe you are expecting to leave here, some day
soon?"

"I really don't know," said Macroy. "I cannot return to the ministry, of course. Or certainly I don't
expect to. I must wait—as I would put it—on the
Lord. And it may be that I belong here."

He caught Zeigler's unsatisfied expression. "Excuse
me. The obvious trouble is, Mr. Zeigler, that every
time they take me into town, as on occasion they do,
sooner or later I stop in my tracks and burst into tears.
Which wouldn't make me very useful in the pulpit,
I'm afraid."

"I guess," said Zeigler, "you've had a pretty rough
deal. In fact, I know you've had, but—"

"No, no," said Macroy. "That's not the point. It
isn't what anyone did to *me*. It's what *I* couldn't do.
And still can't. Of course, here, it is much easier. I
can love these people, almost all of them."

"And you can't help trying to help them, can

you?" Zeigler said, finding himself irresistibly involved. "Why do you say you don't expect to return to the ministry?"

"Oh, that's very simple." Macroy smiled a little ruefully. "I've explained, it seems to me, to a great many people." He sighed.

"I wish you'd explain it to me," said Zeigler earnestly.

"Then of course I'll try," said Macroy. "But I hope you'll understand that, while I must use certain terms, I don't mean to exhort you to become a Christian, for instance."

"I understand," said Zeigler.

"Christians were given two commandments," Macroy began slowly. "You, too, were given much the same ones, I believe, although in a different form."

"Go on," said Zeigler eagerly.

"The first is to love God, which God knows I do. But I was also committed to the second commandment and that one I could not obey. Oh, I longed to—I even thought that I was obeying. But it isn't, I discovered, a thing that you can force yourself to do. And when that Grace—I mean, when it didn't come to me and I simply was not able—"

"To do what, sir?"

"To love them all."

"*All!*" Zeigler's hair stirred.

"That's what He said." Macroy was calm and sure. The voice was beautiful. "Thy neighbor? Thy enemy?"

And Zeigler saw it, suddenly. "You took it literally!" he burst out.

"Yes."

"But listen," said Zeigler in agitation, "that's just too hard. I mean, that's just about impossible!"

"It was certainly too hard for me," said Macroy, sadly, yet smiling.

"But—" Zeigler squirmed. "But that's asking too much of *any* human being. How *can* you love all the rotten people in the whole damn world—excuse me, sir. But surely you realize you were expecting too much of yourself."

"So they keep telling me," said Macroy, still smiling. "And since that's my point, too, I know it very well. What I don't feel they quite understand, and it is so perfectly plain to me—" He turned to Zeigler, mind-to-mind. "Suppose you are committed to follow Him, to feed His sheep, to feed His lambs, to be His disciple, which is a discipline, isn't it?—and suppose you cannot make the grade? Then, when you see that you cannot, mustn't you leave the ministry? How could I be a hypocrite, when He said not to be?

"Let me put it in analogy," Macroy continued, warming to argument. "Some young men who wish to become airplane pilots wash out. Isn't that the term? They just can't make the grade. So they may not be pilots. They would endanger people. They may, of course, work on the ground."

Zeigler was appalled. He could not speak.

"So if I have necessarily left the ministry," said Macroy, "that doesn't mean that I may not love as *many* as I can."

Zeigler saw the image of a ray of light that came straight down, vertical and One-to-one. Suddenly there was a cross-piece, horizontal, like loving arms spread out—but *it* had broken. Zeigler's heart seemed to have opened and out of it flooded a torrent of such pity, such affectionate pity, that he thought he was going to cry.

A thousand schemes began to whirl in his brain. Something should be done. This man *should* be understood. Zeigler would storm into the doctor's office. Or he *would* write a story, after all.

Zeigler said, his voice shaking, "Thanks, Mr. Macroy, for talking to me. And may the Lord lift up His countenance upon you and shine upon you and give you peace."

Macroy looked up. His look made Zeigler turn and almost run away.

Zeigler, speeding along the walk, was glad no one

else had heard him sounding off in singing scripture, like some old rabbi, for God's sakes! Okay, he'd felt like doing it and he had done it and what was it with the human race that you'd better not sound as if you felt something like that?

Maybe that man *is* crazy! But I love him!

Just the same, Zeigler wasn't going back to Doctor Norman's office, not right now. There'd been a reaction, all right, but he didn't care to have it seen all over his face. He'd go see Milly Norman who would give him some coffee and gossip. She always did. He'd take time to cool it. Or figure out how to translate it—

No, let the man alone, let him stay where he was. Why should Zeigler say one word to help get Hugh Macroy back into the stinking world, which would *kill* him. Sure as hell, it would.

Zeigler was blind and he ran slambang into a man and murmured an apology.

"Hey," said the man, moving to impede him further, "hey, Press, you get any good news outta the nutty preacher, hey, Press?"

"Nothing I can use," said Zeigler bitterly. He started off, but he thought, Love them *all*?

So he stopped and looked experimentally at this stranger. Here was a patient. Zeigler didn't doubt it. A middle-aged, foxy-faced, shambling man, with salted red hair, little beady eyes, and soft repellent lips. A more unlovable sight Zeigler had seldom seen.

Just the same, he said aloud and heartily, "Hey, don't you worry about a thing, old-timer," and then, with his eyes stinging, but telling himself to stop being so much the way he *was*, because he'd never make it, anyhow—suddenly it was too much for him and Zeigler sprinted to his car.

In a little while a man shambled up to where Macroy still sat on the bench under the pepper tree.

"Hey, you the Reverend Macroy?"

"I'm Hugh Macroy. Not a Reverend."

"Well—er—my name's Leroy Chase."

"How do you do, Mr. Chase?"

"Yah. Glad to meetcha. Say, listen, there's something I guess I gotta tell you."

"Sit down," said Macroy cordially.

The man sat down. He put his unkept hands through his graying red hair. "I'm kinda nervous."

"You needn't tell me anything."

"Yah, but I wish—I mean, I want to."

"Well, I'm listening."

"Well, see, it's a kinda long story."

"Go ahead."

"Well, see, I was up Salinas this time and I was hitching back down to L.A."

Macroy had turned his body slightly toward his companion.

"Well," the man said, "I guess you know that hitchers can't be choosers. Hah! So I get this ride and this stupe, he takes California One." Chase's little eyes shifted nervously.

Macroy said, "I see."

"So he dumps me in Big Sur, which is nowhere. So when I finally get another hitch south, I figure I'm lucky. Only trouble is, I find out *this* bird is juiced up pretty strong, and when the fog starts rolling in, believe me, I'm scared. So I want out. So I *get* out. So there I am."

The man was speaking in short bursts. "In that fog, what am I? A ghost or something? Who can see a thumb? Nobody is going to take his eye off the white line to look, even. And it gets dark. And what can I do?"

Macroy was listening intently, but he kept silent.

The red-headed man chewed on his own mouth for a moment before he went on. "Well, I got my blanket roll on me, so I figure I'll just bed down and wait out the fog. Why not? So I find this big rock and I nest myself down behind it, where no car is going to plow into me, see? And there I am, dozing and all that.

Then there's this car pulls off the road and stops, right ten, fifteen feet in front of me."

The man leaned suddenly away to blow his nose. Macroy looked away, flexed one ankle, then let it relax. He said nothing.

"So I wonder, should I jump up and beg a ride? But it's all so kinda weird, see—white air, you could say?" Chase was gesturing now, making slashes in the air for emphasis. "A man gets out with a flashlight. It's like a halo. And the other party gets out, see. Well, I dunno what's up. I can't see too good. I know they can't see me. I got a gray blanket. I'm practically another rock. And I'm lying low and thinking, why bother?"

The man's speech became slower, his voice a little deeper. "What's the matter with where I am, I think. It's kinda wild out there that night—the white air and all. And I can hear the sea. I always liked listening to the sea, especially by myself, you know?"

Macroy nodded. His eyes were fixed on the man's face.

"Listen, you know what I'm trying to—"

"I'm listening."

"So when this person starts coming along with the flash, I turn my face, so it won't show—"

"Yes," said Macroy, with a strange placidity.

"Then the light goes down on the ground. It don't fall, see? It's just pointing down. And I'm wondering what the hell—excuse me—when . . ." The voice was getting shrill. "My God, I know what she's gonna do! Listen, no man can take a thing like that, for God's sake!"

The man was crying now, crying. "So I think, 'Oh, no, you don't! Not on *me*, you don't!' So I just give a big heave and, Holy God, it's too close! And over she goes! Oh, listen, I never meant—I never— But who could take a thing like that?"

Chase was now on the edge of the bench. "Before I know what I'm doing, I drag my roll and I'm running up the edgy side, north. My life is in my feet, brother, but I gotta get out of there. It's just instinct, see? I could hear you calling—"

"You heard me?" Macroy was looking at the sky.

"Listen. Listen. So I'm about half, three-quarters of a mile away and now here comes this car going south. So I figure to look like I been going south the whole while. That way, I never *was* there. And damned if this guy don't stop in the fog and pick me up. Well, I soon find out *he* ain't exactly cold sober, but by this time I don't care, I'm so— Then what does he have to do but stop for you? But you tell him to send help and we just—we just went on by."

Chase slumped. He would fall off the bench in a few moments.

"If you had told me then—" Macroy had shut his eyes.

"Oh, listen, Mister, maybe you're some kind of saint or something but I didn't know, not then. Didn't even know you was a preacher."

"And you had two chances."

"Well, I had—well, three really. But look, nobody coulda said I'd done that on purpose. Maybe manslaughter. Who knows? What I couldn't take was the—was the *motive*. See, it's too damned hilarious. What I couldn't take was the big hah-hah. I mean, *I* knew she never saw me. I know that. *She* wouldn't have done a thing like that. But all I thought at the time was 'Hey, this I don't have to take.' If I would have stopped for one second—but here it comes, outta the night, you could say— Who's going to understand? Who? Because what a screaming howl, right?"

Chase was sobbing. He wasn't looking at Macroy. He sobbed into the crook of his own elbow.

Macroy said musingly, "Yes, it is supposed to be quite funny."

"Listen, what I did do." Chase gathered voice. "This happy-boy, he fin'ly gets into that gas station, and he don't even know what day it is. The message is long gone from his mind. So *I* made the call to the Sheriff. That was the third chance. But I chickened out. I hung up. And I say 'so long' to this happy character and go in the café and when I see the cop car rolling I figure I done all I could and maybe she's okay. I'm praying she's okay. It was the best that I could do." He hiccuped.

They were silent then, in the sunshine that had crept around the tree.

Macroy said in a moment or two, "Why are you here?"

Chase mopped his face with his sleeve. "Oh, I fall apart, see?" he said rather cheerfully. "I practically never been what they'd call 'together.' You talk about chances. I had plenty chances. But not me, I wouldn't stay in school. I coulda even gone to college. But I wouldn't go. So I'm forty years old and I'm crying in my wine, when I can get any, like a baby whining after a shining star, too far—" The man controlled his wailing rhyme abruptly. "Well. So. Now they don't know what else to do with me. So I'm a nut. That's okay."

He relaxed against the back of the bench with a thump. "So now," he spoke quietly, "I'll do anything. I mean clear your name? If you want? What can they do to me?"

Macroy didn't speak.

"I wish—" said Chase. "Well, anyhow, now you know it wasn't your fault and it wasn't her fault, either. And it wasn't—" He stopped and seemed to listen, anxiously.

"Excuse me," said Macroy. "I was wondering what I would have done. I'm no saint." Macroy turned his face. "And never was."

"But I didn't know you, Mr. Macroy," Chase began to be agitated again. "You got to remember, for all I knew, you mighta killed me."

Macroy said, "I might have. I *think* not. But I wouldn't have laughed."

Chase drew in breath, an in-going sob. "Ah, you don't know me, either. All I *ever* been is a bum, all my life. I never did no good or been no good."

"But you wish you had? You wish you could?"

"God knows!" The cry came out of him, astonished.

"Yes. And I believe you." Macroy bent his head. "I'm sorry. I'm sorry. That woman was very dear to me. Very dear."

"Don't I believe it?" cried Chase as if his heart had split. "Oh, God, don't I *know*! I heard you calling her. I knew it in your voice." Chase was sobbing. "I remember a thing—what they say in church—I remember. Don't tell me it was good enough, the best I could do. Because it wasn't, and that's what I know."

Chase was on his knees and hanging to the minister's knees, and sobbing. "Oh, listen, listen. I'm sorry. I got a broken heart. Believe me? Please believe me!"

STRAIGHT DOWN THE MIDDLE

Thomas Adcock

"It was a shame to train a brilliant boy like Fredo Suarez in auto shop," said Sister Nell Abbott, A.B., M.A., Ph.D. "Had we had a school like this a few years ago, I feel sure that Fredo would be alive today."

"You can't blame the school altogether, ma'am," said Larry Stein, M.P.D. "Most of these punk kids claim to be misunderstood geniuses."

The old nun's eyes glinted. "Fredo was not a punk, and he was a genius," she said. "The moment he discovered music, all his conflicts with society ended."

"I'm sorry, I don't claim to be a sociologist, ma'am. I'm just trying to find the diamonds."

They were sitting in the principal's office, where an August sun blazed through windows that still bore the glazier's labels. The bookshelves were freshly painted, and the floor was stacked with the nun's books. In the adjoining room, a telephone man was running new wires, and down the hall, expert welders of stainless steel were closing the last seams in the glittering chemistry lab.

The letters after Sister Nell Abbott's name were

trophies of a long teaching career, all of it in the Little
Havana district of Miami. She was a tiny, energetic
woman whose face, in the shadow of her cowl, was a
lacy network of soft wrinkles. It was impossible to tell
how old she was, but one thing was sure—the years
had not slowed her nimble mind, or softened her firm
opinions.

The letters after Larry Stein's name meant Miami
Police Department. He was a detective on the robbery
squad, and a very boyish-looking one, being of the
scientific school of criminology. He was tall, wide-
shouldered, with blue eyes and black hair. He had
come to his job from the top of his class in a college
back in Minnesota; in his way, he was probably as
dedicated to his career as Sister Nell Abbott was to
hers.

The nun was so wrapped up in her new school that
it was hard to get her to talk about an old and hope-
lessly unsolved case. The cardinal himself had laid the
cornerstone a year and a half ago. Next week, His
Eminence would consecrate it, with a sermon in
Spanish.

"Oh yes, the diamonds," the nun said absently.
"Have you talked to Carmen Suarez, Fredo's sister?"

"No, but a lot of officers have," said Stein. "She
doesn't know much. And anyway, you know how loyal
Cubans are to their families."

"What's wrong with that?" the nun snapped.

"Nothing, ma'am, except that it makes our work
harder. Don't misunderstand me. I don't suspect anyone. I don't even expect to find the diamonds, really.
I just happened to finish a case—and they handed me
this one. Every time a man on the squad gets caught
up, they give him this old case just to keep him busy."

He smiled. He was trying to be tactful, having
sensed a rather impatient hostility in the old nun. But
it did not work. Sister Nell said, "Well, I imagine all
this industry would sound very good to the taxpay-
ers—but I'm afraid that to the people involved in the
case, it's just another excuse to roust them around."

Stein blinked. *Roust!* That was a term cops used—or cop-haters. There were plenty of cop-haters in this part of the city, as there were in every part of every city where poor people lived. But he had hardly expected to find one in a Catholic order.

"I give you my word, ma'am, I'm not giving anyone a roust here."

"Well, then, go see Carmen. She'll give you a completely different picture of this tragedy. Even," the nun added significantly, "if she is afflicted by this Cuban idiosyncrasy of being loyal to her family."

"All right," Stein sighed. "But would you mind going over it again yourself? We keep hoping you'll recall some trivial detail that would start us on a new track."

"Oh, very well. The sooner you find the rocks, the sooner you'll take the heat off these people."

Rocks! Heat! Detective Larry Stein was slightly shocked again.

Sister Nell Abbott leaned back, frowning.

"I can date it accurately," she said, "because it was the day our cornerstone was laid. I was here on the school grounds, talking to the construction foreman, when I saw Donny Esposito and Fredo drive up . . ."

Detective Stein kept notes, but there was little she could tell him that was not in the files—very thick files that had accumulated for eighteen long months. Donny Esposito, age twenty-eight and no good, had been out of prison a week. He was walking across the Sixth Street viaduct when he saw a car standing in the middle of the span with a flat tire. It was an expensive car, and in his pocket Donny had a gun. The temptation was too much for him.

He held up the old couple in the car, taking one hundred and fifteen dollars from the man. He hit the woman with the gun when she tried to signal a passing motorist. She fell down, blood flowing freely from her head. Donny took two rings from her hands and tore a brooch from her dress before running across the viaduct.

Then he stole a car from a parking lot and got away clean. It was an inspired daylight job, brilliantly executed. He had a right to feel elated; and he did.

But the woman died.

And within an hour, her husband had identified Donny Esposito from police mug shots. Soon, felony men were searching Little Havana for him. They met several witnesses who had seen him cruising the streets, looking for Fredo Suarez, age sixteen.

"Fredo was very young when Donny caught that five-to-life armed robbery rap a few years back," Sister Nell said briskly. "To all boys that age, Donny was then a neighborhood hero, a sort of Robin Hood. Fredo had, of course, outgrown that. But Donny didn't know it. He thought Fredo would still be his admirer."

"And Donny needed admiration," Stein murmured. "The elation of the robbery was dying by then, he was just a scared rat."

"Of course, I had no idea there had been a robbery and a murder when I saw them," Sister Nell continued. "They went into the sheet metal shop across the street. I would say it was maybe ten minutes later when a police car drove into the schoolyard, passing Donny's car as though they were stone blind. I have never understood how two supposedly competent policemen could overlook a red hot car."

"Well, it wasn't on the hot list yet, ma'am. The owner didn't even know it was stolen until we told him."

"Oh. Well then, a plainclothesman got out of the police car and came over to the foreman and me. The instant he identified himself, I just knew he must be looking for Donny. Then—we heard two shots from inside the shop. I told the plainclothesman that Donny Esposito was in there, but to be careful of Fredo . . ."

Sister Nell added, with sorrow in her voice, "I didn't know, of course, that Fredo, poor boy, was dead. The two officers ran across the street. One covered the front door. The other ran behind the shop. We heard the firing there. Soon some other prowl cars arrived, then the ambulance. And that's about all I can tell you, young man."

The only thing new was to hear it told by a nun, in the cop-hater lingo. Donny Esposito had killed Fredo Suarez, and had then run straight into the arms of the detective covering the back door. They fired simultaneously. The detective died. And Donny lived, to stand trial for three slayings.

But still missing, after eighteen months, were two rings and a brooch—valued at thirty-two thousand dollars. Donny was a tough punk but a cheap one. He had turned pale when told the value of his loot. *"Dios, no es posible!"* he gasped.

Donny swore he had given the jewels to Fredo to hide when they stopped at the Suarez home. He thought Fredo had left them there. He was surprised as well as upset when, in the sheet metal shop, Fredo began talking about making him take them back. *"This stuff is hot!"* Fredo had said, according to Donny. *"You're not unloading it on me."*

That, Donny said, was when he lost his head and shot the kid. He had died last month in the lethal-gas chamber of the Florida State Penitentiary, still swearing that he had not seen the jewels since handing them to Fredo, in Fredo's home. Everything else he said checked out.

"There was one other witness," Detective Stein said to Sister Nell. "And that would be Hector Nicasso, the guy who runs the sheet metal shop."

"Now, you let him alone!" Sister Nell said sharply. "Hector has gone straight for years. Why abuse him, on the word of a self-confessed liar?"

"Donny Esposito confessed to murder, not to lying," Stein said patiently. "When you've been on this job awhile, ma'am, you can tell when a thief is leveling. I didn't talk to him, but others did."

"But Hector Nicasso is a hunchback, and he's half deaf and about half blind. Pick on someone your own size. What are you trying to do—ride him right back to the joint?"

There it was again, the cop-hater jargon. *Joint!* She had probably picked it up the same way a cop did, by close and frequent association with people who talked that way. There were tough characters in Little Havana. And Sister Nell had apparently learned as much as she had taught.

"If Hector's clean, he has nothing to worry about," Stein said, slipping into the same mode of speech. "Sorry I had to bother you, ma'am, when you're so busy with your new school and all. Thank you very much."

He stood up. The nun stood up, too. She came around her new desk and escorted him to the front door. There she stopped and looked up at him, like a veteran principal dealing with a well-meaning but rather stupid schoolboy.

"Find your jewels," she said, "but there must be some better way to do it than to go on bullying the same innocent people. I thought detectives were supposed to be so smart."

"Not necessarily, ma'am. Most of us are pretty dumb."

She almost smiled. "I don't believe that. You just act dumb. Young man, let an old woman give you a word of advice: you've been going at this all wrong. Everything you do is based upon evil—the word of Donny Esposito—and nothing but evil can ever come from evil."

"If Donny lied, then everything I've been taught as a policeman is wrong, ma'am."

"That is quite possible," Sister Nell said serenely. "Now you must stop believing evil and begin anew. Then see if you feel like pushing any more Cubans around."

"I'm not pushing anybody around, ma'am. I'm trying to go straight down the middle on this case. First, I'll have to talk to Hector Nicasso."

She shook a finger at him. "I suppose so, but see that you don't bully him."

He watched her go back down the hall—a tiny, bustling, busy figure; an old woman with many things on her mind. She stopped to flick a speck of dirt from one of her lovely new walls. She shook her head, more in sadness than in anger. She turned a corner, and was gone.

Detective Larry Stein shook his head as well, crossed the ungraded schoolyard and then the street—to the sheet metal shop where Fredo Suarez had been murdered.

Hector Nicasso had learned his craft in prison. So far as the police knew, he had indeed gone straight since then. But ex-convicts did frequent his shop, and his story that he was only helping them get "squared around" might or might not be true.

It was a small shop, and stiflingly hot. Hector had been injured at birth, leaving him dwarfishly deformed, hard of hearing, and almost blind. He snatched off one pair of thick glasses and put on a still thicker pair to study Detective Stein's police identification card. He wiped the sweat from his swarthy face. Then he cupped one hand behind his ear and again changed glasses, to bring Stein's face back into focus.

"A cop," he said flatly. "The jewels again—no?"

"The jewels again, yes," Stein shouted into the hand cupped at Hector's ear.

"Boy, you guys never take your thumb off," Hector said. "You know, cop, any time you want to take your business somewhere else, it's going to be all right by me. Well, here's how it was . . ."

His story had not changed since the last time, or the time before that. He had liked Fredo Suarez. He swore Fredo was a good kid. The only reason Fredo had brought Donny to the shop was that he was scared stiff. He wanted Hector to help him get rid of Donny.

"Donny said they were dime-store jewels he had pinched, but Fredo had a hunch," Hector told Detective Stein. "But he don't know how to shake Donny, see? He knows I'm stir-smart, and if I ain't, who is?"

Hector smiled. It was an oddly warm and attractive smile for such an unsightly man. Stein liked the smile. Stein said, "Well, I guess a guy as mean and rat-scared as Donny was that day would be hard to shake. Go on."

Hector continued, "I'm working on a job when they come in. With a slob like Donny Esposito, there's a time to chime off to him and a time to clam up—you know what I mean, cop?"

"I get it," Stein said.

"I was going to wait until I could say, Donny, cut loose from this punk kid; this is the kind of kid that loses his moxie and flakes out. Well, this is what I was going to say, to help Fredo get rid of him.

"But just then, Donny sees this car stop across the way. Nobody has to wise him up, who it is. Donny can make a cop around a corner in the pitch dark. Also he knows the sister—Sister Nell over to the school there—has got no time for him. Oh, man, that Sister Nell—she was always ratting him out to the priest back when Donny was in school." Hector Nicasso sighed. "Donny Esposito and me—what a pair! And we had one tough priest then. He would wallop the hell out of you for stealing."

"So the two of you were in the school together."

"Oh yeah."

Stein nodded. "Okay. Go on."

"I didn't see Donny's gun because I'm wearing my glasses for close work and I'm blind as a bat two feet off. I didn't hear them arguing—not the words, I mean; just a noise. But even a deaf man can hear a gun go off. He goes bing-bang, twice. He runs out the door. And there is this poor kid Fredo, deader than hell."

"You didn't see the jewels at all?"

"How would I see jewels? I can't see a horse in my own bed with the wrong glasses on."

Stein thought it over. "Hector, you're a lousy witness, but we think you're telling the truth for once."

Nicasso crossed himself. "I can lie. I am human, as who is not? But this time, I swear I'm talking straight—God's witness."

Stein went out. It was only a few blocks to a small, old, but neatly kept house that had been repainted so many times that its crust of paint was almost as thick as the wood siding. A tall woman, dark-skinned and with a crown of white hair piled high on her head, answered his knock. Stein offered his identification card and detective's shield.

She glanced at it quickly and said, "Police?"

"Yes, ma'am. I'd like to see Miss Carmen Suarez."

"Carmen not here. I mother. Carmen no do nothing bad. You go away, *por favor*."

"All right, ma'am," Stein said. "I just promised Sister Nell Abbott I'd talk to her, that's all. It's nothing to worry about."

The nun's name seemed to make a decided difference. "Oh! Carmen work now," her mother said. "You come back tonight, eight o'clock. You see her then, no?"

Stein agreed. He went downtown and spent the rest of the day on still less profitable leads. So far as he could determine, no crooked pawnbroker, no shady jeweler, no known fence in all Miami had handled the jewels. No snitch had ever heard of them floating around the streets for sale. It was the deadest of dead ends.

Stein returned at eight o'clock to the Suarez home. Carmen herself let him in. Every man who had interviewed the dead boy's sister had spoken well of her, and most of them had mentioned how drop-dead gorgeous she was. Stein had expected a pert, chesty, sexy little thing. What he saw confounded that expectation. He saw a tall, dark woman of twenty-two years

whose beauty was many things; pain, for one. Carmen
Suarez still suffered from her brother's death, and it
put shadows in her huge black eyes, and made her
hold her head just a bit higher. Partly her beauty was
serenity; the deep, unshakable kind that comes from
sorrow. And partly, too, it was something warm and
kind and indefinably Cuban, something felt rather
than seen; and from the moment he felt it, nothing
about Larry Stein's job would ever be the same to
him again.

"Please come in," she said, with a smile. "Do you
want to talk to Mother, too? She speaks more English
than you might think, but it's painful to her tongue."

"No, don't bother her," Stein said. "I'm just here
because I promised Sister Nell Abbott."

"I hope I can help you," Carmen said. They sat
down in the small, neat parlor. "It would mean so
much to Mother, to have you find the jewels."

"I'd like to get one thing straight," Stein said. "I
don't suspect anyone, and regardless of what that nun
says, I'm not trying to push people around—Cubans
or anybody else."

Carmen laughed, a soft laugh that crinkled her eyes
and took some of the pain away. "Oh, don't let Sister
Nell upset you. Sister is from Minneapolis, of all
places, but she's more Cuban than us Cubans. I think
she has a complex about us. You know, of course,
what the kids call her to tease her?"

"No, I don't."

"La Panchita."

Stein said, "What does it mean?"

"Little Pancha. It's a sort of baby love-name, from
a *mariache* song—you know, for street musicians. It's
a romantic song, very sad, sometimes very naughty,
always very Cuban. All you had to do, to be kept in
after school, was whistle *La Panchita* where Sister
could hear you."

It was, to Larry Stein, somewhat disconcerting to
learn that the nun came from his own home state of

Minnesota. She was more Cuban than the Cubans, while he, a cop, remained a stranger in the community.

According to the files, Carmen Suarez's father had died when she was fourteen, Fredo twelve. The mother had worked in a poultry slaughterhouse, a nasty but well paid job, until Carmen was out of school and could assume the family's support. And now Carmen was chief statistician for an electronics firm; Stein had been surprised to learn from the files that she made more money than he did.

She was an intelligent young woman, and eager to help, but it was another dead end. She talked freely, but it was mostly about her dead brother. She seemed to want very much for Stein to understand the boy.

"He stole things. He carried a switchblade knife. He was a real punk, and it was his fault and ours and I'm not trying to excuse it. Such things are not really excusable, are they?" Carmen asked.

Stein hedged. "Well, under certain—"

"When he was about fourteen, he suddenly got interested in jazz music. He played clarinet. Then, overnight, he was a different person. Do you know anything about jazz?"

"Well, *I* got through two years of college by playing trumpet in a little band."

She studied him curiously. "And now you're a cop?"

"In music, just good isn't good enough. You've got to be very, very good to make a career of it. And I wasn't very, very good."

"I think Fredo was," Carmen said. "Sister made a tape of some tunes he composed. After Fredo was killed, she gave it to Mother. Would you like to hear it?"

"Yes," Stein said sincerely.

Carmen went out and came back with a cassette player. She slipped in Fredo's tape and the two of them listened; Carmen's eyes never left Stein's face.

The tape had been played many times and was scratchy, and the recording circumstances were not the best. The music itself was undisciplined. Like a teen-age boy, it was always on the verge of being very bad—or very, very good.

Mostly, it was the latter. Mostly this was the strong, original music of a half-trained, reckless kid who did not know how good he was. How could he? He had been trained for life's work in an auto shop. Now he was dead.

The tape ended. Stein said, "If I could play like that, I wouldn't be a cop today."

Carmen's swift smile rewarded him. "And you know music! Oh, Mother will be so proud to know you said that."

He did not want to go yet. He stalled for time. "Would you mind playing it again?"

When he left the house, hours later, he still had no idea where the diamonds were, and he had probably fallen in love with Carmen Suarez. It was an odd love. He did not want to take her to shows, or buy her dinner and flowers, or kiss her—not yet, anyway. That could wait. Even thinking about it could wait.

All he felt was a mystical desire to serve her. In many ways, Larry Stein was just as boyish as he looked. He loved Carmen as he had loved his first sweetheart, in the fourth grade.

But he was a good policeman, trained to face his problem squarely. He went to his apartment down-town and sat in his shorts for a long time, facing his problem with tested police logic learned at the acad-emy. And he could only conclude: something was wrong; someone had lied.

It came down to this—he could believe the cold logic of police science, or the warm loyalty of Sister Nell Abbott and Hector Nicasso and Carmen Suarez. But not both. Both sides in this case, where everything had gone stale but the bitterness, could not be right.

Stein did not sleep well that night. It was humid and hot. The beat of a dead boy's wild music was in his bones; he kept seeing the painfully beautiful face of Carmen Suarez.

He left his apartment house early in the morning. He headed toward the Police Headquarters building, intending to have breakfast somewhere along the way. Then it came to him.

Being of the scientific school of criminology, Larry Stein knew all about the subconscious mind. And how it works in sleep. He was pretty sure that all through the hot, humid night's sleep he had never left his problem for a moment.

He stopped walking and simply stood at a corner, marveling at how simple it was. All the detectives who had ever worked the case had made the same mistake.

Both sides, after all, *could* be right! The men who believed Donny Esposito were right to believe him. But so were Sister Nell and Hector Nicasso and Carmen; they were right to believe as they did.

How this could be, Stein did not yet understand. But with this straight in his head, he saw that he had an entirely new problem. He could stop worrying about the hearts of people, which neither logic nor loyalty could ever know conclusively, and start thinking in terms of *things*. Things had no motives, no feelings. Things were merely things.

Things could be jewels, for instance. Stein picked out the file from the briefcase he carried. It was thick, but he knew his way through it. He licked his thumb and riffled the pages quickly.

He was not halfway through it when it came to him where the jewels were. It was crazy, grotesque, improbable—but it was the only place the things could be, if both sides in this old, bitter case were indeed right.

He threw the file back in his briefcase and started walking again, only back toward his apartment house— and his car, in the basement garage. Then he drove down to Little Havana. It was not yet eight A.M. when he stopped in front of Hector Nicasso's sheet metal

shop, but the door was open. And from the interior of
the shop came the rhythmic thump of Hector's electric
punch press.

Stein went in. He approached warily, not wishing
to startle the hunchback at his machine. Hector, however, had a sixth sense about cops. He snapped the
switch of the punch press, snatched off one pair of
glasses, put the other pair on, and whirled to face
Detective Stein like he was a cornered fox. "Oh, you
again—no?" was all he said.

Stein leaned over to shout into his ear. "Me again,
yes. Look, pal, you can help me."

"Oh yeah?"

"Listen, we keep track of the jewels all the way
from the robbery to the Suarez home. That's where
Donny Esposito says he gave them to Fredo—right?
But we know they're not in that house, because
Donny said Fredo still had them when the two of them
came here. Besides which, we tore that house apart
and couldn't find the diamonds."

Hector shrugged. "Go on," he muttered. "Go on."

"There's a chance that Fredo threw them out between his house and your shop. But Donny says he
still had them when they were here."

"I did not see them," Hector said quickly.

"I believe you. But I think Donny did see them.
They couldn't possibly have left here—yet we've
turned your shop upside down and inside out without
finding any trace of the diamonds."

Hector was tense and suspicious. "Go on," he said.

"Hector, you know what I think? All this kid
wanted was to get rid of those hot rocks. I think he
threw them down on your workbench, and then they
got mixed up in your job. I think we'll find the diamonds in somebody's rear bumper or front fender—
whatever you were working on then, eighteen months
ago. They're just *things*, Hector. They didn't get up
and walk out. They went out of here in a thing of
some kind."

Hector's face whitened. He crossed himself.

"Mother of God—I was sealing the time capsule for the cornerstone of the new school!" he burst out. "You know—a copper box with the things people put under cornerstones. The daily paper. A letter from the mayor. A rosary blessed by the pope. The key to the old school building. You can't solder it shut until the last day, because you have to have the daily paper."

They stared at each other. "Hector," Stein said, "do you know how to reach the sister by phone?"

Again, Hector crossed himself. "Don't call her! The cardinal himself set the stone, blessed it, spread the mortar. Sister would kill us for such sacrilege."

"It's not sacrilege. We're trying to clear a dead boy's name, Hector. We've got to tear that stone out."

Hector shuddered. "I will give you the tools, but you must do it. You're a cop. Maybe your soul is in better shape to carry this sin than mine."

Don't bet on it, Stein thought. He said, "Let's go."

Hector filled a gunny sack with tools, and Stein carried them across the street, to the corner of the new school. He took off his coat and rolled up his sleeves.

It was rich, strong mortar, and the cardinal had been lavish with it. It was an hour before Stein could insert a bar and pry out the big cube of carved granite. He knelt and attacked the mortar in the bottom of the cavity with a small chisel, working slowly and carefully.

In ten more minutes, he lifted it out—a copper casket about the size of a shoebox. He did not try to break Hector's sturdy soldering job. With a knife, he carefully cut a large hole in the soft copper lid.

"Say, what's going on here?" said a sharp voice behind him.

Stein stood up. Sister Nell Abbott had come out of the front door of her new school and was bustling toward them, black robes flying. He had never seen such outraged anger on a human face, and he knew better than to try to explain it to her. Either he was

right or he was not, and if he was not, words would
be no help.

He turned the box upside down over his hand and
shook it. He held the hand out. Sister Nell looked.
She shrank back.

There, among the holy things on Stein's hand, lay
three pieces of stolen jewelry. They had cost thirty-
two thousand dollars retail, and also four lives.

"I told you I was trying to go straight down the
middle to find them," Stein said. "They got mixed up
in these things when Hector sealed the box."

What Sister Nell said rather surprised Stein, at first.
On second thought, it was just what he should have
expected of the nun all the Cuban kids called *La
Panchita*.

"Oh, I'm so glad Donny Esposito did not go to
meet his God with a lie on his soul!" Sister Nell cried.

"So am I, ma'am."

The nun looked ruefully down at the wreckage of
her cornerstone. Then back up at Stein. "Now, this
must all be done over again, after the cardinal himself
set it!" she said.

"I can put it back," Stein said. "I don't know much
about these things, but I don't think this would disturb
the blessing, would it? I mean—"

"No. wait. You must be the one to do it, because
you have done us all a very great service. But wait
until our consecration, and do it then. You must be a
guest of honor. I know the cardinal would want to
meet the young man who has done this thing for us."

Stein's first thought was that Carmen Suarez would
be there, and because he had found the jewels and
restored her brother Fredo's honest name she would
look as he saw her that one brief moment when she
laughed—when some of the pain had been erased
from her face.

"I'd like to, ma'am," Stein said. "But I ought to let
you know that I'm not a Catholic."

"Oh, that's all right," Sister Nell said airily. "The
cardinal goes straight down the middle, too."

DEATH OF AN ALUMNUS

Janet O'Daniel

Sister Maureen had been on the go all day, dashing
between buildings with her short veil flying, checking
off items on a list, seeing to the seating arrangement
on the stage of the auditorium. A big crowd was expected for the dedication of the new building there
on the grounds of St. Margaret's Home. Monsignor
Griffin, Father Dunne, Mr. Hewitt from the bank that
held the mortgage. And then of course Mrs. Frazer
from the Altar Guild and Mr. Allen from the K of C.
Both had been active in fund-raising for the building.
A good many "graduates" would be coming, too.
Boys and girls—but of course they were men and
women now—who had been the orphaned and the
homeless when St. Margaret's took them in. A really
hectic day, but wonderful, too, Sister Maureen reflected. "Who would have thought it would end the
way it did?" Sister Brigid said, only that was much
later.

Sister Brigid had brought soup to her office late in
the day with the early autumn dusk drawing in and
had scolded her for overdoing. "You're wearing yourself out, sister. And I'm sure you skipped lunch. Now
take your shoes off for a minute and close your eyes.

Feel that lovely new carpet under your feet. Oh, I do *love* this room."

"Much too grand," Sister Maureen said. "Carpet indeed."

"Nonsense. The director should have a nice office."

Sister Maureen waved this away. "What about the flowers? Has Roger brought the chrysanthemums from the greenhouse? I wanted twelve pots on the stage."

"All taken care of, sister. Now drink the soup."

"Was he agreeable about it?" Sister Maureen picked up the spoon.

"Oh, well, you know Roger. He doesn't like it when anybody but you tells him to do anything. But I said it was *for* you, and he seemed to get the idea."

Sister Maureen nodded and took a swallow of soup. Roger Mulligan, who had the mind of a child, had lived at the home for so many years that all of them had forgotten how he arrived and where he came from. Roger's talent for gardening went far beyond mere greenness of thumb. He lived and breathed along with the living and breathing of his plants, understanding them in a way that Sister Maureen found bewildering. God's gift, of course, she thought now. The door that opened when another one closed.

She glanced up at Sister Brigid, who stood there with her arms folded, obviously not planning to budge one inch in the matter of the soup. There was a good deal of Attila the Hun in Sister Brigid, she decided. Sister Maureen sighed and drank the soup.

"Very good," Sister Brigid said, a parent rewarding a tractable child. "Now I'll show your visitor in."

"Oh no—" Sister Maureen looked distressed. "I have so many things still to do. I really think I should save all my visiting for after the dedication ceremonies."

"You won't want to save this one," Sister Brigid said with a small, mysterious smile, and went to the door.

The young man who came in was so tall that he

ducked in the doorway. A boyish grin opened his face wide. "Hi, coach."

"Eddie!" Sister Maureen was up from her chair in a flash and flying around the desk. The young man seized her and lifted her off the floor in a huge hug. "I was so hoping you'd come!" she said.

"You didn't think I'd miss it, did you?"

"I know how busy you are. I was watching you on television last night."

He gave a groan. "Not my best game—"

"Well, maybe not. They can't all be best. But at least you pulled it out in overtime."

"Just trying to do what you always taught me, sister. Keep both feet on the floor and fake them out. Hey, you know something—all the time I was here I never asked you how you knew so much about basketball?"

"Five brothers, all over six feet."

"But what about now? No more teaching? No more coaching? This is some office—are you really the new head man around here?"

"Yes, I'm afraid so. And we're getting quite grand. We have two coaches now. Sister Veronica—she works with the girls, and Mr. Byrne, a lay worker, he's the boys' coach."

"Bet they're not up to your style."

"Oh, they're very good—"

"I remember your pins. You always had a lot of big safety pins around you to pin up your skirts and your veil when you were showing us how to make jump shots."

"Well, never mind that. Now tell me if you're getting offers. I heard you were. From the pros."

"Well, some."

"Of course. You were bound to. But you're not making any quick decisions, I hope."

"No—"

"Good. Because the money probably sounds tempting. But you should get your degree first. You still want to be a lawyer, don't you?"

"Oh, sure. And I'm going to be."

"That's all right then." Studying his face—blue eyes, slightly uptilted nose—she was sure he was telling the truth. Eddie Bristow had always had a transparent face. It was one of the things that endeared him to her and had, right from that first day when his older brother Francis had brought him to St. Margaret's and he had stood there, clinging to Francis's hand, nose running, eyes wide, trying hard not to cry. "It's not that I don't want him, sister," Francis had said. "But with both our folks gone now—and I'm in construction, see. I move around a lot. As soon as I get settled, I'll be glad to have him. If you could just keep him here for a few months—" In the actual event it had been eight years, all the years of his growing up, and Sister Maureen had tried not to fault Francis, who she was sure had meant well.

She gave him another look and wondered whether it was her imagination or whether some shade of uneasiness was clouding those wide-open blue eyes.

"Is everything all right with you, Eddie?" she asked gently. "I mean—" A thought lurched into her head, alarming her. "You haven't had anything to do with drugs, have you? So many athletes you hear about—"

"No, Lord, no. Not my style, sister. I'm fine. Hey, you know who I was thinking about? Old Roger. How's he doing? Still in his greenhouse?"

A little too deliberate a change of subject, Sister Maureen thought, but she answered, "Same as ever. And yes, still there. Why don't we stop over and see him before the program? Roger always liked you." Eddie had never teased and tormented him as some of the others had, that was why.

"Can you spare the time? Who's on the program, by the way? The monsignor, I bet. Trot out that speech of his about the golden opportunities of youth?"

She gave him a poke. "I'll take the time. And don't get wise. Yes, the monsignor. Also Mr. Hewitt from the bank."

"Oh, boy. His are always about the cards being stacked against you and the odds being long—"

"You're dreadful. Now look, maybe I'll introduce you from the audience. You wouldn't mind that, would you? I mean, we don't have that many illustrious alumni to point to." Seeing his frown she assured him, "You won't have to make a speech, you know. Just stand up and wave. Like a prizefighter."

"All right. I'll do it for you, sister." He grinned down at her. Sister Maureen remembered those two front teeth, one always toeing out slightly in front of the other.

"It's so good to *see* you, Eddie." She put a hand on his arm as they started out the door. "Speaking of illustrious alumni, I thought I saw Artie Hoffman when I was crossing the lawn earlier."

Something went tense in his arm. She felt it through the tweed of his jacket. "Artie Hoffman—"

"Yes. Last one I'd have expected to show up today. That is—of course I think kindly of all our boys and girls, only Artie *was* one of the difficult ones."

"A creep."

"Now, now. Charity, Eddie. Only it did puzzle me a bit, seeing him, because I'd been thinking he was—away."

"In the slammer. He was. For illegal gambling. He's been out for a while, though."

"Oh. Well, that explains it. Now let's go see Roger. We'll catch up on all the news later."

It was not quite dark, but a little wind had started up, blowing leaves across their path. Sister Maureen felt a small chill. Autumn, of course. One had to expect it. They left the old brick administration building and started across the lawn toward the greenhouse. Far beyond stretched the fifty acres of St. Margaret's with its residence cottages, convent, chapel, school building, barn. And as a centerpiece now the big new all-purpose building, dominating everything. Once the place had been a farm, and even now the spreading-out of the city into suburbs had not quite reached it.

Sister Maureen glanced up at the tall figure striding along beside her, remembering times when a small Eddie had tagged along at her heels with his rapid-fire questions and young enthusiasms. She thought about rewards and how great they could be sometimes. More than she deserved, certainly, but she would try to accept them humbly and be grateful.

Soft, moist warmth greeted them as they pushed open the door of the greenhouse. They walked down an aisle surrounded by trembling green leaves and extravagant blooms. Pale pink cyclamen, bronze chrysanthemums, African daisies. At the end of the aisle Roger Mulligan, in work shirt and jeans that were carefully folded up six inches, stood at a potting table planting freesia bulbs in light soil. He moved his head from side to side as he worked, humming in a low tuneless drone. His plaid shirt was slightly pulled out over his jeans in back. He was putting on weight, Sister Maureen thought. Too many of the sisters slipped him goodies on the sly. She would have to speak to them.

"Roger, look who's here," she said. She reached up and pushed a strand of hair back from his forehead. One or two gray hairs there, she noticed with surprise. She still thought of him as one of the children—they all did. "Do you remember Eddie? He used to be a friend of yours."

Roger gave him a sideways look, tucking his chin in shyly and then wagging his head even more rapidly from side to side.

"Hi, Roger." Eddie Bristow stuck out his hand. Roger regarded it warily for a moment, then took it in his own hand, which had a fair amount of potting soil clinging to it. He smiled the trusting smile which had always melted Sister Maureen's heart.

"Eddie's come to the program, Roger. The one in the auditorium where you sent the flowers."

"Mums," Roger said. "I sent mums."

"You're doing a good job, Roger," Eddie said. "Everything looks first-rate around here."

Roger's head wagged harder than ever.

"May I have a couple of pots of those African daisies, too?" Sister Maureen asked. "I know everyone will admire them."

"Okay."

"Will you walk along with us and bring them?"

"Okay."

Roger led the way and started out the door with a flowerpot in each hand, but then stopped so short that Eddie and Sister Maureen nearly bumped into him.

"What is it, Roger old man?" Eddie asked, and then both of them saw someone walking across the lawn away from the greenhouse. Someone looking in? Sister Maureen wondered. One of the guests doing a bit of sightseeing? She felt the autumn chill again. The figure turned toward them, a thin outline in the dusk. Plaid jacket, wingtip shoes, a cigarette in one hand. While they watched he spun the cigarette away in a bright arc, then stood there dimly silhouetted, the night wind blowing leaves around his feet. But now familiar. Sister Maureen peered into the shadows. "Artie Hoffman? Is that you? Hello, Artie."

"Hi, sister." He lifted one finger to his forehead in a little salute. "Just looking the old place over."

"So glad you came. It's almost time for the program."

"See you there," he said, and walked away from them.

Roger stood in the doorway, looking anxious.

"Come along, Roger. We'll walk with you. No one's going to bother you," Sister Maureen said.

"I don't like him," Roger said quite clearly.

Of course he wouldn't, she thought. Artie had always been one of his tormentors when they were younger. "Come on. Eddie and I will be with you." Roger edged along slowly, and Sister Maureen turned to glance up at Eddie Bristow. His expression indicated quite clearly that he didn't like Artie Hoffman either. Currents, Sister Maureen thought. Those childhood currents that ran underneath everything and never quite disappeared.

"Come on, you two," she said firmly, as if they were both sixth-graders.

She helped Roger place the daisies on the stage of the brightly lighted, paint-smelling auditorium, then turned to Eddie.

"We've about fifteen minutes before the program starts. Go ahead and look around if you want to. The cafeteria's through that door, kitchen beyond. Upstairs is the library. Study rooms. Over that way—" she pointed "—is the new gym and swimming pool. They're on the other side of the building. Only don't be late getting back. Oh—there's the monsignor—got to run."

"Come on, Roger, let's beat it," Eddie said, and Roger, grinning and wagging, followed him out.

After that, everyone arrived at once as they were bound to do, Sister Maureen thought. Monsignor Griffin first, along with Father Dunne. She hurried over to greet them. They were a study in contrasts, the monsignor tall and magisterial—but really he was very kindhearted, Sister Maureen reminded herself— it was just that he looked so *imposing* in his long cassock. His gray hair was brushed back to make a leonine frame for distinguished, gaunt features. Father Dunne, St. Margaret's own priest, was short and round-faced, his hair thinning. The bulbous tips of his shoes turned upward.

"This is your day, sister," Monsignor Griffin said, smiling at her. "We owe it all to your tenacity."

She hoped not too many people would say that to her—she would be in mortal danger of succumbing to vanity.

"Not at all, monsignor," she insisted. "Everyone contributed so much. And of course it was God's help more than anything that saw it through."

"We all acknowledge that," the monsignor smiled. "But you are certainly St. Margaret's staunchest champion."

"We all acknowledge that, too, don't we?" someone

said close to her ear, and Sister Maureen turned to see Mr. Hewitt from the bank, gray-haired, solid—but natty, too, in his navy blazer and french cuffs—the lights catching on the metal frames of his glasses. She had lost track of how many hours she had spent in his office at the bank going over figures.

"Oh, Mr. Hewitt, how good of you to come. And we're looking forward to a few words from you. I know you won't mind that—you're very good at thinking on your feet." Out of the corner of her eye she could see the fifth-graders who were going to sing. They were wiggling like a nest of eels at one side of the auditorium. And where was Sister Angela, who was to play the piano? Sister Maureen had an inspiration. "Father Dunne, why don't you take Monsignor and Mr. Hewitt on a little tour before the program starts? Fifteen minutes—no more now. You're all to be on the stage, of course." She herded them off and turned to be confronted by Mrs. Frazer from the Altar Guild, who had wafted heavily into the auditorium on a cloud of Emeraude.

"Sister Maureen, how absolutely wonderful everything looks. Now do put me right to work, I'm at your disposal."

"Mrs. Frazer! I knew we could count on you." Uncharitably, Sister Maureen wished Mrs. Frazer had not chosen this moment to "help." Things were confused enough. Inspiration struck. "Perhaps you might see if the tables are set up for the refreshments later. In the cafeteria?"

"Oh, by all means, sister." Mrs. Frazer bustled off, weighty with importance, and Sister Maureen offered up a small prayer that Sister Brigid, who was in charge of refreshments and an impeccable organizer, would forgive her.

The auditorium was starting to fill up. People were making their way in in ones and twos and groups. She recognized most of those who had once been residents at St. Margaret's—familiar faces which she had known as child faces, and in most cases the thing that had

been there then was still present, only refined or
sharpened or thrown into a new focus. But still there.
What was central remained. Now they were adults and
drawn back here by some curious mix of nostalgia
and—what? Affection, she hoped. Of course, remembrance was bound to be a mixed bag of pain and happiness. But perhaps today they were remembering the
good parts.

Things got under way at last, and only twenty minutes
behind schedule. She saw Eddie return to the auditorium and take a seat in the back. She tried to catch
his eye; she would have liked him somewhere in the
middle, since she planned to introduce him. Per-
versely, he refused to catch her signal. Then Father
Dunne returned, shepherding the monsignor.

"Splendid, sister. Splendid," the monsignor said as
he took his seat on the platform. "Golden opportunities for the young people in every room."

"That is *quite* a swimming pool," Mr. Hewitt said
admiringly, strolling in after them. "And the exercise
equipment! I assure you, some of my friends wouldn't
mind spending a lunch hour there."

"All in order," Mrs. Frazer said in loud bell tones.
"And such sweet centerpieces on the tables—"

"Wonderful," Sister Maureen said, and got up to
stand at the podium.

"Friends—" she said a little shakily. "We're so
happy to see you all here today." The noisy hum of
talk faded to silence. Feet shuffled, throats were
cleared, and the program got under way.

It was when the fifth-graders were singing that she
caught sight of Sister Brigid, all the way in the back.
She had pushed the auditorium door open cautiously
and now she stood there looking toward the stage, her
face white and terrified.

Quietly Sister Maureen left the stage by the side
steps and walked up the aisle to the back. She could
feel eyes on her. " 'For amber waves of grain,' " the
fifth-graders sang doggedly.

"What is it, sister?" she whispered, and Sister Brigid shook her head wordlessly and lifted a hand to the door. Sister Maureen followed her out into the corridor.

"What's wrong?"

"Out in the back. By the back entrance," Sister Brigid said in a faint, tight voice.

The body lay in the autumn-brown tulip bed that had been newly planted near the door. Brightly illuminated by outdoor spotlights, the soft, friable earth was trampled, and several of the little yellow marking sticks were knocked about. Queen of Bartigon, Sister Maureen read. Holland Beauty. She made herself look at the plaid sports jacket, the wingtip shoes. At the contorted face, the dead, staring eyes. And at the Japanese weeding knife, black and wicked-looking, sticking out of Artie Hoffman's chest. She crossed herself.

"Sister, go get somebody," she said. Her voice had a faraway sound in her own ears. "Sheriff Burke's in there, I saw him earlier. And tell Father Dunne. Oh dear, the monsignor, too. Well, do your best."

Sister Brigid hurried inside as someone else slipped out the door. Sister Maureen looked up. "Oh, Eddie—"

"I saw you leave." But he was looking past her, at the body. "Artie Hoffman."

She nodded. "Oh, Eddie, who would do such a thing—" She stopped, suddenly cold with fear. "Eddie, go over to the greenhouse and find Roger. Stay with him until I can get there."

He stared at her. "Roger! You certainly don't think he did this. He'd never hurt anybody."

"No, I'm sure he wouldn't. I'm sure of it. Only—" She hesitated and looked back toward the body. "That's Roger's knife."

She heard him swear softly, under his breath, and then without another word set off at a loping run. He would be gentle with Roger; she knew she could count on him. But what good was gentleness if Roger really had done it? What would they do to him? Lock him away in some dreadful institution?

The door crashed open again. Sheriff Burke, with one of his uniformed men who had been helping to keep an eye on traffic and parking. Father Dunne, his round face pale, his thinning hair standing up around it, was right behind them. Monsignor Griffin stood in the doorway, his handsome head framed against the indoor light. Father Dunne took an involuntary step toward the body and Sheriff Burke said sharply, "Stay back. Everyone. And keep everyone inside for now. I'll have questions to ask." He surveyed the scene, the sprawled body, the trampled earth now blood-soaked. Someone—she realized it was Mr. Hewitt—helped Sister Maureen to her feet.

"Whose knife is that?" the sheriff asked.

In Sister Maureen's office the little group sat uneasily. Sheriff Burke paced. He was wearing a suit today instead of the flannel shirt and corduroy trousers Sister Maureen was used to. "We'll have to wait and see what the M.E. says, but it must have been only an hour or so ago. You'd think someone would have seen something."

"Everyone was inside for the program," Sister Maureen said.

"Not everyone, obviously," the sheriff said. She noticed he had loosened his tie, but he still looked uncomfortable in the suit. "Hoffman was apparently hanging around out there. Maybe he was waiting to see someone."

"Here?" Sister Maureen's eyes were wide.

The sheriff did not answer. He swung around to face Eddie Bristow. "You said that fellow Roger was with you."

"He was, yes. That is, we left the auditorium together. He went back to the greenhouse."

"Know that for a fact?"

"I saw him start across the lawn toward it. Yes, I'm sure that's where he went."

"After the sisters here found the body, you went there looking for him. How come you did that?"

"I told him to," Sister Maureen said quickly. "I was—we all feel concern about Roger because he's not—like the rest."

"And besides, that was his knife, right?"

Sister Maureen dodged the question. "Where is he now?"

"He's there in the greenhouse. I've got Deputy Poole with him."

"Oh dear." Sister Maureen pressed her hands together. "I hope he doesn't frighten Roger. Of course, anyone could have picked up that knife, sheriff. Roger's always leaving tools around."

Mr. Hewitt, sitting next to her, said thoughtfully, "And that someone could have figured Roger would be blamed, only they wouldn't send him to prison because of the way he is."

"Oh, but that would be an awful thing to do," Sister Maureen said, "To take advantage of a poor soul like Roger—"

"Murder itself is an awful thing," Father Dunne said gently, and Sister Maureen sat back guiltily, her hands in her lap.

"After you saw Roger leave for the greenhouse, Mr. Bristow, what did you do?" the sheriff asked.

"Took a short tour of the building—Sister thought I might be interested."

"Others were doing that, too?"

"Everybody was doing it—milling around, looking in the rooms."

"Did you talk to any of them? Any of those you saw?"

"I might have waved or nodded to one or two—faces that looked familiar. I didn't stop and talk to anybody."

"You must have known many of the people here today. You grew up here, didn't you?"

"Yes. But I knew the program was coming up in

a few minutes. I figured I'd see people later, at the reception."

"They must have recognized you, though. St. Margaret's superstar," Sheriff Burke said with a chilly smile.

Eddie Bristow's face reddened.

"What do you think of the new facilities here?" the sheriff asked suddenly. "The gym and pool and all that."

Eddie stared at him, eyes narrowed. He shrugged. "Great."

"You looked that area over pretty carefully, did you?"

"Not carefully, just stuck my head in."

"Anybody there when you did that?"

"I didn't see anybody."

"Back door from the gym leads right out to where he was found. If you were planning to meet him there, that'd be the way to go, I should think."

"I wasn't planning to meet him."

Sheriff Burke pursed his lips, stuck both hands in his pants pockets. The pants themselves had worked down to just under a slight paunch.

The monsignor said, "What about those people waiting in the auditorium, sheriff?" His voice had a clear, authoritative ring. The sheriff might be in charge, but there could be no mistaking whose bailiwick this was.

"I'll want to talk to them—some of them anyway. Monsignor, would you go and speak to them? Explain—well, the best you can, and ask them to be patient for a few minutes more?"

Monsignor Griffin's handsome head dipped in a brief nod and he went out. The sheriff turned back to Eddie. "I saw you play against State last night."

Sister Maureen frowned. Basketball? At a time like this?

"Had me worried there for a while when it went into overtime, but you managed to pull it out." Eddie said nothing. "Just lucky?"

"Yes, I suppose."

"Or maybe something else? Artie Hoffman was a gambler. Gamblers have gotten to college athletes before, haven't they? Maybe Artie approached you, offered you money to hold the point spread down. Then he could have reneged, backed out of the deal—"

"Sheriff Burke, what a thing to say!" Sister Maureen flared. "Eddie would never do something dishonest. He grew up here at St. Margaret's. I'm the one who taught him basketball. I know him."

Sheriff Burke turned to her. "All due respect, sister, but we don't always know people as well as we think we do. And, of course, Artie Hoffman grew up here, too, didn't he? Now what about this Roger fellow? He's retarded, you say."

"He is, yes. But he's the gentlest soul—I mean, he cares for the greenhouse and does the planting, and he'd never hurt anyone."

"You know him, too, I take it." The polite irony was not lost on Sister Maureen.

"I feel that I do, yes," she said, struggling mightily to maintain a respectful tone.

"Did he know Artie Hoffman?"

"Yes, he knew him."

"They weren't friends."

"Not—really."

"Enemies?"

"Goodness, Roger doesn't have enemies."

"He liked Hoffman then."

Sister Maureen squeezed her hands together. "No, he didn't really like him. He was kind of—afraid of him. That's another reason why he'd never have gone near him. Artie Hoffman used to tease him—some of the children did that, thoughtlessly."

"He might not have gone near him intentionally, but if he happened to run into Hoffman, and if he happened to have that knife with him, it might have given him courage."

Sister Maureen shook her head firmly but said nothing.

The sheriff turned back to Eddie. "I heard there was pretty heavy betting on that game with State."

Eddie shrugged.

"Artie Hoffman did approach you, didn't he?"

Sister Maureen opened her mouth to speak but then snapped it shut. She glanced at Eddie. There were two spots of color in his cheeks.

"Yes."

Sister Maureen gasped. The sheriff's eyebrows went up and his mouth twitched slightly. If he were a cat he'd be purring, Sister Maureen thought angrily. "That certainly doesn't mean—" she began, but no one was listening.

"How much did he offer?" the sheriff asked.

Eddie hesitated. "Five thousand dollars. As you say, there was heavy betting on the game."

"And the money looked pretty good to you."

"No!"

"All you had to do was keep the point spread down—which you managed pretty neatly—only maybe Artie went back on his word, weaseled out of paying. And when you saw him here tonight you figured you'd threaten him, or put some muscle on him—"

"No! I never did any of that. Because I never made a deal with him. I told him to go to hell. Whether you believe it or not, I played the best I could last night."

Sister Maureen was looking from one to the other, thinking hard, thinking back.

"He was always a penny ante sort of person," she said.

"Who?" Sheriff Burke turned to her.

"Artie Hoffman. I was just remembering what he was like when he was here with us at St. Margaret's. He used to pay the littler boys a penny to find him discarded bottles. Then he'd return them for the nickel. You know, things like that."

"Yes, I'm sure he was, sister—"

"I think fondly of all our boys and girls, of course, only Artie was always—enterprising. And as I say, penny ante. Small time. I can't imagine him ever of-fering five thousand dollars to anyone."

"Even if he stood to make a lot more?"

"Even then. It wasn't in his makeup. Of course, someone else might have been behind him. Maybe he was only a go-between. And maybe that other person was the one he quarreled with." The room had gone silent. Sister Maureen said, "Sister Brigid, do you sup-pose you could scout out some coffee for us? I think we all need—" She paused at the sight of Sister Brig-id's long, plain face, still pale with shock but now staring in horror at the floor. Sister Maureen followed the look and so did Sheriff Burke and Eddie Bristow. Father Dunne cleared his throat uncomfortably. Mr. Hewitt shifted in his chair and looked down. A smear of black dirt was grinding itself into the pale beige carpet under his feet. Some of it still clung to his shoes, and a faint earth smell came with it.

"My my," he said. "I seem to have—"

Sister Maureen said thoughtfully, "Nobody has planting soil like Roger's. He keeps his own compost heap. And he'd just done the tulip bed. All that fresh dirt."

Mr. Hewitt's face began to look mottled. "Now wait a minute. What's going on here?"

"People want a banker to be above reproach, don't they?" Sister Maureen said. "I mean—rather like one of us. Artie was only a messenger, but he could have been holding you up for a bigger cut, couldn't he? And threatening to let everyone know just how much of a gambler you really were? Father Dunne, Mr. Hewitt didn't stay with you and Monsignor when you went on your little sight-seeing tour, did he?"

"Monsignor was interested in the library," the little priest said worriedly. "Mr. Hewitt wanted to take a look at the facilities on the first floor. The pool, the gymnasium—"

"And returned to the auditorium at the last minute. In fact, everyone else was seated by that time, weren't they?" she added, almost apologetically. She gave the banker a scrutinizing look. "You've changed your jacket, Mr. Hewitt. Where's that lovely blue blazer you were wearing?"

"Now wait a minute," Mr. Hewitt said. "Now just wait a minute here."

"That one's rather wrinkled. Is it one you keep in your car—for emergencies, perhaps? Or did your wife remind you to drop it off at the dry cleaner's and you forgot? I imagine your other one would have got blood on it—"

"Look here," Mr. Hewitt said.

"And so careless of Roger to leave his weeding knife out that way."

"I think we'd better talk this over," Sheriff Burke said.

"Was it just the dirt on the carpet? And that business about the jacket?" Sister Brigid had found Sister Maureen on her hands and knees early the next morning, smoothing the tulip bed at the back of the new building. The grounds were quiet, the air clear and autumn bright. Sister Maureen's veil was slightly askew, her hands black with the soft dirt.

"I wanted to straighten this out before Roger noticed," she explained, sticking a Holland Beauty marker back in place. "I may be mixing these up some, but I don't think he'll be too upset. I suspect he had them a little mixed up himself." She shaded her eyes with one hand and looked up at Sister Brigid. "No—or only partly those things. Earlier Eddie'd made fun of all the speeches we were going to hear— you know he was always a wicked mimic that way. And he remembered how Mr. Hewitt's were usually about changing the odds and about the cards being stacked against you, all that kind of thing."

"Gambling talk," Sister Brigid said sagely.

"Of course it didn't mean anything—it was just in fun, only it stuck in my mind, you see, even though I scolded Eddie. And there wasn't any other way his shoes could have picked up all that dirt, was there?

The sheriff kept everybody back, even Father Dunne, didn't he?"

Sister Brigid shook her head sadly. "I've been brushing your carpet," she said.

"Well." Sister Maureen sat back on her heels and smiled a rueful, one-sided smile. "Both of us down on our knees. I think after yesterday that's fairly appropriate, don't you, sister?"

THE PRICE OF LIGHT

Ellis Peters

Hamo FitzHamon of Lidyate held two fat manors in the northeastern corner of the county, towards the border of Cheshire. Though a gross feeder, a heavy drinker, a self-indulgent lecher, a harsh landlord, and a brutal master, he had reached the age of sixty in the best of health, and it came as a salutary shock to him when he was at last taken with a mild seizure, and for the first time in his life saw the next world yawning before him, and awoke to the uneasy consciousness that it might see fit to treat him somewhat more austerely than this world had done.

Though he repented none of them, he was aware of a whole register of acts in his past which heaven might construe as heavy sins. It began to seem to him a prudent precaution to acquire merit for his soul as quickly as possible. Also as cheaply, for he was a grasping and possessive man. A judicious gift to some holy house should secure the welfare of his soul. There was no need to go so far as endowing an abbey, or a new church of his own. The Benedictine abbey of Shrewsbury could put up a powerful assault of prayers on his behalf in return for a much more modest gift.

The thought of alms to the poor, however ostentatiously bestowed in the first place, did not recommend itself. Whatever was given would be soon consumed and forgotten, and a ragtag of beggarly blessings from the indigent could carry very little weight, besides failing to confer a lasting luster upon himself. No, he wanted something that would continue in daily use and daily respectful notice, a permanent reminder of his munificence and piety.

He took his time about making his decision, and when he was satisfied of the best value he could get for the least expenditure, he sent his law-man to Shrewsbury to confer with abbot and prior, and conclude with due ceremony and many witnesses the charter that conveyed to the custodian of the altar of St. Mary, within the abbey church, one of his free tenant farms, the rent to provide light for Our Lady's altar throughout the year. He promised also, for the proper displaying of his charity, the gift of a pair of fine silver candlesticks, which he himself would bring and see installed on the altar at the coming Christmas feast.

Abbot Heribert, who after a long life of repeated disillusionments still contrived to think the best of everybody, was moved to tears by this penitential generosity. Prior Robert, himself an aristocrat, refrained, out of Norman solidarity, from casting doubt upon Hamo's motives, but he elevated his eyebrows all the same. Brother Cadfael, who knew only the public reputation of the donor and was sceptical enough to suspend judgment until he encountered the source, said nothing, and waited to observe and decide for himself. Not that he expected much; he had been in the world fifty-five years and learned to temper all his expectations, bad or good.

It was with mild and detached interest that he observed the arrival of the party from Lidyate on the morning of Christmas Eve. A hard, cold Christmas it was proving to be, all bitter black frost and grudging snow, thin and sharp as whips before a withering east wind. The weather had been vicious all the year, and the harvest a disaster. In the villages, people shivered and starved, and Brother Oswald the almoner fretted and grieved the more that the alms he had to distribute were not enough to keep all those bodies and souls together.

The sight of a cavalcade of three good riding horses, ridden by travelers richly wrapped up from the cold and followed by two pack-ponies, brought all the wretched petitioners crowding and crying, holding out hands blue with frost. All they got out of it was a single perfunctory handful of small coin, and when they hampered his movements FitzHamon used his whip as a matter of course to clear the way. Rumor, thought Brother Cadfael, pausing on his way to the infirmary with his daily medicines for the sick, had probably not done Hamo FitzHamon any injustice.

Dismounting in the great court, the knight of Lidyate was seen to be a big, over-fleshed, topheavy man with bushy hair and beard and eyebrows, all grey-streaked from their former black, and stiff and bristling as wire. He might well have been a very handsome man before indulgence purpled his face and pocked his skin and sank his sharp black eyes deep into flabby sacks of flesh. He looked more than his age, but still a man to be reckoned with.

The second horse carried his lady, pillion behind a groom. A small figure she made, even swathed almost to invisibility in her woollens and furs, and she rode snuggled comfortably against the groom's broad back, her arms hugging him round the waist. And a very well looking young fellow he was, this groom, a strapping lad barely twenty years old, with round, ruddy cheeks and merry, guileless eyes, long in the legs, wide in the shoulders, everything a country youth should be, and attentive to his duties into the bargain, for he was down from the saddle in one lithe leap and reaching up to take the lady by the waist, every bit as heartily as she had been clasping him a moment before, and lift her lightly down. Small gloved hands rested on his shoulders a brief moment longer than was necessary. His respectful support of her continued until she was safe on the ground and sure of her footing; perhaps a few seconds more. Hamo FitzHamon was occupied with Prior Robert's ceremonious welcome and the attentions of the hospitaler, who had made the best rooms of the guest-hall ready for him.

The third horse also carried two people but the woman on the pillion did not wait for anyone to help her down, but slid quickly to the ground and hurried to help her mistress off with the great outer cloak in which she had traveled. A quiet, submissive young woman, perhaps in her middle twenties, perhaps older, in drab homespun, her hair hidden away under a coarse linen wimple, her face was thin and pale, her skin dazzlingly fair, and her eyes, reserved and weary, were of a pale, clear blue, a fierce color that ill suited their humility and resignation.

Lifting the heavy folds from her lady's shoulders, the maid showed a head the taller of the two, but drab indeed beside the bright little bird that emerged from the cloak. Lady FitzHamon came forth graciously smiling on the world in scarlet and brown, like a robin, and just as confidently. She had dark hair braided about a small, shapely head, soft full cheeks flushed rosy by the chill air, and large dark eyes assured of their charm and power.

She could not possibly have been more than thirty, probably not so much. FitzHamon had a grown son somewhere, with children of his own, and waiting, some said, with little patience for his inheritance. This girl must be a second or a third wife, a good deal younger than her stepson, and a beauty at that. Hamo was secure enough and important enough to keep himself supplied with wives as he wore them out. This one must have cost him dear, for she had not the air of a poor but pretty relative sold for a profitable alliance; rather she looked as if she knew her own status very well indeed and meant to have it acknowledged. She would look well presiding over the high table at Lidyate, certainly, which was probably the main consideration.

The groom behind whom the maid had ridden was an older man, lean and wiry, with a face like the bole of a knotty oak. By the sardonic patience of his eyes, he had been in close and relatively favored attendance on FitzHamon for many years, knew the best and the worst his moods could do, and was sure of his own ability to ride the storms. Without a word, he set about unloading the pack-horses and followed his lord to the guest-hall, while the young man took FitzHamon's bridle and led the horses away to the stables.

Cadfael watched the two women cross to the doorway, the lady springy as a young hind, with bright eyes taking in everything around her, the tall maid keeping always a pace behind, with long steps curbed to keep her distance. Even thus, frustrated like a mewed hawk, she had a graceful gait. Almost certainly of villein stock, like the two grooms. Cadfael had long practice in distinguishing the free from the unfree. Not that the free had any easy life, often they were worse off than the villeins of their neighborhood; there were plenty of free men, this Christmas, gaunt and hungry, forced to hold out begging hands among the throng round the gatehouse. Freedom, the first ambition of every man, still could not fill the bellies of wives and children in a bad season.

FitzHamon and his party appeared at Vespers in full glory, to see the candlesticks reverently installed upon the altar in the Lady Chapel. Abbot, prior, and brothers had no difficulty in sufficiently admiring the gift, for they were indeed things of beauty, two fluted stems ending in the twin cups of flowering lilies. Even the veins of the leaves showed delicate and perfect as in the living plant. Brother Oswald the almoner, himself a skilled silversmith when he had time to exercise his craft, stood gazing at the new embellishments of the altar with a face and mind curiously torn between rapture and regret, and ventured to delay the donor for a moment as he was being ushered away to sup with Abbot Heribert in his lodging.

"My lord, these are of truly noble workmanship. I have some knowledge of precious metals, and of the most notable craftsmen in these parts, but I never saw any work so true to the plant as this. A countryman's eye is here, but the hand of a court craftsman. May we know who made them?"

FitzHamon's marred face curdled into deeper purple, as if an unpardonable shadow had been cast upon his hour of self-congratulation. He said brusquely: "I commissioned them from a fellow in my own service. You would not know his name—a villein born, but he had some skill." And with that he swept on, avoiding further question, and wife and menservants and maid trailed after him. Only the older groom, who seemed less in awe of his lord than anyone, perhaps by reason of having so often presided over the ceremony of carrying him dead-drunk to his bed, turned back for a moment to pluck at Brother Oswald's sleeve and advise him in a confidential whisper: "You'll find him short to question on that head. The silversmith—Alard, his name was—cut and ran from his service last Christmas, and for all they hunted him as far as London, where the signs pointed, he's never been found. I'd let that matter lie if I were you."

And with that he trotted away after his master, and left several thoughtful faces staring after him.

"Not a man to part willingly with any property of his," mused Brother Cadfael, "metal or man, but for a price, and a steep price at that."

"Brother, be ashamed!" reproved Brother Jerome at his elbow. "Has he not parted with these very treasures for pure charity?"

Cadfael refrained from elaborating on the profit Fitz-Hamon expected for his benevolence. It was never worth arguing with Jerome, who in any case knew as well as anyone that the silver lilies and the rent of one farm were no free gift. But Brother Oswald said grievingly: "I wish he had directed his charity better. Surely these are beautiful things, a delight to the eyes, but well sold they could have provided money enough to buy the means of keeping my poorest petitioners alive through the winter, some of whom will surely die for the want of them."

Brother Jerome was scandalized. "Has he not given them to Our Lady herself?" he lamented indignantly. "Beware of the sin of those apostles who cried out with the same complaint against the woman who brought the pot of spikenard and poured it over the Saviour's feet. Remember Our Lord's reproof to them, that they should let her alone, for she had done well!"

"Our Lord was acknowledging a well meant impulse of devotion," said Brother Oswald with spirit. "He did not say it was well advised! 'She hath done what she could' is what he said. He never said that with a little thought she might not have done better. What use would it have been to wound the giver after the thing was done? Spilled oil of spikenard could hardly be recovered."

His eyes dwelt with love and compunction upon the silver lilies, with their tall stems of wax and flame. For these remained, and to divert them to other use was still possible, or would have been possible if the donor had been a more approachable man. He had, after all, a right to dispose as he wished of his own property.

"It is sin," admonished Jerome sanctimoniously, "even to covet for other use, however worthy, that which has been given to Our Lady. The very thought is sin."

"If Our Lady could make her own will known," said Brother Cadfael drily, "we might learn which is the graver sin, and which the more acceptable sacrifice."

"Could any price be too high for the lighting of this holy altar?" demanded Jerome.

It was a good question, Cadfael thought, as they went to supper in the refectory. Ask Brother Jordan, for instance, the value of light. Jordan was old and frail, and gradually going blind. As yet he could distinguish shapes, but like shadows in a dream, though he

knew his way about cloisters and precincts so well that
his gathering darkness was no hindrance to his freedom of movement. But as every day the twilight
closed in on him by a shade, so did his profound love
of light grow daily more devoted, until he had for-
saken other duties and taken upon himself to tend all
the lamps and candles on both altars, for the sake of
being always irradiated by light, and sacred light at
that. As soon as Compline was over this evening, he
would be busy devoutly trimming the wicks of candle
and lamp, to have the steady flames smokeless and
immaculate for the Matins of Christmas Day. It was
doubtful if he would go to his bed at all until Matins
and Lauds were over. The very old need little sleep,
and sleep is itself a kind of darkness. But what Jordan
treasured was the flame of light, and not the vessel
holding it; and would not those splendid two-pound
candles shine upon him just as well from plain wooden
sconces?

Cadfael was in the warming-house with the rest of
the brothers about a quarter of an hour before Compline when a lay brother from the guest-hall came
enquiring for him.

"The lady asks if you'll speak with her. She's com-
plaining of a bad head and that she'll never be able
to sleep. Brother Hospitaler recommended her to you
for a remedy."

Cadfael went with him without comment, but with
some curiosity, for at Vespers the Lady FitzHamon
had looked in blooming health and sparkling spirits.
Nor did she seem greatly changed when he met her
in the hall, though she was still swathed in the cloak
she had worn to cross the great court to and from
the abbot's house and had the hood so drawn that it
shadowed her face. The silent maid hovered at her
shoulder.

"You are Brother Cadfael? They tell me you are
expert in herbs and medicines, and can certainly help
me. I came early back from the lord abbot's supper

with a headache and have told my lord that I shall go early to bed. But I have such disturbed sleep, and with this pain how shall I be able to rest? Can you give me some draught that will ease me? They say you have a perfect apothecarium in your herb-garden, and all your own work, growing, gathering, drying, brewing, and all. There must be something there that can soothe pain and bring deep sleep."

Well, thought Cadfael, small blame to her if she sometimes sought a means to ward off her old husband's rough attentions for a night, especially for a festival night when he was likely to have drunk heavily. Nor was it Cadfael's business to question whether the petitioner really needed his remedies. A guest might ask for whatever the house afforded.

"I have a syrup of my own making," he said, "which may do you good service. I'll bring you a vial of it from my workshop store."

"May I come with you? I should like to see your workshop." She had forgotten to sound frail and tired. The voice could have been a curious child's. "As I already am cloaked and shod," she said winningly. "We just returned from the lord abbot's table."

"But should you not go in from the cold, madam? Though the snow's swept here in the court, it lies on some of the garden paths."

"A few minutes in the fresh air will help me," she said, "before trying to sleep. And it cannot be far."

It was not far. Once away from the subdued lights of the buildings, they were aware of the stars, snapping like sparks from a cold fire, in a clear black sky just engendering a few tattered snow-clouds in the east. In the garden, between the pleached hedges, it seemed almost warm, as though the sleeping trees breathed tempered air as well as cutting off the bleak wind. The silence was profound. The herb-garden was walled, and the wooden hut where Cadfael brewed and stored his medicines was sheltered from the worst of the cold. Once inside and a small lamp kindled, Lady FitzHamon forgot her invalid role in wonder and

delight, looking round her with bright, inquisitive
eyes. The maid, submissive and still, scarcely turned
her head, but her eyes ranged from left to right and
a faint color touched life into her cheeks. The many
faint, sweet scents made her nostrils quiver and her
lips curve just perceptibly with pleasure.

Curious as a cat, the lady probed into every sack
and jar and box, peered at mortars and bottles, and
asked a hundred questions in a breath.

"And this is rosemary, these little dried needles?
And in this great sack—is it grain?" She plunged her
hands wrist-deep inside the neck of it, and the hut was
filled with sweetness. "Lavender! Such a great harvest
of it! Do you, then, prepare perfumes for us women?"

"Lavender has other good properties," said Cadfael. He was filling a small vial with a clear syrup he
made from eastern poppies, a legacy of his crusading
years. "It is helpful for all disorders that trouble the
head and spirit, and its scent is calming. I'll give you
a little pillow filled with that and other herbs that shall
help to bring you sleep. But this draught will ensure
it. You may take all that I give you here and get no
harm, only a good night's rest."

She had been playing inquisitively with a pile of
small clay dishes he kept by his work-bench, rough
dishes in which the fine seeds sifted from fruiting
plants could be spread to dry out, but she came at
once to gaze eagerly at the modest vial he presented
to her. "Is it enough? It takes much to give me sleep."

"This," he assured her patiently, "would bring sleep
to a strong man. But it will not harm even a delicate
lady like you."

She took it in her hand with a small, sleek smile of
satisfaction. "Then I thank you indeed! I will make a
gift—shall I?—to your almoner in requital. Elfgiva,
you bring the little pillow. I shall breathe it all night
long. It should sweeten dreams."

So her name was Elfgiva. A Norse name. She had
Norse eyes, as he had already noted, blue as ice, and
pale fine skin worn finer and whiter by weariness.

All this time she had noted everything that passed, motionless, and never said a word. Was she older or younger than her lady? There was no guessing. The one was so clamant and the other so still.

He put out his lamp and closed the door, and led them back to the great court just in time to take leave of them and still be prompt for Compline. Clearly the lady had no intention of attending. As for the lord, he was just being helped away from the abbot's lodging, his grooms supporting him one on either side, though as yet he was not gravely drunk. They headed for the guest-hall at an easy roll. No doubt only the hour of Compline had concluded the drawn-out supper, probably to the abbot's considerable relief. He was no drinker and could have very little in common with Hamo FitzHamon. Apart, of course, from a deep devotion to the altar of St. Mary.

The lady and her maid had already vanished within the guest-hall. The younger groom carried in his free hand a large jug, full, to judge by the way he held it. The young wife could drain her draught and clutch her herbal pillow with confidence; the drinking was not yet at an end, and her sleep would be solitary and untroubled. Brother Cadfael went to Compline mildly sad, and obscurely comforted.

Only when service was ended, and the brothers on the way to their beds, did he remember that he had left his flask of poppy syrup unstoppered. Not that it would come to any harm in the frosty night, but his sense of fitness drove him to go and remedy the omission before he slept.

His sandaled feet, muffled in strips of woollen cloth for warmth and safety on the frozen paths, made his coming quite silent, and he was already reaching out a hand to the latch of the door, but not yet touching, when he was brought up short and still by the murmur of voices within. Soft, whispering, dreamy voices that made sounds less and more than speech, caresses rather than words, though once at least words surfaced for a moment. A man's voice, young, wary, saying:

"But how if he *does*?" And a woman's soft, suppressed laughter: "He'll sleep till morning, never fear!" And her words were suddenly hushed with kissing, and her laughter became huge, ecstatic sighs, the young man's breath heaving triumphantly. But still, a moment later, the note of fear again, half enjoyed: "Still, you know him. He *may*—" And she, soothing: "Not for an hour at least—then we'll go. It will grow cold here—"

That, at any rate, was true; small fear of them wishing to sleep out the night here, even two close-wrapped in one cloak on the bench-bed against the wooden wall.

Brother Cadfael withdrew very circumspectly from the herb-garden and made his way back in chastened thought towards the dortoir. Now he knew who had swallowed that draught of his, and it was not the lady. In the pitcher of wine the young groom had been carrying? Enough for a strong man, even if he had not been drunk already. Meantime, no doubt, the body-servant was left to put his lord to bed, somewhere apart from the chamber where the lady lay supposedly nursing her indisposition and sleeping the sleep of the innocent. Ah, well, it was no business of Cadfael's, nor had he any intention of getting involved. He did not feel particularly censorious. Doubtful if she ever had any choice about marrying Hamo; and with this handsome boy forever about them, to point the contrast—

A brief experience of genuine passion, echoing old loves, pricked sharply through the years of his vocation. At least he knew what he was condoning. And who could help feeling some admiration for her opportunist daring, the quick wit that had procured the means, the alert eye that had seized on the most remote and adequate shelter available?

Cadfael went to bed, and slept without dreams, and rose at the Matin bell some minutes before midnight. The procession of the brothers wound its way down the night stairs into the church, and into the soft, full glow of the lights before St. Mary's altar.

Withdrawn reverently some yards from the step of the altar, old Brother Jordan, who should long ago have been in his cell with the rest, kneeled upright with clasped hands and ecstatic face, in which the great veiled eyes stared full into the light he loved. When Prior Robert exclaimed in concern at finding him there on the stones, and laid a hand on his shoulder, he started as if out of a trance, and lifted to them a countenance itself all light.

"Oh, brothers, I have been so blessed! I have lived through a wonder! Praise God that ever it was granted to me! But bear with me, for I am forbidden to speak of it to any for three days. On the third day from today I may speak—!"

"Look, brothers!" wailed Jerome suddenly, pointing. "Look at the altar!"

Every man present, except Jordan, who still serenely prayed and smiled, turned to gape where Jerome pointed. The tall candles stood secured by drops of their own wax in two small clay dishes such as Cadfael used for sorting seeds. The two silver lilies were gone from the place of honor.

Through loss, disorder, consternation, and suspicion, Prior Robert would still hold fast to the order of the day. Let Hamo FitzHamon sleep in happy ignorance till morning, still Matins and Lauds must be properly celebrated. Christmas was larger than all the giving and losing of silverware. Grimly he saw the services of the church observed, and despatched the brethren back to their beds until Prime, to sleep or lie wakeful and fearful, as they might. Nor would he allow any pestering of Brother Jordan by others, though possibly he did try in private to extort something more satisfactory from the old man.

Clearly the theft, whether he knew anything about it or not, troubled Jordan not at all. To everything he said only: "I am enjoined to silence until midnight of the third day." And when asked by whom, he smiled seraphically, and was silent.

It was Robert himself who broke the news to Hamo FitzHamon in the morning, before Mass. The uproar, though vicious, was somewhat tempered by the after-effects of Cadfael's poppy draught, which dulled the edge of energy if not of malice. His body-servant, the older groom, Sweyn, was keeping well back out of reach, even with Robert still present, and the lady sat somewhat apart, too, as though still frail and possibly a little out of temper. She exclaimed dutifully, and apparently sincerely, at the outrage done to her husband, and echoed his demand that the thief should be hunted down and the candlesticks recovered.

Prior Robert was just as zealous in the matter. No effort should be spared to regain the princely gift, of that they could be sure. He had already made certain of various circumstances which should limit the hunt. There had been a brief fall of snow after Compline, just enough to lay down a clean film of white on the ground. No single footprint had as yet marked this pure layer. He had only to look for himself at the paths leading from both parish doors of the church to see that no one had left by that way. The porter would swear that no one had passed the gatehouse; and on the one side of the abbey grounds not walled, the Meole brook was full and frozen but the snow on both sides of it was virgin. Within the enclave, of course, tracks and cross-tracks were trodden out everywhere; but no one had left the enclave since Compline, when the candlesticks were still in their place.

"So the miscreant is still within the walls?" said Hamo, glinting vengefully. "So much the better! Then his booty is still here within, too, and if we have to turn all your abode doors out of dortoirs, we'll find it! It, and him!"

"We will search everywhere," agreed Robert, "and question every man. We are as deeply offended as your lordship at this blasphemous crime. You may yourself oversee the search if you will."

*   *   *

So all that Christmas Day, alongside the solemn rejoicings in the church, an angry hunt raged about the precincts in full cry. It was not difficult for all the monks to account for their time to the last minute, their routine being so ordered that brother inevitably extricated brother from suspicion; and such as had special duties that took them out of the general view, like Cadfael in his visit to the herb-garden, had all witnesses to vouch for them. The lay brothers ranged more freely, but tended to work in pairs, at least. The servants and the few guests protested their innocence, and if they had not, all of them, others willing to prove it, neither could Hamo prove the contrary.

When it came to his own two grooms, there were several witnesses to testify that Sweyn had returned to his bed in the lofts of the stables as soon as he had put his lord to bed, and certainly empty-handed; and Sweyn, as Cadfael noted with interest, swore unblinkingly that young Madoc, who had come in an hour after him, had nonetheless returned with him, and spent that hour, at Sweyn's order, tending one of the pack-ponies below, which showed signs of a cough, and that otherwise they had been together throughout.

A villein instinctively closing ranks with his kind against his lord, wondered Cadfael? Or does Sweyn know very well where that young man was last night, or at least what he was about, and is he intent on protecting him from a worse vengeance? No wonder Madoc looked a shade less merry and ruddy than usual this morning, though on the whole he kept his countenance very well, and refrained from even looking at the lady, while her tone to him was cool, sharp, and distant.

Cadfael left them hard at it again after the miserable meal they made of dinner, and went into the church alone. While they were feverishly searching every corner for the candlesticks he had forborne from taking part, but now that they were elsewhere he might find something of interest there. He would not be looking

for anything so obvious as two large silver candlesticks. He made obeisance at the altar and mounted
the step to look closely at the burning candles. No
one had paid any attention to the modest containers
that had been substituted for Hamo's gift; and just as
well, in the circumstances, that Cadfael's workshop
was very little visited, or these little clay pots might
have been recognized as coming from there. He
moulded and baked them himself as he wanted them.
He had no intention of condoning theft, but neither
did he relish the idea of any creature, however sin-
ful, falling into Hamo FitzHamon's mercies.

Something long and fine, a thread of silver-gold,
was caught and coiled in the wax at the base of one
candle. Carefully he detached candle from holder, and
unlaced from it a long, pale hair. To make sure of
retaining it, he broke off the imprisoning disc of wax
with it and then hoisted and turned the candle to see
if anything else was to be found under it. One tiny
oval dot showed; with a fingernail he extracted a single seed of lavender. Left in the dish from beforetime?
He thought not. The stacked pots were all empty. No,
this had been brought here in the fold of a sleeve,
most probably, and shaken out while the candle was
being transferred.

The lady had plunged both hands with pleasure into
the sack of lavender, and moved freely about his
workshop investigating everything. It would have been
easy to take two of these dishes unseen, and wrap
them in a fold of her cloak. Even more plausibly, she
might have delegated the task to young Madoc when
they crept away from their assignation. Supposing,
say, they had reached the desperate point of planning
flight together and needed funds to set them on their
way to some safe refuge . . . yes, there were possibili-
ties. In the meantime, the grain of lavender had given
Cadfael another idea. And there was, of course, that
long, fine hair, pale as flax, but brighter. The boy was
fair. But so fair?

He went out through the frozen garden to his herbarium, shut himself securely into his workshop, and opened the sack of lavender, plunging both arms to the elbow and groping through the chill, smooth sweetness that parted and slid like grain.

They were there, well down. His fingers traced the shape first of one, then a second. He sat down to consider what must be done.

Finding the lost valuables did not identify the thief. He could produce and restore them at once, but Fitz-Hamon would certainly pursue the hunt vindictively until he found the culprit and Cadfael had seen enough of him to know that it might cost life and all before this complainant was satisfied. He needed to know more before he would hand over any man to be done to death.

Better not leave the things here, however. He doubted if they would ransack his hut, but they might. He rolled the candlesticks in a piece of sacking and thrust them into the center of the pleached hedge where it was thickest. The meager, frozen snow had dropped with the brief sun. His arm went in to the shoulder, and when he withdrew it the twigs sprang back and covered all, holding the package securely. Whoever had first hidden it would surely come by night to reclaim it, and show a human face at last.

It was well that he had moved it, for the searchers, driven by an increasingly angry Hamo, reached his hut before Vespers, examined everything within it while he stood by to prevent actual damage to his medicines, and went away satisfied that what they were seeking was not there. They had not, in fact, been very thorough about the sack of lavender; the candlesticks might well have escaped notice even if he had left them there. It did not occur to anyone to tear the hedges apart, luckily. When they were gone, to probe all the fodder and grain in the barns, Cadfael restored the silver to its original place. Let the bait lie safe in the trap until the quarry came to claim it, as he surely would, once relieved of the fear that the hunters might find it first.

Cadfael kept watch that night. He had no difficulty in absenting himself from the dortoir once everyone was in bed and asleep. His cell was by the night stairs and the prior slept at the far end of the long room, and slept deeply. And bitter though the night air was, the sheltered hut was barely colder than his cell, and he kept blankets there for swathing some of his jars and bottles against frost. He took his little box with tinder and flint, and hid himself in the corner behind the door. It might be a wasted vigil; the thief, having survived one day, might think it politic to venture yet another before removing his spoils.

But it was not wasted. He reckoned it might be as late as ten o'clock when he heard a light hand at the door. Two hours before the bell would sound for Matins, almost two hours since the household had retired. Even the guest-hall should be silent and asleep by now. The hour was carefully chosen.

Cadfael held his breath and waited. The door swung slowly open, a shadow stole past him, light steps felt their way unerringly to where the sack of lavender was propped against the wall. Equally silently, Cadfael swung the door to again and set his back against it. Only then did he strike a spark, and hold the blown flame to the wick of his little lamp.

She did not start or cry out or try to rush past him and escape into the night. The attempt would not have succeeded, and she had had long practice in enduring what could not be cured. She stood facing him as the small flame steadied and burned taller, her face shadowed by the hood of her cloak, the candlesticks clasped possessively to her breast.

"Elfgiva," said Brother Cadfael gently. And then: "Are you here for yourself or for your mistress?" But he thought he knew the answer already. That frivolous young wife would never really leave her rich husband and easy life, however tedious and unpleasant Hamo's attentions might be, to risk everything with her penniless villein lover. She would only keep him to enjoy in secret whenever she felt it safe. Even when the old man died, she would submit to marriage at an overlord's will to another equally distasteful. She was not the stuff of which heroines and adventurers are made. This was another kind of woman.

Cadfael went close and lifted a hand gently to put back the hood from her head. She was tall, a hand's-breadth taller than he, and erect as one of the lilies she clasped. The net that had covered her hair was drawn off with the hood and a great flood of silver-gold streamed about her in the dim light, framing the pale face and startling-blue eyes. Norse hair! The Danes had left their seed as far south as Cheshire, and planted this tall flower among them. She was no longer plain, tired, and resigned. In this dim but loving light, she shone in austere beauty. Just so must Brother Jordan's veiled eyes have seen her.

"Now I see!" said Cadfael. "You came into the Lady Chapel and shone upon our half-blind brother's darkness as you shine here. You are the visitation that brought him awe and bliss, and enjoined silence upon him for three days."

The voice he had scarcely heard speak a word until then, a voice level, low, and beautiful, said: "I made no claim to be what I am not. It was he who mistook me. I did not refuse the gift."

"I understand. You had not thought to find anyone there; he took you by surprise as you took him. He took you for Our Lady herself, disposing as she saw fit of what had been given her. And you made him promise you three days' grace." The lady had plunged her hands into the sack, yes, but Elfgiva had carried the pillow and a grain or two had filtered through the muslin to betray her.

"Yes," she said, watching him with unwavering blue eyes.

"So in the end you had nothing against him making known how the candlesticks were stolen." It was not an accusation, he was pursuing his way to understanding. But at once she said clearly: "I did not steal them. I took them. I will restore them—to their owner."

"Then you don't claim they are yours?"

"No," she said, "they are not mine. But neither are they FitzHamon's."

"Do you tell me," said Cadfael mildly, "that there has been no theft at all?"

"Oh, yes!" said Elfgiva, and her pallor burned into a fierce brightness, and her voice vibrated like a harp-string. "Yes, there has been a theft, and a vile, cruel theft, too, but not here, not now. The theft was a year ago, when FitzHamon received these candlesticks from Alard who made them, his villein, like me. Do you know what the promised price was for these? Manumission for Alard, and marriage with me, what we had begged of him three years and more. Even in villeinage we would have married and been thankful. But he promised freedom! Free man makes free wife, and I was promised, too. But when he got the fine works he wanted, then he refused the promised price. He laughed! I saw, I heard him! He kicked Alard away from him like a dog. So what was his due and denied him, Alard took. He ran! On St. Stephen's Day he ran!"

"And left you behind?" said Cadfael gently.

"What chance had he to take me? Or even to bid me farewell? He was thrust out to manual labor on FitzHamon's other manor. When his chance came, he took it and fled. I was not sad! I rejoiced! Whether I live or die, whether he remembers or forgets me, he is free. No, but in two days more he will be free. For a year and a day he will have been working for his living in his own craft, in a charter borough, and after that he cannot be haled back into servitude, even if they find him."

"I do not think," said Brother Cadfael, "that he will have forgotten you! Now I see why our brother may speak after three days. It will be too late then to try to reclaim a runaway serf. And you hold that these

exquisite things you are cradling belong by right to
Alard who made them?"

"Surely," she said. "Seeing he never was paid for
them, they are still his."

"And you are setting out tonight to take them to
him. Yes! As I heard it, they had some cause to pursue him towards London . . . indeed, into London,
though they never found him. Have you had better
word of him? *From* him?"

The pale face smiled. "Neither he nor I can read or
write. And whom should he trust to carry word until
his time is complete and he is free? No, never any
word."

"But Shrewsbury is also a charter borough, where
the unfree may work their way to freedom in a year
and a day. And sensible boroughs encourage the coming of good craftsmen and will go far to hide and
protect them. I know! So you think he may be here
. . . and the trail laid towards London a false trail.
True, why should he run so far, when there's help so
near? But, daughter, what if you do not find him in
Shrewsbury?"

"Then I will look for him elsewhere until I do. I
can live as a runaway, too. I have skills, I can make
my own way until I do get word of him. Shrewsbury
can as well make room for a good seamstress as for a
man's gifts, and someone in the silversmiths' craft will
know where to find a brother so talented as Alard. I
shall find him!"

"And when you do? Oh, child, have you looked
beyond that?"

"To the very end," said Elfgiva firmly. "If I find
him and he no longer wants me, no longer thinks of
me, if he is married and has put me out of his mind,
then I will deliver him these things that belong to him,
to do with as he pleases, and go on my own way and
make my own life as best I may without him. And
wish well to him as long as I live."

Oh, no . . . small fear she would be forgotten, not

in a year, not in many years. "And if he is utterly glad of you, and loves you still?"

"Then," she said, gravely smiling, "if he is of the same mind as I, I have made a vow to Our Lady, who lent me her semblance in the old man's eyes, that we will sell these candlesticks where they may fetch their proper price, and that price shall be delivered to your almoner to feed the hungry. And that will be our gift, Alard's and mine, though no one will ever know it."

"Our Lady will know it," said Cadfael, "and so shall I. Now, how were you planning to get out of this enclave and into Shrewsbury? Both our gates and the town gates are closed until morning."

She lifted eloquent shoulders. "The parish doors are not barred. And even if I leave tracks, will it matter, provided I find a safe hiding-place inside the town?"

"And wait in the cold of the night? You would freeze before morning. No, let me think. We can do better for you than that."

Her lips shaped *"we?"* in silence, wondering, but quick to understand. She did not question his decisions, as he had not questioned hers. He thought he would long remember the slow, deepening smile, the glow of warmth mantling her cheeks. "You believe me!" she said.

"Every word. Here, give me the candlesticks, let me wrap them, and do you put up your hair again in net and hood. We've had no fresh snow since morning. The path to the parish door is well trodden; no one will know your tracks among the many. And, girl, when you come to the town end of the bridge there's a little house off to the left, under the wall, close to the gate. Knock there and ask for shelter over the night till the gates open, and say that Brother Cadfael sent you. They know me; I doctored their son when he was sick. They'll give you a warm corner and a place to lie, for kindness' sake, and ask no questions, and answer none from others, either. And likely they'll know where to find the silversmiths of the town, to set you on your way."

She bound up her pale, bright hair and covered her head, wrapping the cloak about her, and was again the maidservant in homespun. She obeyed without question his every word, moved silently at his back round the great court by way of the shadows, halting when he halted, and so he brought her to the church, and let her out by the parish door into the public street, still a good hour before Matins. At the last moment, she said, close at his shoulder within the half open door: "I shall be grateful always. Someday I shall send you word."

"No need for words," said Brother Cadfael, "if you send me the sign I shall be waiting for. Go now, quickly, there's not a soul stirring."

She was gone, lightly and silently, flitting past the abbey gatehouse like a tall shadow, towards the bridge and the town. Cadfael closed the door softly and went back up the night stairs to the dortoir, too late to sleep but in good time to rise at the sound of the bell and return in procession to celebrate Matins.

There was, of course, the resultant uproar to face next morning, and he could not afford to avoid it, there was too much at stake. Lady FitzHamon naturally expected her maid to be in attendance as soon as she opened her eyes, and raised a petulant outcry when there was no submissive shadow waiting to dress her and do her hair. Calling failed to summon and search to find Elfgiva, but it was an hour or more before it dawned on the lady that she had lost her accomplished maid for good.

Furiously, she made her own toilet unassisted and raged out to complain to her husband, who had risen before her and was waiting for her to accompany him to Mass. At her angry declaration that Elfgiva was nowhere to be found and must have run away during the night, he first scoffed, for why should a sane girl take herself off into a killing frost when she had warmth and shelter and enough to eat where she was?

Then he made the inevitable connection and let out a roar of rage.

"Gone, is she? And my candlesticks gone with her, I dare swear! So it was *she*! The foul little thief! But I'll have her yet, I'll drag her back, she shall not live to enjoy her ill-gotten gains!"

It seemed likely that the lady would heartily endorse all this; her mouth was already open to echo him when Brother Cadfael, brushing her sleeve close as the agitated brothers ringed the pair, contrived to shake a few grains of lavender onto her wrist. Her mouth closed abruptly. She gazed at the tiny things for the briefest instant before she shook them off, she flashed an even briefer glance at Brother Cadfael, caught his eye, and heard in a rapid whisper: "Madam, softly! Proof of the maid's innocence is also proof of the mistress's."

She was by no means a stupid woman. A second quick glance confirmed what she had already grasped, that there was one man here who had a weapon to hold over her at least as deadly as any she could use against Elfgiva. She was also a woman of decision, and wasted no time in bitterness once her course was chosen. The tone in which she addressed her lord almost as sharp as that in which she had complained of Elfgiva's desertion.

"She your thief, indeed! That's folly, as you should very well know. The girl is an ungrateful fool to leave me, but a thief she never has been, and certainly is not this time. She can't possibly have taken the candlesticks. You know well enough when they vanished, and you know I was not well that night and went early to bed. She was with me until long after Brother Prior discovered the theft. I asked her to stay with me until you came to bed. *As you never did*," she ended tartly. "You may remember!"

Hamo probably remembered very little of that night; certainly he was in no position to gainsay what his wife so roundly declared. He took out a little of his ill-temper on her, but she was not so much in awe of him that she dared not reply in kind. Of course, she was certain of what she said! *She* had not drunk herself stupid at the lord abbot's table, she had been nursing a bad head of another kind, and even with Brother Cadfael's remedies she had not slept until after midnight, and Elfgiva had then been still beside her. Let him hunt a runaway maidservant, by all means, the thankless hussy, but never call her a thief, for she was none.

Hunt her he did, though with less energy now that it seemed clear he would not recapture his property with her. He sent his grooms and half the lay servants off in both directions to enquire if anyone had seen a solitary girl in a hurry. They were kept at it all day, but they returned empty-handed.

The party from Lidyate, less one member, left for home next day. Lady FitzHamon rode demurely behind young Madoc, her cheek against his broad shoulders; she even gave Brother Cadfael the flicker of a conspiratorial smile as the cavalcade rode out of the gates and detached one arm from round Madoc's waist to wave as they reached the roadway. So Hamo was not present to hear when Brother Jordan, at last released from his vow, told how Our Lady had appeared to him in a vision of light, fair as an angel, and taken away with her the candlesticks that were hers to take and do with as she would, and how she had spoken to him and enjoined on him his three days of silence. And if there were some among the listeners who wondered whether the fair woman had not been a more corporeal being, no one had the heart to say so to Jordan, whose vision was comfort and consolation for the fading of the light.

That was at Matins, at midnight of the day after St. Stephen's. Among the scattering of alms handed in at the gatehouse next morning for the beggars, there was a little basket that weighed surprisingly heavily. The porter could not remember who had brought it, taking it to be some offerings of food or old clothing, like all the rest. But when it was opened it sent Brother Oswald, almost incoherent with joy and wonder, running to Abbot Heribert to report what seemed to be a miracle. For the basket was full of good coin, to the value of more than a hundred marks. Well used, it would ease all the worst needs of his poorest petitioners until the weather relented.

"Surely," said Brother Oswald devoutly, "Our Lady has made her own will known. Is not this the sign we have hoped for?"

Certainly it was for Cadfael, and earlier than he had dared to hope for it. He had the message that needed no words. She had found him and been welcomed with joy. Since midnight Alard the silversmith had been a free man, and free man makes free wife. Presented with such a woman as Elfgiva, he could give as gladly as she, for what was gold, what was silver, by comparison?

A FACE TO REMEMBER

Mary Amlaw

"May I speak with you, Mother?"

Small and stooped with age, Sister Gabriela paused respectfully by the prioress' desk. Normally she wore a smile that radiated joy, but she was not smiling today. On the contrary, she seemed unusually agitated. An ordinary person might not have detected Gabriela's emotion, for the Daughters of Elias had learned in pre-Vatican II days to conceal anything that seemed negative, but Mary Dominic noticed the line that kept reappearing between Gabriela's eyebrows and the small sigh that escaped her unsmiling lips.

With a small gesture Mary Dominic invited Gabriela to sit down. Mary Dominic was the elected superior of the community, charged not only with the care of souls but with the overall well-being of the nuns. Keeping eighteen women in harmony—Mary Dominic already thought of little Sharon Diaz as one of themselves—taxed her innate understanding of people far more than handling the needs of scores of retreatants. They returned to the outside world within a few days. The community remained.

Mary Dominic smiled at Gabriela. "Yes, sister?" Gabriela was ninety-two, a meek soul tending towards scruples. A gifted artist, her eyes were still sharp and her hands still able to wield the brush, although more slowly than before.

Gabriela whispered, "Mother, I've sinned against charity. Oh, such a stupid offense! I hardly know how to tell you."

Mary Dominic had never known a scruple in her life. A vibrant woman, she embraced life whole-heartedly, and had a knack for restoring minor difficulties to their proper perspective. But she had a soft spot for Gabriela, so timid and loving, and nodded to encourage her to speak.

"I was assigned to one of our retreatants, Mrs. Prestavolta. Mother, I've been praying earnestly for guidance on how best to help her. Her face struck me the moment I saw her, when she registered. There is no peace in it. I went to her room this morning to inquire about when she would like to make an appointment for spiritual discussion. Her door was partly open, and music was coming out."

Gabriela unconsciously wrinkled her forehead in dismay. "Not religious music, Mother. That loud noise the youngsters seem to enjoy. She didn't hear my knock, but it made the door swing open wider. Poor Mrs. Prestavolta—poor thing!—" Gabriela's eyes filled with tears of compassion. "She was *shaving*, Mother. I had a relative once with the same problem, and it made her life a misery. I understood then why Mrs. Prestavolta has been so withdrawn. She doesn't want her secret known, poor woman."

Mary Dominic was more amused than she wanted Gabriela to know. "Did she see you, sister?"

"Oh, no, Mother. I drew the door nearly shut, as it had been, and left without speaking to her. But I clumsily intruded on that woman's privacy, Mother, and now I know her secret which I have no right to know."

Mary Dominic managed to sound as solemn as the situation warranted. "Dear sister, please do not upset yourself so. Our dear Lord would not desire it. Who knows, perhaps He allowed you to learn this secret for some purpose of His own. I know you won't say anything of her affliction. That would be truly uncharitable."

"But there's more fault on my part," Gabriela said. "I had meant to instruct her about our regard for silence. I understood too late that she had the radio playing so loudly to cover the noise of the razor. If I hadn't been so quick to judge—"

"Life is full of ifs," Mary Dominic soothed her. "Put it behind you, sister. You meant no harm, and where there is no ill intent, there is no sin."

Gabriela left Mary Dominic's presence only partially consoled. Tact suggested she avoid Mrs. Prestavolta unless the woman approached her; conscience urged that she keep a watchful eye on Mrs. Prestavolta from a distance in an effort to anticipate any of the poor woman's desires. Mrs. Prestavolta had little to say to her fellow retreatants. She had not requested spiritual guidance and didn't seem drawn to the chapel, but she did spend many hours on the grounds by herself. Gabriela considered that Mrs. Prestavolta was communing with God among the trees, alone and in silence. That was what a retreat was for—solitude and silence with God. Mrs. Prestavolta was surely in need of God. Her features haunted Gabriela. So shallow a face! No peace, no joy, no love resided there.

Perhaps God had allowed Gabriela to blunder because He wanted to reach the woman in His own way. He would touch her, and then she would wish to speak to Gabriela. Until then, Gabriela would remain at a distance, watching and praying.

Sharon Carmelita Diaz sat at the small desk in her narrow cell. The community had informed her after morning prayer that she had been accepted. She had been with the Daughters of Elias twelve months; first as a retreatant, then as postulant and novice. Now she was to choose her profession day, when she would dress like a bride to make her solemn vows. Then she would retire and be dressed in the dark blue habit of the sisters. Thereafter she would be called by her name in religion, Sister Mary Magdalen—a name she had chosen as being eminently suitable.

She had won. Twelve months of prayer, of obedience, of uninspired meals. Twelve months laboring without pay, without crossing the iron gates of the convent into the outside world. Twelve months of behaving like the most docile applicant ever to approach a community.

At first she barely survived from hour to hour. Only the thought of Big Luke's vengeance had helped her persist. He thought she had agreed to testify against him when he was picked up for the murder of a local politician who had been making trouble for Luke and his colleagues.

She would never doublecross a man like Luke, but he had been looking for a scapegoat and he would never believe her. He picked her up six months before when she was working Las Vegas as a stripper, and he was already tired of her.

Sharon never knew her mother. Her grandmother died when she was five, and her father, a migrant farm worker, had no way to raise her. By the time she was fourteen she'd lived in seven foster homes and two residences. Her body was her fortune. She took to the streets, then to the lounges. She'd been doing just fine when Luke picked her up. If he hadn't been arrested, the affair would have fizzled out without any danger. As it was, she thought flight her best chance to live, even though she knew it sealed her guilt in Luke's eyes.

She went to the Daughters of Elias, a continent away in Boston, Massachusetts, as an ordinary retreatant. The scores of weary people seeking the peace and solace of God made her feel safe. Three days after arriving, she lied, saying that she felt an attraction to the religious life; would the Daughters of Elias accept her as a postulant?

The nuns seemed like children to her. They ac-

cepted her lies as truth, and she assumed the outward
shell of their life as a protective disguise.

A year had gone. Luke must have forgotten her by
now, or given up the search. She knew she could leave
for the city at last. She had five hundred dollars and
jewelry the nuns didn't know about. That was nothing
given the way she spent in the old days, but it would
get her a room for a few days while she found an
income. With her dark eyes, creamy skin, and sexy
figure that wouldn't be hard. Twelve months of convent life hadn't killed her skill with men, she was sure.

Time to resume the excitement of her old life. The
habit of prayer would soon be overcome by pleasure,
the remembrance of solitude and silence swamped by
headier joys.

She had played her part perfectly for twelve long
months, amused and then intrigued by the existence
of such an unworldly thing as a community of women
who took God so seriously they had vowed to devote
their lives to Him.

Maybe she had played her part too perfectly. The
lie had become truth: she was attracted to this life.
But in spite of the morning's good news, she was most
certainly not acceptable; the nuns thought her an orphan who had been a good little mouse from birth.
Would they want her if they knew she had been a
hooker, a stripper, a criminal's girl?

There was only one way to find out. Sharon pulled
a piece of stationery towards her and began to write.
"Dear Mother Mary Dominic, I have not been honest
with you and the community."

She wrote quickly, without pausing to phrase her
words more tactfully, sealed the letter without reread-
ing it, and took it at once to Mary Dominic's cell.
Then she went to her work in the garden.

Once Mary Dominic read that letter, Sharon feared
she would be asked to leave. She did not want to
leave. And others had applied who were not very
good material on the face of it; at least one boasted
a past nearly as colorful as Sharon's. The nuns made

her welcome, to Sharon's surprise. "Some of God's greatest saints began as notorious sinners," Mary Dominic told her. "If God calls souls here, we must give them their chance." But the life proved too foreign and she left within weeks.

The white rhododendron needed attention. Sharon concentrated on debriding the leaves of last year's dead stalks. She made a perfect target as she stretched to reach the top of the bush.

White rhododendrons, Ouzo noted. Expensive. The Daughters of Elias must have money somewhere.

He looked around carefully. The retreatants were attending the late morning conference, the nuns were at their household tasks, the garden below was empty except for Sharon. A wall surrounded the grounds, and trees grew near the wall, protecting him from the street. He was on the fire escape outside the women's wing, just beyond the lilac hedge that separated the retreatants' garden from the small area reserved for the nuns.

He aimed without hurry. The bullet had only to graze her. It had been treated with a nicotine solution that would poison her after he had gone. The bullet reached its mark; she slapped at her neck and looked about as if a bee had stung her. Good. Maybe she'd realize Big Luke had caught up with her before she died. He watched her resume breaking the spikes of the dead flowerets as if nothing had happened and smiled, a lengthening of the upper lip and a glint in the eyes that boded no good. Soon the poison would work; she might feel faint and excuse herself from recreation, or keel over unexpectedly in choir. She might think it was flu. The nuns might never know otherwise; and if they came to realize it was murder, they would surely want to hush it up. From what he had learned, that Mary Dominic had the clout to do it.

It had gone well. Luke would be pleased.

Ouzo slid the gun into the purse at his feet. Now

he would leave by the front gate in the same guise in which he had entered—a retreatant. At the corner he would walk boldly into St. Anthony's church. Only the side door nearest the rectory was left open nowadays—symbolic of the neighborhood's deteriorating respectability—but he could leave by any door; it would lock behind him. An old lady or two might be huddled in one of the pews, saying her beads. He would walk by, lock himself in the restroom near the sacristy, shed wig and dress, and emerge as a male. His disguise would join the bundles of clothes collected monthly for the poor.

Purse in hand, he turned to find two dark eyes peering at him from the wall. A black kid, about eight or nine. The child gave a startled gasp and leaped for the ground. Ouzo heard him pounding down the sidewalk.

How much had the kid seen? Was he there when Ouzo fired? No. He had checked. At most, the kid had seen an aging woman fumbling with her purse. Even if he had glimpsed the gun, what harm would it do? This was a neighborhood where people kept shootings and brawls and drugdealing to themselves. If Ouzo had thought there was any danger, he would have hunted the kid down and killed him. It wasn't mercy that spared the boy's life, but cocksureness. Ouzo never made mistakes.

He checked to make sure nothing had been left in his room, hefted his overnight bag, and walked down the stairs to the front lobby in the slightly dragging gait of a weary, arthritic woman. He even gave a nod to the elderly nun who appeared from nowhere to open the door for him.

Beyond the iron gates of the convent, the street was clear. At night it would be a different story: every stoop and porch crowded with people escaping the heat inside. Radios blaring, teens necking in the shadows and flaunting themselves on the street.

By then Ouzo would be far away. Even if the murder got out and some smart cop tied it up to Luke's trial, there was no way to connect it with Ouzo. He smiled as he made his way into the dim coolness of St. Anthony's. He was pleased with himself.

Zebulon Williams leaned on the buzzer that would eventually bring a nun to the door. When the neighborhood had been middle-class Irish and Italian, the door had opened at the slightest touch and the caller could wait in a vestibule furnished with comfortable chairs. Now the vestibule was bare, and the doors that led from it were kept locked.

Zeb danced with impatience. He had just run from his third-floor apartment down the street, where he had watched the gun-toting old lady head downhill to St. Anthony's. He had waited until she was gone before coming to tell Mother Mary Dominic his story. She'd know what to do. She always did.

The door was opened by Sister Vincent. Zeb didn't like her. Sister Vincent had joined the Daughters of Elias in the palmy days when a single family owned an entire house now converted to six apartments and all the neighbors were white. Nuns were considered a spiritual luxury then, a jewel in the crown of the parish, for the Daughters of Elias were not teaching nuns. They were spiritual directors. The convent was a house of prayer for all who felt the need.

In those days, people who requested spiritual favors came laden with welcome gifts. Delicacies the nuns never purchased for themselves appeared to brighten feast days. Fine linens, warm sweaters, expensive chocolates, imported liqueurs—all were accepted gratefully, for when God moved hearts to generosity, it would be churlish not to accept with joy.

But as urban blight took over, the fine old houses with their molded ceilings and paneled rooms housed the refuse of the city. The fall from middle to lower class to racially-mixed impoverished happened in a decade. Now the only white faces to be seen were within the convent walls.

Seldom now was the plain convent fare broken with delicacies. The neighbors rarely asked for prayers.

They wanted help with landlords who shut off the heat, with children dealing drugs, with intemperate or disappearing spouses.

Sister Vincent found the change most contrary to her idea of the calling of a Daughter of Elias. Mary Dominic, on the other hand, thrived on it. She knew all the neighbors by name. They held her in reverence, not knowing how she managed to get faulty plumbing fixed and exorbitant rents reduced; where she found scholarships for students who would otherwise have to leave school. Some said when Mary Dominic spoke, the very demons of hell jumped to obey.

Zebulon looked up at the imposing height and scowling face of Sister Vincent and grimaced. "I want Sister Mary Dominic, please."

"She is busy," Sister Vincent said loftily. She considered it a scandal that Mary Dominic allowed everyone such easy access to her office.

"But we are not a cloistered community," Mary Dominic explained patiently to Vincent. "We embody the ideals of the contemplative *and* the active life. Would Our Lord have turned His back on the need of these people? He is our model. Our life has no meaning if it is not patterned on His."

Sister Vincent was silenced but not convinced. In her opinion, a reasonable community would have followed their supporters to the suburbs and not let the inner city surround them; but having made the initial mistake of staying, they might at least hold themselves separate from the riffraff around them.

"It's important," Zeb said urgently.

"I will be the judge of that." Vincent's tone was frosty. "What do you wish to tell her, young man?"

Zebulon considered. He could always scale the convent wall and hide in the garden until Mary Dominic appeared for her evening exercise. Meantime he would leave his message.

"One of the old ladies who was in here has a gun," Zebulon said. "She shot one of the sisters."

"Yes, of course she did," Vincent sniffed. "Run along now. I'll see that your message is delivered."

"Yes'm. Only when Sister Mary Dominic sees me, she gives me a chocolate chip cookie."

"Indeed." Vincent's voice conveyed her disapproval. She closed the door, her sense of righteousness strengthened. One of the retreatants shooting a nun, indeed! What a tale! Obviously the result of too much television. How people as poor as these could afford TV—and color at that—was just one indication of how wrong things were in the world.

In Vincent's day, the poor were decently humble. They didn't spend their meager resources on TV and cigarettes. Altogether, the world was far better in the old days.

Sister Vincent went back to mopping floors. She would convey Zebulon's message as she had promised, but at a suitable time—recreation, when the whole community could enjoy the tale.

Sharon felt too ill for lunch. "I think it's flu," she told Sister Angela, mistress of novices. "If I could lie down—"

"Of course," Angela, a sweet-faced, kind-tempered woman, agreed promptly. "Don't try to come to choir or evening prayer. I'll look in on you a bit later to see how you are."

Sharon thanked her. She felt very odd. She had always been strong physically. Even the flu rarely laid her low for more than a day or two. Perhaps she was coming down with one of the new strains; her legs and arms felt heavy and her head was swimming. Had Mary Dominic read her letter yet? she wondered. At any rate, the nuns wouldn't be able to put her out sick. She'd have a little longer with them, at least.

Mary Dominic remained in the chapel after Night Prayer, interceding for the well-being of the community. Tonight she was especially concerned about Sharon. Mary Dominic had doubted her fitness for the religious life from the beginning; but as the months passed, Sharon had shown an astonishing progress in prayer and understanding of what it meant to live in community. She had a sweet, complaisant nature that became more evident as the months went on, yet she was stubborn when injustice showed itself. Like Mary Dominic herself, she seemed to have a deeper appreciation of the needs of the neighborhood than some of the nuns who felt prayer was everything, older nuns with little use for the more recent thrust of the church towards social justice.

The community had voted to accept Sharon, and Mary Dominic had agreed, but she sensed difficulties ahead.

She was interrupted by Sister Angela. "Mother, please come. It's Sharon." Sister Angela was pale.

Mary Dominic rose at once and followed Angela down the long corridor to the novices' wing. It had been built for twenty girls; now there was only Sharon, and three of the older nuns, including Gabriela, who found the stairs to the upper cells difficult.

Sharon seemed to be sleeping peacefully under the single blanket on her straw mattress. On her face was a look of utter peace, as if she were experiencing a splendidly consoling dream. Her hair, not yet cropped, spread thick and dark around her, a rich halo.

"She didn't feel well at lunchtime," Angela said. "I gave her permission to rest in her cell. I looked in on her before going to bed. She doesn't seem to be breathing."

Mary Dominic laid her hand on Sharon's forehead. It was cool.

"I tried to wake her before I came to you," Angela said. Her eyes met Mary Dominic's. Death was no intruder in their lives but only the final earthly tryst of the soul with God. "Send for Dr. Richards and for Father Lowell," Mary Dominic said. "I can't understand it. Sharon seemed like such a healthy girl."

"Perhaps her heart," Sister Angela suggested. "She

seemed overcome when we told her she had been accepted. So much excitement. So much joy."

After doctor and priest fulfilled their offices, the community would gather at the bedside with lighted candles and invoke the angels to lead Sharon's soul to paradise. "Shall I call the others now?" Angela asked.

Some instinct prompted Mary Dominic to say, "Not just yet, sister. We'll wait for the doctor."

Dr. Richards was a distant cousin of Mary Dominic's, a distinguished physician with well-to-do patients. He made himself available to the nuns out of kindness and the strong sense of kinship that had always united the family. When he left Sharon's cell, his face was as gray as his hair.

"I'm afraid this is a police matter," he told his cousin. "There has to be an autopsy." And as Mary Dominic stared at him, uncomprehending, he added gently, "There's a bullet graze beneath the left ear."

"Police?" Only years of searching every event for the will of God kept Mary Dominic's voice under control. She was thinking of the nuns. Vincent would be difficult. Gabriela and some of the older nuns would be frightened into fits. "Are you saying a shot killed her? Sharon was murdered here, in a house of prayer?"

"It may have been an accident," Richards said. "One of the neighborhood kids trying target practice from the wall. Would you prefer to call the police yourself, or would you like me to do it for you?"

"You, please," Mary Dominic said. She wasn't sure she would be coherent if she phoned.

Police calls were common in the neighborhood, but never before at the convent of the Daughters of Elias. Medical examiner, photographer, technicians, investigators—a nightmare. The nuns must be questioned and the retreatants as well, according to Sergeant Mike Maguire.

"I would like to protect the community as much as

possible," Mary Dominic said in her most charming manner. "Some of the nuns are quite elderly—"

She didn't expect to be rounded on like a common criminal by that redheaded upstart of a sergeant. "I know who you are, Mary Dominic Hughes. I know your father was ambassador to France. Your uncle is a congressman. One of your brothers is married to a Hollywood superstar and one of your sisters to a European prince. None of it matters to me. I'm here to find a killer and I won't let you charm me or bribe me out of it."

Mary Dominic wasn't often taken aback, but Mike Maguire had managed it. "Surely you don't think one of us is a murderer."

"I keep an open mind until all the evidence is in," Mike said like a defiant schoolboy. "One of you may have seen or heard something we should know."

The nuns tried hard to remain serene and cooperative, but as Mary Dominic had feared, the older ones were terribly upset, and Clare Francis, the cook, asked if she might do some extra baking to calm her nerves. "I can't settle, Mother," she complained, "and I know I won't sleep. I might as well be useful."

They might have managed without difficulty if there had been only one questioning, but Mike Maguire's parting words were "I'll be back."

It was midnight when Mary Dominic climbed the staircase to her third floor cell and found Sharon's letter. Often newly accepted members found themselves overwhelmed with feelings of unworthiness, or a terrible longing to return to the world, and shared this in imprudent letters that Mary Dominic later returned after long discussions. She expected Sharon's to be of that kind and would have waited to read it until morning except for the circumstances of her death.

She read quickly. Then she folded the letter and put it back in the envelope. Mike Maguire should be told, she knew, but she didn't want him using Sharon's history to intimidate the community. Whatever the girl had been, during her months with the Daughters of Elias God had touched her heart. She had behaved well, in defiance of her past. She had been loved. Mary Dominic could imagine Mike Maguire using Sharon's history as a bludgeon to assault everything the community believed in. She was determined to prevent it. And she knew more than Mike Maguire—she knew the motive.

"It's absurd to think one of us harmed Sister Sharon," she told the community early the next day, choosing her words to jog their memories without alarming them. "It's almost as absurd to think one of our retreatants could have acted so wrongfully. But people do make enemies, and it's possible that someone who disliked Sister Sharon or bore her a grudge could have come here pretending to be a retreatant. I think it would be wise for us to consider everything that happened yesterday. If any of you recall something out of the ordinary, no matter how small or how remote it may seem, I wish to be told."

She had hardly left for her office than Sister Vincent hurried after her. "Mother," she gasped. "I forgot to give you Zebulon's message." And Vincent poured out her tale. "It sounded so farfetched, I was sure he'd seen it on television. A woman shooting one of the nuns indeed!"

A woman? From Sharon's letter, Mary Dominic would have expected a man.

And then she remembered Gabriela's shaving woman.

"Sister Vincent, ask the community to pray for a speedy conclusion to this matter," she said. "Please ask Sister Gabriela to come to my office, and tell Zebulon I'd like to see him this afternoon."

When Gabriela arrived at the office, her radiant smile once more in evidence despite the upset of having the police in and out, Mary Dominic asked, "That woman you spoke of to me yesterday, Mrs. Prestavolta. Did you see her face clearly?"

Gabriela's smile dimmed. "Oh, yes, Mother. I noticed her when she registered—such a terrible face. So empty. There was no peace in that face, Mother. No joy. And I saw her clearly while she was shaving. Her back was to me but her face was reflected in the mirror. Fortunately I was standing out of range of the mirror or she would have noticed me." Gabriela's smile faded entirely. "I felt bad that she left without wanting any spiritual direction."

"Could you draw her face, do you think?"

"Yes, of course, Mother."

"I would like you to do so. And also draw the face of our foundress from her portrait in the upper hallway. And one other, of your own choosing. Then I would like you to draw the same faces, but with men's haircuts. And then once again, with men's haircuts and beards. Could you have the drawings ready by lunchtime?"

"Yes, Mother, if I don't labor over them."

"They needn't be finished to perfection," Mary Dominic said, "as long as the features are recognizable."

Gabriela nodded and left at once to execute her task. There was something to be said for pre-Vatican II training, Mary Dominic thought. No question, no argument, no hesitation—just a simple "Yes." Gabriela probably didn't even wonder why she had been asked to make the drawings. If she did wonder, she would most likely assume it was a kind of penance for her "sin" of the day before.

Mary Dominic had the drawings when Mike Maguire showed up that afternoon. She greeted him with a beautiful smile. "Before we call the community for questioning, something has been brought to my attention that I think you should share."

"I'm not in the mood for games, sister," Mike said, glowering at her from his six foot four height. "Once upon a time I might have agreed that all nuns were angels. Now I know better. They're just people, and people are capable of surprising things."

"Once upon a time," Mary Dominic echoed softly. "Does that mean you no longer believe in God?"

Mike glared. "That has nothing to do with this investigation."

"I see." Mary Dominic made a mental note to put Mike Maguire on the prayer list. "Mr. Maguire, one of the sisters came to me with a fantastic tale. One of the neighborhood children apparently saw the shooting. He's waiting in the parlor. I haven't heard his story yet. I thought you'd like to be present." She swept out with great dignity, leaving Mike to follow.

Zebulon was waiting in a rose-colored Queen Anne chair, a platter of chocolate chip cookies and a pitcher of lemonade at his side and a beatific expression on his face. He rose when Mary Dominic entered and cast a curious look at Mike. "Is he police?" he asked Mary Dominic.

"Yes, Zebulon. This is Sergeant Mike Maguire. Sergeant, meet Zebulon, one of our friends. Now if you'll tell me what you told Sister Vincent, Zeb—"

Zebulon enjoyed telling his tale. He had seen it all; the grayhaired woman checking her surroundings, aiming and firing the gun, hiding it afterwards in her purse.

"She didn't see me. I was in a tree up high," Zeb confided. "When I saw her aim the gun, I scooted down. She saw me after she put the gun away, but I ran." He frowned. "That was a funny kind of lady."

"Most ladies don't shoot people," Mary Dominic agreed.

"Different funny," Zebulon persisted. "If I could take some of these cookies home with me, I might remember more."

"You may take all of them," Mary Dominic agreed. "What was funny about the lady?"

"The pocketbook. She held it funny. Like she wasn't used to having one."

Mike Maguire was letting Mary Dominic run the show. "Zebulon, I have some pictures here I'd like you to look at." She unfolded the three drawings of women. Gabriela had included St. Therese as her choice. Mary Dominic held back a chuckle. It was probably the first time the saint had been included in a rogues' gallery.

Zebulon stabbed Mrs. Prestavolta's picture instantly. "That's her! That's the lady with the gun."

"Thank you, Zeb. Now, Mr. Maguire, if you'd care to look at these—" and Mary Dominic showed him the men's pictures, three clean-shaven, three bearded. He passed over St. Therese and the foundress. The drawings of "Mrs. Prestavolta" held his attention.

"You know him," Mary Dominic guessed.

He looked as if he'd like to swear. Instead he said, "Everyone knows him. Frank 'Ouzo' Ferrante. A dozen aliases. Suspected of numerous crimes. I don't think we can nail him. He's slippery."

"Zebulon, please show the sergeant Mrs. Prestavolta's picture."

Zeb was pleased to do so, and even more pleased to be dismissed with the bulging bag of cookies clutched safely in his hand.

"Prestavolta-Ouzo shot Sister Sharon, it seems." Mary Dominic handed Maguire Sharon's letter. "And this explains why."

"The bullet itself didn't kill her," Mike said. "She was poisoned by it. It was treated with nicotine. A single drop of the pure stuff is lethal." He thrust his fingers through his hair, standing it up like a peacock's tail. "Where did you get the drawings?"

"Our Sister Gabriela is a talented artist. She doesn't know her Mrs. Prestavolta is a man. Perhaps now you might not need to question the whole community again today? And the retreatants might be allowed to leave?"

Mike knew when he was licked. "I'll want to see this Sister Gabriela and Sister Vincent. That should do it."

"We've been asking God to provide a speedy solution," Mary Dominic said. She had remembered Mike Maguire when he ruffled his hair. He had been an altar boy at her father's funeral twenty years before.

"In my book, a real God would blast that scum off the face of the earth," he said.

" 'Let the wheat and tares grow up together until the harvest,' " Mary Dominic reminded him, " 'lest in pulling up the tares, the young wheat come, too.' "

The second questioning went far more graciously than the first. Mike Maguire and Mary Dominic parted on sufficiently friendly terms for him to call her several weeks later.

"I guess there's some kind of justice in the world after all," he said. "Ouzo was killed in a freak accident. A bridge he was traveling on alone collapsed under him. No one else was hurt."

"Indeed," Mary Dominic murmured. Mike cleared his throat.

"I was wondering if you nuns had been praying about it."

Mary Dominic smiled. "We always pray for God's mercy," she said.

THE MAN IN THE PASSAGE

G. K. Chesterton

Two men appeared simultaneously at the two ends of a sort of passage running along the side of the Apollo Theater in the Adelphi. The evening daylight in the streets was large and luminous, opalescent and empty. The passage was comparatively long and dark, so each man could see the other as a mere black silhouette at the other end. Nevertheless, each man knew the other, even in that inky outline, for they were both men of striking appearance, and they hated each other.

The covered passage opened at one end on one of the steep streets of the Adelphi, and at the other on a terrace overlooking the sunset-colored river. One side of the passage was a blank wall, for the building it supported was an old unsuccessful theater restaurant, now shut up. The other side of the passage contained two doors, one at each end. Neither was what was commonly called the stage door; they were a sort of special and private stage doors, used by very special performers, and in this case by the star actor and actress in the Shakespearean performance of the day. Persons of that eminence often like to have such private exits and entrances, for meeting friends or avoiding them.

The two men in question were certainly two such friends, men who evidently knew the doors and counted on their opening, for each approached the door at the upper end with equal coolness and confidence. Not, however, with equal speed; but the man who walked fast was the man from the other end of the tunnel, so they both arrived before the secret stage door almost at the same instant. They saluted each other with civility, and waited a moment before one of them, the sharper walker, who seemed to have the shorter patience, knocked at the door.

In this and everything else each man was opposite and neither could be called inferior. As private persons, both were handsome, capable, and popular. As public persons, both were in the first public rank. But everything about them, from their glory to their good looks, was of a diverse and incomparable kind. Sir Wilson Seymour was the kind of man whose importance is known to everybody who knows. The more you mixed with the innermost ring in every polity or profession, the more often you met Sir Wilson Seymour. He was the one intelligent man on twenty unintelligent committees—on every sort of subject, from the reform of the Royal Academy to the project of bimetallism for Greater Britain. In the arts especially he was omnipotent. He was so unique that nobody could quite decide whether he was a great aristocrat who had taken up art, or a great artist whom the aristocrats had taken up. But you could not meet him for five minutes without realizing that you had really been ruled by him all your life.

His appearance was "distinguished" in exactly the same sense; it was at once conventional and unique. Fashion could have found no fault with his high silk hat; yet it was unlike anyone else's hat—a little higher, perhaps, and adding something to his natural height. His tall, slender figure had a slight stoop, yet it looked the reverse of feeble. His hair was silver-gray, but he did not look old; it was worn longer than the common, yet he did not look effeminate; it was curly, but it did not look curled. His carefully pointed beard made him look more manly and militant rather than otherwise, as it does in those old admirals of Velasquez with whose dark portraits his house was hung. His gray gloves were a shade bluer, his silver-knobbed cane a shade longer than scores of such gloves and canes flapped and flourished about the theaters and the restaurants.

The other man was not so tall, yet would have struck nobody as short, but merely as strong and handsome. His hair also was curly, but fair and cropped close to a strong, massive head—the sort of head you break a door with, as Chaucer said of the Miller's. His military mustache and the carriage of his shoulders showed him a soldier, but he had a pair of those peculiar, frank, and piercing blue eyes which are more common in sailors. His face was somewhat square, his jaw was square; his shoulders were square, even his jacket was square. Indeed, in the wild school of caricature then current, Mr. Max Beerbohm had represented him as a proposition in the fourth book of Euclid.

For he also was a public man, though with quite another sort of success. You did not have to be in the best society to have heard of Captain Cutler, of the siege of Hong-Kong and the great march across China. You could not get away from hearing of him wherever you were; his portrait was on every other post card; his maps and battles in every other illustrated paper; songs in his honor in every other music-hall turn or on every other barrel organ. His fame, though probably more temporary, was ten times more wide, popular, and spontaneous than the other man's. In thousands of English homes he appeared enormous above England, like Nelson. Yet he had infinitely less power in England than Sir Wilson Seymour.

The door was opened to them by an aged servant or "dresser," whose broken-down face and figure and black, shabby coat and trousers contrasted queerly with the glittering interior of the great actress's dress-

ing room. It was fitted and filled with looking glasses
at every angle of refraction, so that they looked like
the hundred facets of one huge diamond—if one could
get inside a diamond. The other features of luxury—
a few flowers, a few colored cushions, a few scraps of
stage costume—were multiplied by all the mirrors into
the madness of the Arabian Nights, and danced and
changed places perpetually as the shuffling attendant
shifted a mirror outwards or shot one back against the
wall.

They both spoke to the dingy dresser by name, calling him Parkinson, and asking for the lady as Miss
Aurora Rome. Parkinson said she was in the other
room, but he would go and tell her. A shade crossed
the brow of both visitors; for the other room was the
private room of the great actor with whom Miss Aurora was performing, and she was of the kind that
does not inflame admiration without inflaming jeal-
ousy. In about half a minute, however, the inner door
opened, and she entered as she always did, even in
private life, so that the very silence seemed to be a
roar of applause, and one well deserved. She was clad
in a somewhat strange garb of peacock green and peacock blue satins, that gleamed like blue and green
metals, such as delight children and esthetes, and her
heavy, hot brown hair framed one of those magic faces
which are dangerous to all men, but especially to boys
and to men growing gray. In company with her male
colleague, the great American actor, Isidore Bruno,
she was producing a particularly poetical and fantastic
interpretation of *Midsummer Night's Dream*, in which
the artistic prominence was given to Oberon and Tita-
nia, or in other words to Bruno and herself.

Set in dreamy and exquisite scenery, and moving
in mystical dances, the green costume, like burnished
beetle wings, expressed all the elusive individuality of
an elfin queen. But when personally confronted in
what was still broad daylight, a man looked only at
her face.

She greeted both men with the beaming and baffling

smile which kept so many males at the same just dangerous distance from her. She accepted some flowers from Cutler, which were as tropical and expensive as his victories; and another sort of present from Sir Wilson Seymour, offered later on and more nonchalantly by that gentleman. For it was against his breeding to show eagerness, and against his conventional unconventionality to give anything so obvious as flowers. He had picked up a trifle, he said, which was rather a curiosity; it was an ancient Greek dagger of the Mycenean Epoch, and might have been well worn in the time of Theseus and Hippolyta. It was made of brass like all the Heroic weapons, but, oddly enough, sharp enough to prick anyone still. He had really been attracted to it by the leaflike shape; it was as perfect as a Greek vase. If it was of any interest to Miss Rome or could come in anywhere in the play, he hoped she would—

The inner door burst open and a big figure appeared, who was more of a contrast to the explanatory Seymour than even Captain Cutler. Nearly six-foot-six, and of more than theatrical thews and muscles, Isidore Bruno, in the gorgeous leopard skin and golden-brown garments of Oberon, looked like a barbaric god. He leaned on a sort of hunting spear, which across a theater looked a slight, silvery wand, but which in the small and comparatively crowded room looked as plain as a pikestaff—and as menacing. His vivid, black eyes rolled volcanically, his bronze face, handsome as it was, showed at that moment a combination of high cheekbones with set white teeth, which recalled certain American conjectures about his origin in the Southern plantations.

"Aurora," he began, in that deep voice like a drum of passion that had moved so many audiences, "will you—"

He stopped indecisively because a sixth figure had suddenly presented itself just inside the doorway—a figure so incongruous in the scene as to be almost comic. It was a very short man in the black uniform of the Roman secular clergy, and looking (especially in such a presence as Bruno's and Aurora's) rather like the wooden Noah out of an ark. He did not, however, seem conscious of any contrast, but said with dull civility, "I believe Miss Rome sent for me."

A shrewd observer might have remarked that the emotional temperature rather rose at so unemotional an interruption. The detachment of a professional celibate seemed to reveal to the others that they stood round the woman as a ring of amorous rivals; just as a stranger coming in with frost on his coat will reveal that a room is like a furnace. The presence of the one man who did not care about her increased Miss Rome's sense that everybody else was in love with her, and each in a somewhat dangerous way: the actor with all the appetite of a savage and a spoiled child; the soldier with all the simple selfishness of a man of will rather than mind; Sir Wilson with that daily hardening concentration with which old Hedonists take to a hobby; nay, even the abject Parkinson, who had known her before her triumphs, and who followed her about the room with eyes or feet, with the dumb fascination of a dog.

A shrewd person might also have noted a yet odder thing. The man like a black wooden Noah (who was not wholly without shrewdness) noted it with a considerable but contained amusement. It was evident that the great Aurora, though by no means indifferent to the admiration of the other sex, wanted at this moment to get rid of all the men who admired her and be left alone with the man who did not—did not admire her in that sense, at least; for the little priest did admire and even enjoy the firm feminine diplomacy with which she set about her task. There was, perhaps, only one thing that Aurora Rome was clever about, and that was one half of humanity—the other half. The little priest watched, like a Napoleonic campaign, the swift precision of her policy for expelling all while banishing none. Bruno, the big actor, was so babyish that it was easy to send him off in brute sulks, banging

the door. Cutler, the British offer, was pachyderma-
tous to ideas, but punctilious about behavior. He
would ignore all hints, but he would die rather than
ignore a definite commission from a lady. As to old
Seymour he had to be treated differently; he had to
be left to the last. The only way to move him was to
appeal to him in confidence as an old friend, to let
him into the secret of the clearance. The priest did
really admire Miss Rome as she achieved all these
three objects in one selected action.

She went across to Captain Cutler and said in her
sweetest manner, "I shall value all these flowers because they must be your favorite flowers. But they
won't be complete, you know, without *my* favorite
flower. *Do* go over to that shop around the corner
and get me some lilies-of-the-valley and then it will be
quite lovely."

The first object of her diplomacy, the exit of the
enraged Bruno, was at once achieved. He had already
handed his spear in a lordly style like a scepter to the
piteous Parkinson, and was about to assume one of
the cushioned seats like a throne. But at this open
appeal to his rival there glowed in his opal eyeballs
all the sensitive insolence of the slave; he knotted his
enormous brown fists for an instant, and then, dashing
open the door, disappeared into his own apartments
beyond. But meanwhile Miss Rome's experiment in
mobilizing the British Army had not succeeded so simply as seemed probable. Cutler had indeed risen stiffly
and suddenly, and walked towards the door, hatless,
as if at a word of command. But perhaps there was
something ostentatiously elegant about the languid figure of Seymour leaning against one of the looking
glasses, that brought him up short at the entrance,
turning his head this way and that like a bewildered
bulldog.

"I must show this stupid man where to go," said
Aurora in a whisper to Seymour, and ran out to the
threshhold to speed the parting guest.

Seymour seemed to be listening, elegant and unconscious as was his posture, and he seemed relieved when he heard the lady call out some last instructions to the Captain, and then turn sharply and run laughing down the passage towards the other end, the end on the terrace above the Thames. Yet a second or two after, Seymour's brow darkened again. A man in his position has so many rivals, and he remembered that at the other end of the passage was the corresponding entrance to Bruno's private room. He did not lose his dignity; he said some civil words to Father Brown about the revival of Byzantine architecture in the Westminster Cathedral, and then, quite naturally, strolled out himself into the upper end of the passage. Father Brown and Parkinson were left alone, and they were neither of them men with a taste for superfluous conversation. The dresser went round the room, pulling out looking glasses and pushing them in again, his dingy dark coat and trousers looking all the more dismal since he was still holding the festive fairy spear of King Oberon. Every time he pulled out the frame of a new glass, a new black figure of Father Brown appeared; the absurd glass chamber was full of Father Browns, upside down in the air like angels, turning somersaults like acrobats, turning their backs to everybody like very rude persons.

Father Brown seemed quite unconscious of this cloud of witnesses, but followed Parkinson with an idly attentive eye till he took himself and his absurd spear into the farther room of Bruno. Then he abandoned himself to such abstract meditations as always amused him—calculating the angles of the mirrors, the angles of each refraction, the angle at which each must fit into the wall . . . when he heard a strong but strangled cry.

He sprang to his feet and stood rigidly listening. After the same instant Sir Wilson Seymour burst back into the room, white as ivory. "Who's that man in the passage?" he cried. "Where's that dagger of mine?"

Before Father Brown could turn in his heavy boots, Seymour was plunging about the room looking for the weapon. And before he could possibly find that weapon or any other, a brisk running of feet broke upon the pavement outside, and the square face of Cutler was thrust into the same doorway. He was still grotesquely grasping a bunch of lilies-of-the-valley. "What's this?" he cried. "What's that creature down the passage? Is this some of your tricks?"

"My tricks!" exclaimed his pale rival, and made a stride towards him.

In the instant of time in which all this happened, Father Brown stepped out into the top of the passage, looked down it, and at once walked briskly towards what he saw.

At this the other two men dropped their quarrel and darted after him, Cutler calling out, "What are you doing? Who are you?"

"My name is Brown," said the priest sadly, as he bent over something and straightened himself again. "Miss Rome sent for me, and I came as quickly as I could. I have come too late."

The three men looked down, and in one of them at least the life died in that late light of afternoon. It ran along the passage like a path of gold, and in the midst of it Aurora Rome lay lustrous in her robes of green and gold, with her dead face turned upwards. Her dress was torn away as in a struggle, leaving the right shoulder bare, but the wound from which the blood was welling was on the other side. The brass dagger lay flat and gleaming a yard or so away.

There was a blank stillness for a measurable time; so that they could hear far off a flower girl's laugh outside Charing Cross, and someone whistling furiously for a taxicab in one of the streets off the Strand. Then the Captain, with a movement so sudden that it might have been passion or play-acting, took Sir Wilson Seymour by the throat.

Seymour looked at him steadily without either fight or fear. "You need not kill me," he said, in a voice quite cold. "I shall do that on my own account."

The Captain's hand hesitated and dropped; and the

other added with the same icy candor, "If I find I haven't the nerve to do it with that dagger, I can do it in a month with drink."

"Drink isn't good enough for me," replied Cutler, "but I'll have blood for this before I die. Not yours— but I think I know whose."

And before the others could appreciate his intention he snatched up the dagger, sprang at the other door at the lower end of the passage, burst it open, bolt and all, and confronted Bruno in his dressing room. As he did so, old Parkinson tottered in his wavering way out of the door and caught sight of the corpse lying in the passage. He moved shakily towards it; looked at it weakly with a working face; then moved shakily back into the dressing room again, and sat down suddenly on one of the richly cushioned chairs. Father Brown instantly ran across to him, taking no notice of Cutler and the colossal actor, though the room already rang with their blows and they began to struggle for the dagger. Seymour, who retained some practical sense, was whistling for the police at the end of the passage.

When the police arrived it was to tear the two men from an almost apelike grapple; and, after a few formal inquiries, to arrest Isidore Bruno upon a charge of murder, brought against him by his furious opponent. The idea that the great national hero of the hour had arrested a wrongdoer with his own hand doubtless had its weight with the police, who are not without elements of the journalist. They treated Cutler with a certain solemn attention, and pointed out that he had got a slight slash on the hand. Even as Cutler bore him back across tilted chair and table, Bruno had twisted the dagger out of his grasp and disabled him just below the wrist. The injury was really slight, but till he was removed from the room the half-savage prisoner stared at the running blood with a steady smile.

"Looks a cannibal sort of chap, don't he?" said the constable confidentially to Cutler.

Cutler made no answer, but said sharply a moment after, "We must attend to the . . . the death . . ." and his voice escaped from articulation.

"The two deaths," came in the voice of the priest from the farther side of the room. "This poor fellow was gone when I got across to him." And he stood looking down at old Parkinson, who sat in a black huddle on the gorgeous chair. He also had paid his tribute, not without eloquence, to the woman who had died.

The silence was first broken by Cutler, who seemed not untouched by a rough tenderness. "I wish I was him," he said huskily. "I remember he used to watch her wherever she walked more than—anybody. She was his air, and he's dried up. He's just dead."

"We are all dead," said Seymour in a strange voice, looking down the road.

They took leave of Father Brown at the corner of the road, with some random apologies for any rudeness they might have shown. Both their faces were tragic, but also cryptic.

The mind of the little priest was always a rabbit warren of wild thoughts that jumped too quickly for him to catch them. Like the white tail of a rabbit, he had the vanishing thought that he was certain of their grief, but not so certain of their innocence.

"We had better all be going," said Seymour heavily. "We have done all we can to help."

"Will you understand my motives," asked Father Brown quietly, "if I say you have done all you can to hurt?"

They both started as if guiltily, and Cutler said sharply, "To hurt?"

"To hurt yourselves," answered the priest. "I would not add to your troubles if it weren't common justice to warn you. You've done nearly everything you could do to hang yourselves, if this actor should be acquitted. They'll be sure to subpoena me; I shall be bound to say that after the cry was heard each of you rushed into the room in a wild state and began quarreling about a dagger. As far as my words on oath can go, either of you might have done it. You hurt yourselves with that; and then Captain Cutler must hurt himself with the dagger."

"Hurt myself!" exclaimed the Captain, with contempt. "A silly little scratch."

"Which drew blood," replied the priest, nodding. "We know there's blood on the brass now. And so we shall never know whether there was blood on it before."

There was a silence; and then Seymour said, with an emphasis quite alien to his daily accent, "But I saw a man in the passage."

"I know you did," answered the cleric Brown, with a face of wood; "so did Captain Cutler. That's what seems so improbable."

Before either could make sufficient sense of it even to answer, Father Brown had politely excused himself and gone stumping up the road with his stumpy old umbrella.

As modern newspapers are conducted, the most honest and most important news is the police news. If it be true that in the twentieth century more space was given to murder than to politics, it was for the excellent reason that murder is a more serious subject. But even this would hardly explain the enormous omnipresence and widely distributed detail of "The Bruno Case," or "The Passage Mystery," in the Press of London and the provinces. So vast was the excitement that for some weeks the Press really told the truth; and the reports of examination and cross-examination, if interminable, even if intolerable, are at least reliable, coincidence of persons. The victim was a popular actress; the accused a popular actor; and the accused had been caught red-handed, as it were, by the most popular soldier of the patriotic season. In those extraordinary circumstances the Press was paralyzed into probity and accuracy; and the rest of this somewhat singular business can practically be recorded from the reports of Bruno's trial.

The trial was presided over by Mr. Justice Monk-house, one of those who are jeered at as humorous judges, but who are generally much more serious than the serious judges, for their levity comes from a living impatience of professional solemnity; while the serious judge is really filled with frivolity, because he is filled with vanity. All the chief actors being of a worldly importance, the barristers were well balanced; the prosecutor for the Crown was Sir Walter Cowdray, a heavy but weighty advocate of the sort that knows how to seem English and trustworthy, and how to be rhetorical with reluctance. The prisoner was defended by Mr. Patrick Butler, K.C., who was mistaken for a mere *flâneur* by those who misunderstand the Irish character—and those who had not been examined by him. The medical evidence involved no contradictions, said the doctor whom Seymour had summoned on the spot, agreeing with the eminent surgeon who had later examined the body. Aurora Rome had been stabbed with some sharp instrument such as a knife or dagger; some instrument, at least, of which the blade was short. The wound was just over the heart, and she had died instantly. When the first doctor saw her she could hardly have been dead for twenty minutes. Therefore, when Father Brown found her, she could hardly have been dead for three.

Some official detective evidence followed, chiefly concerned with the presence or absence of any proof of a struggle: the only suggestion of this was the tear-ing of the dress at the shoulder, and this did not seem to fit in particularly well with the direction and finality of the blow. When these details had been supplied, though not explained, the first of the important wit-nesses was called.

Sir Wilson Seymour gave evidence as he did every-thing else that he did at all—not only well, but per-fectly. Though himself much more of a public man than the judge, he conveyed exactly the fine shade of self-effacement before the King's Justice; and though everyone looked at him as they would at the Prime

Minister or the Archbishop of Canterbury, they could have said nothing of his part in it but that it was that of a private gentleman, with an accent on the noun. He was also refreshingly lucid, as he was on the committees. He had been calling on Miss Rome at the theater; he had met Captain Cutler there; they had been joined for a short time by the accused, who had then returned to his own dressing room; they had then been joined by a Roman Catholic priest, who asked for the deceased lady and said his name was Brown. Miss Rome had then gone just outside the theater to the entrance of the passage, in order to point out to Captain Cutler a flower shop at which he was to buy her some more flowers; and the witness had remained in the room, exchanging a few words with the priest. He had then distinctly heard the deceased, having sent the Captain on his errand, turn round laughing and run down the passage towards its other end, where was the prisoner's dressing room. In idle curiosity as to the rapid movements of his friends, he had strolled out to the head of the passage himself and looked down it towards the prisoner's door. Did he see anything in the passage? Yes, he saw something in the passage.

Sir Walter Cowdray allowed an impressive interval, during which the witness looked down, and for all his usual composure seemed to have more than his usual pallor. Then the barrister said in a lower voice, which seemed at once sympathetic and creepy, "Did you see it distinctly?"

Sir Wilson Seymour, however moved, had his excellent brains in full working order. "Very distinctly as regards its outline, but quite indistinctly—indeed not at all—as regards the details inside the outline. The passage is of such length that anyone in the middle of it appears quite black against the light at the other end." The witness lowered his steady eyes once more and added, "I had noticed the fact before, when Captain Cutler first entered it." There was another silence, and the judge leaned forward and made a note.

"Well," said Sir Walter patiently, "what was the outline like? Was it, for instance, like the figure of the murdered woman?"

"Not in the least," answered Seymour quietly.

"What did it look to you like?"

"It looked to me," replied the witness, "like a tall man."

Everyone in court kept his eyes riveted on his pen or his umbrella handle or his book or his boots or whatever he happened to be looking at. They seemed to be holding their eyes away from the prisoner by main force; but they felt his figure in the dock, and they felt it as gigantic. Tall as Bruno was to the eye, he seemed to swell taller and taller when all eyes had been torn away from him.

Cowdray was resuming his seat with his solemn face, smoothing his black silk robes and white silk whiskers. Sir Wilson was leaving the witness box, after a few final particulars to which there were many other witnesses, when the counsel for the defense sprang up and stopped him.

"I shall only detain you a moment," said Mr. Butler, who was a rustic-looking person with red eyebrows and an expression of partial slumber. "Will you tell his lordship how you knew it was a man?"

A faint, refined smile seemed to pass over Seymour's features. "I'm afraid it is the vulgar test of trousers," he said. "When I saw daylight between the long legs I was sure it was a man, after all."

Butler's sleepy eyes opened as suddenly as some silent explosion. "After all!" he repeated slowly. "So you did think first it was a woman?" The red brows quivered.

Seymour looked troubled for the first time. "It is hardly a point of fact," he said, "but if his lordship would like me to answer for my impression, of course I shall do so. There was something about the thing that was not exactly a woman and yet was not quite a man; somehow the curves were different. And it had something that looked like long hair."

"Thank you," said Mr. Butler, K.C., and sat down suddenly, as if he had got what he wanted.

Captain Cutler was a far less plausible and composed witness than Sir Wilson, but his account of the opening incidents was solidly the same. He described the return of Bruno to his dressing room, the dispatching of himself to buy a bunch of lilies-of-the-valley, his return to the upper end of the passage, the thing he saw in the passage, his suspicion of Seymour, and his struggle with Bruno. But he could give little artistic assistance about the black figure that he and Seymour had seen. Asked about its outline, he said he was no art critic—with a somewhat too obvious sneer at Seymour. Asked if it was a man or a woman, he said it looked more like a beast—with a too obvious snarl at the prisoner. But the man was plainly shaken with sorrow and sincere anger, and Cowdray quickly excused him from confirming facts that were already fairly clear.

The defending counsel also was again brief in his cross-examination; although (as was his custom) even in being brief, he seemed to take a long time about it. "You used a rather remarkable expression," he said, looking at Cutler sleepily. "What do you mean by saying that it looked more like a beast than a man or a woman?"

Cutler seemed seriously agitated. "Perhaps I oughtn't to have said that," he said, "but when the brute has huge humped shoulders like a chimpanzee, and bristles sticking out of its head like a pig—"

Mr. Butler cut short his curious impatience in the middle. "Never mind whether its hair was like a pig's," he said. "Was it like a woman's?"

"A woman's!" cried the soldier. "Great Scott, no!"

"The last witness said it was," commented the counsel, with unscrupulous swiftness. "And did the figure have any of those serpentine and semi-feminine curves to which eloquent allusion has been made? No? No feminine curves? The figure, if I understand you, was rather heavy and square than otherwise?"

"He may have been bending forward," said Cutler, in a hoarse and rather faint voice.

"Or again, he may not," said Mr. Butler, and sat down suddenly for the second time.

The third witness called by Sir Walter Cowdray was the little Catholic clergyman, so little compared with the others, that his head seemed hardly to come above the box, so that it was like cross-examining a child. But unfortunately Sir Walter had somehow got it into his head (mostly by some ramifications of his family's religion) that Father Brown was on the side of the prisoner, because the prisoner was wicked and foreign and even partly black. Therefore, he took Father Brown up sharply whenever that proud pontiff tried to explain anything; and told him to answer yes or no, and merely tell the plain facts. When Father Brown began, in his simplicity, to say who he thought the man in the passage was, the barrister told him that he did not want his theories.

"A black shape was seen in the passage. And you say you saw the black shape. Well, what shape was it?"

Father Brown blinked as under rebuke; but he had long known the literal nature of obedience. "The shape," he said, "was short and thick, but had two sharp, black projections curved upwards on each side of the head or top, rather like horns, and—"

"Oh, the devil with horns, no doubt," ejaculated Cowdray, sitting down in triumphant jocularity.

"No," said the priest dispassionately. "I know who it was."

Those in court had been wrought up to an irrational but real sense of some monstrosity. They had forgotten the figure in the dock and thought only of the figure in the passage. And the figure in the passage, described by three capable and respectable men who had all seen it, was a shifting nightmare: one called it a woman, and the other a beast, and the other a devil . . .

The judge was looking at Father Brown with level

and piercing eyes. "You are a most extraordinary witness," he said, "but there is something about you that makes me think you are trying to tell the truth. Well, who was the man you saw in the passage?"

"He was myself," said Father Brown.

Butler, K.C., sprang to his feet in an extraordinary stillness, and said quite calmly, "Your lordship will allow me to cross-examine?" And then, without stopping, he shot at Brown the apparently disconnected question, "You have heard about this dagger; you know the experts say the crime was committed with a short blade?"

"A short blade," assented Brown, nodding solemnly like an owl, "but a very long hilt."

Before the audience could quite dismiss the idea that the priest had really seen himself doing murder with a short dagger with a long hilt (which seemed somehow to make it more horrible), he had himself hurried on to explain.

"I mean daggers aren't the only things with short blades. Spears have short blades. And spears catch at the end of the steel just like daggers, if they're that sort of fancy spear they have in theaters; like the spear poor old Parkinson killed his wife with, just when she'd sent for me to settle their family troubles—and I came just too late, God forgive me! But he died penitent—he just died of being penitent. He couldn't bear what he'd done."

The general impression in court was that the little priest, who was gabbling away, had literally gone mad in the box. But the judge still looked at him with bright and steady eyes of interest; and the counsel for the defense went on with his questions, unperturbed.

"If Parkinson did it with that pantomime spear," asked Butler, "he must have thrust from four yards away. How do you account for signs of struggle, like the dresss dragged off the shoulder?" He had slipped into treating this mere witness as an expert; but no one noticed it now.

"The poor lady's dress was torn," said the witness,

"because it was caught in a panel that slid to just behind her. She struggled to free herself, and as she did so Parkinson came out of the prisoner's room and lunged with the spear."

"A panel?" repeated the barrister in a curious voice.

"It was a looking glass on the other side," explained Father Brown. "When I was in the dressing room I noticed that some of them could probably be slid out into the passage."

There was another vast and unnatural silence, and this time it was the judge who spoke. "So you really mean that, when you looked down that passage, the man you saw was yourself—in a mirror?"

"Yes, my lord; that was what I was trying to say," said Brown, "but they asked me for the shape; and our hats have corners just like horns, and so I—"

The judge leaned forward, his old eyes yet more brilliant, and said in specially distinct tones, "Do you really mean to say that when Sir Wilson Seymour saw that wild what-you-call-him with curves and a woman's hair and a man's trousers, what he saw was Sir Wilson Seymour?"

"Yes, my lord," said Father Brown.

"And you mean to say that when Captain Cutler saw that chimpanzee with humped shoulders and hog's bristles, he simply saw himself?"

"Yes, my lord."

The judge leaned back in his chair with a luxuriance in which it was hard to separate the cynicism and the admiration. "And can you tell us why," he asked, "you should know your own figure in a looking glass, when two such distinguished men don't?"

Father Brown blinked even more painfully than before; then he stammered, "Really, my lord, I don't know . . . unless it's because I don't look at it so often."

JUSTINA

Dorothy Salisbury Davis

Mary Ryan was certainly not homeless. She had lived in the Willoughby for forty-three years. Once it had been a residential hotel occupied mainly by show folk, people who worked in or about the theater at subsistence or slightly higher level. Recently it had been renovated into a stylish cooperative, but with a few small inside pockets, you might say, of people like Mrs. Ryan, who were allowed to remain on as renters by the grace of a qualified managerial charity: after all, what can you put in an inside pocket? Besides tax rebates.

The neighborhood—the West Forties of Manhattan—had gone, in Mrs. Ryan's time, from respectable working-class to shabby and drug-pocked misery and back again to a confusing mix of respectability, affluence, and decay. But through all the changes, the area had remained a neighborhood, with people who had lived there all their lives loyal to one another, to the shops who served them, to church and school, and who were, by and large, tolerant of the unfortunates and the degraded who came and went among them with the inevitability of time and tide.

As Mrs. Ryan got out of the elevator that January morning, she saw the nun backing off from the door-

man. Louis seemed to be trying to persuade her to go
out of the building by demonstrating how it could be
done. He would prance three or four feet ahead of
her toward the door and beckon her to follow him.
The nun would take a step away from him deeper into
the lobby.

Mrs. Ryan had seen the nun in the building before,
and she had seen her on the street, always hurrying,
always laden with nondescript bundles and shopping
bags. She was tall and lean and wore a habit such as
most orders had stepped out of years before. Nor
could Mrs. Ryan associate her garb with that of any
order in her long religious acquaintanceship. "Is there
any way I can help you, Sister?" she asked when she
came abreast of the nun and the doorman.

"Better you can help me," Louis said, pleading with
empty hands. "The super says she's not to come in,
but she is in."

"You ought to show respect, Louis. A Sister is a
Sister. You don't speak of her as *she*."

The nun gazed at Mrs. Ryan with large china-blue
eyes that were full of pleading. "Can he put me out
if I'm waiting for a friend?"

"Certainly not," Mrs. Ryan said.

Louis started to walk away in disgust and then
turned back. "Miss Brennan left the building an hour
ago in her nurse's uniform. Wouldn't you say it would
be a long wait till she comes back, Mrs. Ryan?"

"Sheila Brennan is a friend of mine," Mrs. Ryan
said. "If she said she'll be back, she'll be back. Would
you like to come up to my place for a cup of tea,
Sister? We can phone down to Louis and see if she
comes in."

"How very kind of you, Mrs. Ryan. I would love a
cup of tea." Moving with more grace than would be
thought possible in the heavy, square-toed shoes, the
nun collected two shopping bags from among the poin-
settias. Mrs. Ryan hadn't noticed them. Whether
Louis had, she couldn't know. He was standing, his

back to them, looking out onto the street and spring-
ing up and down on his toes.

In the elevator, Mrs. Ryan surveyed her guest sur-
reptitiously. She wore a full black skirt all the way to
her shoe-tops and a jacket that seemed more Chinese
than Christian. It buttoned clear up under her chin.
The crucifix she wore was an ivory figure on what
looked to be a gold or bronze cross. It put Mrs. Ryan
in mind of one she had once noticed on a black man
who, according to her friend Julie Hayes, was a pimp.
For just that instant she wondered if she had done the
right thing in inviting the nun upstairs. What reassured
her was an association from her youth in Ireland:
there was a smell to the nun only faintly unpleasant,
as of earth or the cellar, but remembered all Mrs.
Ryan's life from the Sisters to whom she had gone in
infant school. Alas, it was the smell of poverty.

Over her head of shaggy brown hair, the nun wore
a thin veil that came down to her breast. It was not
much of a veil, but there was not much breast to her,
either. She said her name was Sister Justina and her
order was the Sisters of Our Lady of Hope, of whom
there were so few left each was allowed to choose her
own ministry: most, Sister Justina said, worked among
the poor and the illiterate, and often lived with them,
as she herself did.

What Mrs. Ryan called her apartment was a single
room into which she had crammed a life, and which
she had for many years shared with a dachshund recently gone to where the good dogs go. A life-size
picture of Fritzie hung on the wall among a gallery
of actors and directors and theater entrepreneurs.
"There's not a face up there you'd recognize today,
but I knew them all," she said, coming out of the
bathroom where she'd put the kettle on to boil on the
electric plate.

The nun was gazing raptly at the faded photographs.
"Were you an actor?"

"I was an usher," Mrs. Ryan said proudly.

"Theater people are the most generous I've ever

begged from. I am a beggar, you know," Justina said
with a simplicity that touched Mrs. Ryan to the core.
There was something luminous about her. She spoke
softly, her voice throaty and low, but an educated
voice.

"The Franciscans—I always give to the Franciscans," Mrs. Ryan said. It was the only begging order
she knew.

"I feel closer to St. Francis myself than to any other
saint," Sister Justina said. "Sometimes I pray for a
mission among birds and animals, and then I'm reminded that pigeons are birds, and that rats and mice
must have come off the ark as well as the loftier crea-
tures. But I think I do my best work among the poor
who ought never to have come to the city at all. They
are the really lost ones." She was sitting at the foot
of the daybed, rubbing her hands together. The color
had risen to her cheeks.

Mrs. Ryan thought of tuberculosis. "Don't you have
a shawl, Sister?"

"I'm warm enough inside, thank you. I have so
many calls to make, would you think it ungrateful of
me to run off without waiting for tea?"

Or Sheila Brennan, Mrs. Ryan thought. But she
had grown accustomed to visitors finding her apartment both claustrophobic and too warm. "The electric
plate is terrible slow," she said, making an excuse for
her guest's departure.

"You're very kind," the nun said. Her eyes welled
up. "God bless!" She gathered a shopping bag in each
hand and want flapping down the hall like a bird that
couldn't get off the ground.

A few minutes later Mrs. Ryan was downstairs
again, about to resume her trip to the Sentinal Thrift
Shop. She lingered near the elevators until Louis went
outdoors to look for a cab for one of the tenants with
liquid assets, as Sheila Brennan liked to say of the co-
op owners. She was not in the mood for a lecture
from Louis, who couldn't stand street people, even if
they belonged to a religious order. She was almost to

the corner of Ninth Avenue when a gust of wind came up, whirling the dust before it. She turned her back, and so it was that she saw Sister Justina emerge from the service or basement entrance of the Willoughby. She clutched her veil against the wind and hurried toward Eighth Avenue, the opposite direction from Mrs. Ryan. And without her shopping bags.

Julie had the feeling that Mrs. Ryan had been waiting for her—not exactly lying in wait, but keeping an eye out for her to appear, either coming to or going from her ground-floor apartment on Forty-fourth Street. Theirs was a friendship of several years, recently broken and more recently mended. Julie still kept the tin box of dog biscuits in case the old lady appeared one day with another Fritzie in tow.

Mrs. Ryan came halloing across the street ahead of a rush of traffic. "Do you have a few minutes, Julie? There's something I need your advice on."

Julie had a few minutes. She was of the conviction that a gossip columnist hustled best who hustled least. Her visit to the rehearsal of *Uptown Downtown* could wait. She unlocked the door and led the way back into her apartment-office.

"Do you remember the day we put down the deposit here, Julie?"

Julie remembered, but it seemed a long time ago, her brief sortie into reading and advising. Sheer mischief, she'd say of it now. Now "the shop," as she'd always called it, was comfortable to live in and equipped as well with the electronics of her trade. She had learned to use the computer and rarely went near the *New York Daily* office at all.

"Friend Julie," Mrs. Ryan said, her voice lush with reminiscence. Then: "You have such good instincts about people. I want to tell you about a nun I met this morning, a beautiful person, the most spiritual eyes you ever saw." Mrs. Ryan didn't exactly proselyte, but she did propagate the faith.

"I'm not great on nuns," Julie said, and the phrase

"a nun and a neck" popped into her mind. Where it had come from she had no idea.

"They're not much different from you and me," Mrs. Ryan said.

Julie raised her eyebrows.

"Her name is Sister Justina," Mrs. Ryan said, and told the story of their encounter.

"Are you sure she's a nun?" was Julie's first question.

"I'd swear to it."

"What does Miss Brennan say about her?"

"Sheila's on the day shift this week—I wouldn't go to the hospital looking for her about this. It's the shopping bags that bother me. What did she do with them?"

"And what was in them? You've got to think about drugs, Mrs. Ryan."

"It crossed my mind, may the Lord forgive me, and I suppose, to be honest, I'd have to say that's why I've come to you."

"It would seem she wanted most to get into the Willoughby," Julie reconstructed. "She tried to make it on Miss Brennan's name and then you came along. It looks as though her purpose was to deliver the shopping bags, but without the doorman or you knowing who she was delivering them to."

Mrs. Ryan agreed reluctantly.

"How did she get past the doorman in the first place?"

"She must have slipped in the way I slipped out—when he was handing someone into a cab."

"Were the bags heavy or light?"

"They flopped along, not heavy, not light."

"And why go out the basement door? Why not sail past the doorman with her head in the air?"

"Ah, she wasn't the type. She told me right out that she was a beggar—but in the way St. Francis was a beggar."

"Funny about that cross," Julie said. "I saw Goldie

the other day. 'Miz Julie, I'm straight as a flagpole,' "
she mimicked. "He even gave me his business card."

"Was he wearing the crucifix?" Mrs. Ryan asked
disapprovingly.

Julie grinned. "I doubt it. He was wearing Brooks
Brothers." She took a mug of tea from the micro-
oven and set it before the older woman.

"Fancy," Mrs. Ryan said, "and me still using an
electric plate." The tea was "instant" and she hated
it.

Julie wondered how many like Mrs. Ryan and
Sheila Brennan were still living in the Willoughby.
"What was the name of your actor friend? Remember
he took us down to the basement that time to look
up his old notices in the trunk room?"

"Jack Carroll. He's gone now, God rest him. He
was a lovely man but a terrible bore." Mrs. Ryan
drank the tea down, trying not to taste it.

"That was one spooky place," Julie said. "Cobwebs
and leaky pipes, and the smell of mold and old clothes
when he opened the trunk."

"It's all changed down there now with the renova-
tion. The old part's been sealed off. There's brand
new washers and dryers in the new section and it's as
bright as daylight."

"She wouldn't be stealing from the dryers, would
she? To give to the poor, of course."

"She would not," Mrs. Ryan said indignantly.
Then, having to account to herself for the shopping
bags, she added, "Besides, she'd be taking a terrible
chance of being caught."

"But wouldn't that account for her going out without the bags—the fear that someone had seen her?"

"Oh, dear, I hope she doesn't come looking for me
now to let her back in," Mrs. Ryan said. "I could
be out in the cold myself. I'm on severance with the
management. They pretend not to know I cook in my
room."

"Mrs. Ryan," Julie said, "why don't you forget I
said that? It's wild. I have a wicked imagination. And

I'd stop worrying about the nun if I were you. She got into the building before you came along—she's not your responsibility."

Mrs. Ryan looked at her reproachfully. Then her face lit up. "Julie, I'd love you to meet her. I'll bring her around someday if I can get her to come and let you judge for yourself."

Sheila Brennan stuck her stockinged feet out for Mrs. Ryan to see. "Will you look at my ankles? You'd think it was the height of summer." The ankles were indeed swollen.

"It's being on them all day," Mrs. Ryan said. "Put them up on the couch while I pour the tea."

Sheila was younger than Mrs. Ryan, a plain, solid woman who dreaded the day of her retirement from St. Jude's Hospital. "The first I saw of Sister Justina was when she visited someone brought into the hospital with frostbite during that bad spell in December. You know the woman who tries to sell yesterday's newspapers on the corner of Fifty-first Street? The police brought her in half frozen. I told the nun that if she'd come to the Willoughby when I got off duty, and if she could promise me the woman would wear it, I'd give her a fisherman's shirt my brother brought me from Donegal. It was foolish of me to put a condition to it and what she said made me ashamed of myself. 'If she doesn't wear it, I will,' she said. I've been asking around of this one and that one to give her their castoffs ever since."

"So she's on the up and up," Mrs. Ryan said and put the teacup and saucer in her friend's hand. "But what was she doing in the Willoughby basement?"

"God knows, Mary. She may just have pushed the wrong elevator-button and wound up there."

Julie and her imagination, Mrs. Ryan thought.

Sheila Brennan's explanation satisfied Mrs. Ryan because she wanted to be satisfied with it. And she did believe the nun to be a true sister to the poor.

She saw her again later that week. Mrs. Ryan was herself in the habit now of taking her principal meal at the Seniors Center in St. Malachy's basement, where she got wholesome food in a cheerful environment at a price she could afford. Afterward, that afternoon, she went upstairs to the Actors Chapel and there she encountered Sister Justina kneeling in a back pew, her shopping bags at her sides.

"Sister—" Mrs. Ryan whispered hoarsely.

The nun jumped as though startled out of deep meditation and upset one of the shopping bags. Out tumbled a variety of empty plastic cups.

Mrs. Ryan went into the pew and helped her collect them, saying how sorry she was to have startled her. The containers, she noted, were reasonably clean, but certainly not new. "All I wanted to say," she explained, "is that I have a friend who would like to meet you. Her name is Julie Hayes. She's a newspaper columnist. She writes about all kinds of people, and she's very good to the needy."

"I've heard of her," the nun said without enthusiasm.

Mrs. Ryan realized she had taken the wrong tack. "Do you mind coming out to the vestibule for a minute? I can't get used to talking in church."

In the vestibule, she modified her description of Julie. "It's true that she helps people. She's even helped the police now and then. I know of at least two murders she's helped them solve. It would take me all day to tell you about her. But, Sister, she's as needy in her way as you are in yours. You both have a great deal to give, but what would you do if you didn't have takers?"

The nun laughed and then clutched at her throat to stop the cough the laugh had started. "Someday," she said when she could get her breath.

"Someday soon," Mrs. Ryan said. "She lives a few doors from the Actors Forum. You know where that is. I helped her find the place. In those days she called herself Friend Julie."

"Friend Julie," the nun repeated with a kind of recognition. **Then:** "I must hurry, Mrs. Ryan. They throw **out the** food if I don't get there in time." She ran down the steps with her bags of containers to collect the leftovers from the Seniors' midday meal.

"Nowadays it's just plain Julie Hayes," Mrs. Ryan called after her.

Julie never doubted that Mrs. Ryan would arrive one day with the nun by the hand, but what she hadn't expected was the nun's arrival alone. She didn't like unannounced visitors, but the ring of the doorbell was urgent and came with a clatter she presently attributed to the nun's use of the cross as a knocker. In fact, it was by the cross—an ivory figure on gold—that she recognized her as Mrs. Ryan's friend. She took off the safety latch and opened the door.

"Friend Julie, I need your help."

"Has something happened to Mrs. Ryan?"

"No," the nun said. "Please?"

Julie relocked the door after the nun and led the way through the apartment. She was trying to remember the nun's name.

"Mrs. Ryan has nothing to do with this, I give my word," the nun said. "She said you wanted to meet me, but that's not why I'm here. I'm Sister Justina."

Julie motioned her into a chair and seated herself across the coffee table from her. She didn't say anything. She just waited for the pitch. It was those big blue eyes, she thought, that had got to Mrs. Ryan.

"All I need to tell you about my mission, I think, is that I try to find temporary shelter for street people who are afraid of institutional places. It's a small person-to-person endeavor, but I've had very good luck until now. I've been keeping two people hidden away at night and in bad weather in an abandoned section of the Willoughby basement."

"You're kidding," Julie said.

"I wish I were." The nun thrust her clasped hands between her knees. "I went to leave them a meal this afternoon." She took a deep breath. "One man was gone and the other one was dead. His skull was smashed in!" Her amazing eyes were filling.

"You're lucky it wasn't you, Sister."

"I don't consider myself lucky."

"Have you gone to the police?"

Justina shook her head. "That's why I came to you. Mrs. Ryan said you've helped the police—"

"Let's forget what Mrs. Ryan says. *You* have to go to the police. You can't just close up that part of the basement again on a dead man as though it was a tomb."

"I don't want to do that. I only wish I could have got poor Tim out of the city in time. He wanted to go, but he was afraid." She looked at Julie pleadingly. "I want to do what I have to do, but I can't."

"I'll go with you if that will help," Julie offered.

"Would you go *for* me?"

"No. If you don't show up and take the responsibility for trespassing or whatever it was, Mrs. Ryan and Miss Brennan could be evicted, and where would they find a place to live?"

Justina shook her head. "Nothing like this has ever happened to me."

"I'll say it again, then: you're lucky."

"Yes, I suppose I am," the nun said with what sounded like heavy irony. "The habit I wear has been my salvation, my hope in life." She drew a long shuddering breath. "Julie, I'm a man."

For a while Julie said nothing. She was remembering where the phrase "a nun and a neck" had come from—the poet Rilke commenting on one of Picasso's acrobats: "The son of a nun and a neck."

"You can use the phone there on my desk if you want to, Sister," she said.

"Thank you," Justina said. She got up. "Who do I call?"

"Try nine-one-one," Julie said.

The nun identified herself to the police dispatcher as Sister Justina, told of a body in the basement of the Willoughby Apartments, and promised to wait herself at the service entrance to the building. She gave them the address.

When Mrs. Ryan dropped in at Billy McGowan's pub for her afternoon glass of lager, Detective Dom Russo was telling of the down-and-outer his detail had taken into custody that afternoon for trying to pass a kinky hundred-dollar bill. Nobody had seen its like since before World War Two. Billy had the first dollar he made in America framed and hung above the bar. He pointed it out to the custom.

"They don't make 'em like that any more," the detective said, wanting to get on with his story. "This gingo claimed first off that he found it, just picked it up off the street. We turned him loose and put a tail on him. You know where the old railroad tracks used to run under Forty-fourth Street? He made a beeline for a hole in the fence, slid down the embankment, and led us straight to where he'd hidden three plastic containers in an old burnt-out stove. I don't need to tell you—the containers were stuffed with all this old-fashioned money."

Someone down the bar wisecracked that that was the best kind. But at the mention of plastic containers, Mrs. Ryan could not swallow her beer.

"We took him in again. This time around, he said he found the money right there in the oven of this old stove. He intended to turn it over to the police, of course," Russo repeated sarcastically, "only first he wanted to look more respectable and went to a thrift shop with one of the C-notes—a silver certificate, they used to call them."

"He should have gone right to the bank," someone else down the bar said. "They'd trade it in—dollar for dollar."

"No questions asked?" someone wanted to know.

"He should have gone to a collector and made himself some real money," Billy said.

"Look," Russo told them, "you're acting like this guy was kosher. Maybe the *money's* kosher, but he's not. I don't believe for a minute he lucked into all that old cash. Anyway, we'll hold him till we hear from the Feds."

"A developing story, as they say." McGowan moved down the bar to Mrs. Ryan. "Drink up, Mary, and I'll put a head on it for you."

"I'll take a rain check, Billy," she told him. "I've got terrible heartburn." She eased herself off the stool, and by ancient habit looked under it, half expecting Fritzie to be curled up there. Out on the street, she drew several deep breaths of the wintry air. Plastic cups, she told herself, weren't such a rare commodity.

It was almost dark and there were misty halos around the streetlights—and when she turned the corner she could see rainbows of revolving color: police activity outside the Willoughby. She approached near enough to see that the action was concentrated around the basement entrance, whereupon she reversed herself and headed for Julie's as fast as her legs would carry her.

Julie was short on patience at the arrival of Mrs. Ryan. For one thing, she was uneasy about not having followed up on the nun's story. After all, she was in the newspaper business. She ought at least to have called the city desk on a breaking story. Or covered it herself. But she had wanted to give Justina a chance to confront the police on her own. She certainly didn't want to be the person to blow her cover.

When Mrs. Ryan finished giving out her jigsaw of a tale, Julie asked her if she'd seen Sister Justina after they'd met at St. Malachy's.

"I haven't."

"Well, she's been here this afternoon, Mrs. Ryan. The police are at the Willoughby to investigate a murder that took place there in the basement. It's highly possible they'll connect it with your man with the money in the plastic cups."

"Holy Mother of God," Mrs. Ryan said.

"And they'll be looking for witnesses, for accessories."

"Sister Justina?"

"And *her* accessories," Julie said. "Your doorman isn't about to take credit for letting her into the building, is he?"

Mrs. Ryan sat a long while in silence. "Would you mind walking me home, dear? My legs are so weak I'm not sure they'll carry me."

Julie pulled on her coat, put the phone on "Service," and fastened her press card onto the inside flap of her shoulderbag.

Mrs. Ryan got weaker and weaker on the way. She suggested they stop for a brief rest at McGowan's, but Julie put a firm hand beneath the older woman's elbow and propelled her homeward.

By then word of police activity at the Willoughby had reached McGowan's and most of the patrons were there to see what was going on. Julie spotted Detective Russo as he came out of the building on the run. She planted Mrs. Ryan among her McGowan's cronies at the barricade and caught up with him as he was climbing into the back of a squad car.

"Okay if I come along?" she asked, halfway into the car behind him. They were on pretty good terms, considering that they weren't always on the same side.

"Why not?" he said ironically.

By the time they reached the precinct house, she knew how the victim and his assailant had got into that part of the Willoughby. The Environmental Protection Department had ordered a removal of old sewage pipes and part of the wall had been removed, a temporary partition put up in its place. "Like everything else in this town," Russo said, "they get the job half done and move on to the next one."

No mention of the nun. "How did they get into the building in the first place, Dom?" Julie asked.

"How the hell do I know? Somebody must've left the door open. And no wonder. It stinks to high heaven down back where they were. They buried their own shit like animals. That's how they found the body—and the tin box with the money in it."

"The money in the plastic cups you found earlier this afternoon. Do you think there's a connection?"

"You better believe it," Russo said. "The victim had one clutched in his hand when he was clobbered with the tin box."

"How did you know to go to the Willoughby in the first place?"

"We had a phone call," Russo said. "But the complainant didn't show. We'd begun to think it was a hoax—but the smell led us to him. A whole section of the wall—we just leaned on it and Jericho!"

"Jericho," Julie said. "That's nice."

So Justina had vanished. No problem: just get out of the habit and grow a beard. Until now she had carried Justina's confession of identity as a confidence, as though it had been told under a seal. It hadn't, of course, but since Detective Russo and company had the suspect in custody and enough evidence to detain him for a while, she decided to keep the matter on hold.

Mrs. Ryan and Sheila Brennan were waiting for Julie when she arrived at Mrs. Ryan's apartment. They seemed less chastened than she thought they ought to be, but there hadn't yet been time for the police to get to them.

"We're expecting them any minute," Mrs. Ryan said. "And we've decided to tell them the truth about Sister."

"And that is?"

"How she got into the building in the first place. How she used us."

Julie felt she was being used herself—that this was a dress rehearsal. "Okay."

"But she would have used anybody to help those she thought needed help." Mrs. Ryan drew a deep breath. "Julie, who would you say all that money belongs to?"

"I wouldn't say." But she was beginning to see a light.

"Sheila and I have a story to tell you. Remember you mentioned Jack Carroll the other day, and his trunk in the basement? Jack lived here for years before Sheila and I ever heard of the Willoughby and he loved to tell stories of the old days—the circus people, the vaudevillians, and the chorus girls. One of his best stories, and God knows he practiced to make it perfect, was about Big Frankie Malloy. When Frankie moved in, the management renovated a whole suite for him. He had tons of money. He had his own barber sent in every day to shave him, he had his meals catered, he was always sending out for this or that, he was a lavish tipper. And the girls, there were plenty of them. But there was something wrong about big Frankie. After he moved in, he never went outdoors again—except once.

"Madge Delaney was his favorite of the girls, and she got booked into the Blue Diamond nightclub just down the street. Frankie went out the night she opened. It was said afterward that the only reason she got the booking was to lure him out. He was shot dead before he ever got to the Blue Diamond."

"Wow," Julie said.

"Don't you think it could be his money that's been hidden away all these years?"

"It's a real possibility," Julie agreed.

"You see why I asked you who it belongs to now."

"I do see," Julie assured her.

Julie's story made page 3 of the bulldog edition of the *New York Daily* and the police, discovering there was no such religious order as the Sisters of Our Lady of Hope, put out an alert for Sister Justina. The Willoughby claimed all of that very old money. It also threatened to sue the contractor whose procrastination made that part of the basement available to Sister Justina and her friends.

Mrs. Ryan's faith in the nun remained steadfast: she

might herself have got the name of the order wrong. Julie thought about looking up Goldie, the reformed pimp, to ask him what became of the gold-and-ivory cross he used to wear. But she decided not to. It was one more thing she didn't have to know.

IN THE CONFESSIONAL

Alice Scanlan Reach

Blue slipped in through the side door of St. Brigid's and stood motionless in the shadow of the Confessional. Opposite him loomed the statue of the Blessed Virgin treading gently on a rising bank of vigil lights. Blue's eyes, darting to the ruby fingers of flame flickering around the marble feet, saw that the metal box nearby with the sign *Candles—10¢* had not yet been replenished. Only a few wax molds remained. Had the box been full, Blue would have known he was too late—that Father Crumlish, on depositing a fresh supply, had opened the drawer attached to the candle container and emptied it of the past week's silver offerings.

So all was well! Once again, all unknowingly, the House of God would furnish Blue with the price of a jug of wine.

Now, from his position in the shadow, Blue's red-rimmed eyes shifted to the altar where Father Crumlish had just turned the lock in the Sacristy door, signaling the start of his nightly nine-o'clock lock-up routine.

Blue knew it by heart.

First, the closing and locking of the weather-weary stained glass windows. Next, the bolting of the heavy oaken doors in the rear of the church. Then came the dreaded moment. Tonight, as every night, listening to Father Crumlish make fast the last window and then approach the Confessional, Blue fought the panic pushing against his lungs—the fear that the priest would give the musty interior of the Confessional more than a quick, casual glance.

Suppose tonight it occurred to Father Crumlish to peer into the Confessional's shadow to see if someone were lurking—

Blue permitted himself a soft sigh of blessed relief. He was safe! The slow footsteps were retreating up the aisle. To be sure, there were torturing hours ahead, but that was the price he had to pay. Already he could almost feel his arms cradling the beloved bottle, his fingers caressing the gracefully curved neck. He could almost taste the soothing, healing sweetness . . .

It was almost too much to bear.

Now came what Blue, chuckling to himself, called "the floor show."

Extinguishing the lights in the rear of the church and thus leaving it, except for candlelight, in total darkness, Father Crumlish, limping a little from the arthritis buried deep in his ancient roots, climbed the narrow, winding stairway to the choir loft.

Blue, hearing the first creaking stair, moved noiselessly and swiftly. In the space of one deep breath he flickered out of the shadow, entered the nearest "sinners' " door of the Confessional, and silently closed it behind him. Then he knelt in cramped darkness, seeing nothing before him but the small closed window separating him from the Confessor's sanctuary.

By now Father Crumlish had reached the choir loft and the "show" began. Believing himself alone with his God and Maker, the descendant of a long line of shillelagh wielders ran his arthritic fingers over the organ's keys and poured out his soul in song. Presently the church rafters rang with his versions of *When Irish*

Eyes Are Smilin', Come Back To Erin, and *The Rose of Tralee.*

It was very pleasant and Blue didn't mind too much that his knee joints ached painfully from their forced kneeling position. As a matter of fact, he rather enjoyed this interlude in the evening's adventure. It gave him time to think, a process which usually eluded him in the shadowy, unreal world where he existed. And what better place to think than this very church where he had served as an altar boy forty—fifty?—how many years ago?

That was another reason he never had the slightest qualm about filching the price of a bottle from the Blessed Virgin's vigil-light offering box. "Borrowing," Blue called it. And who had a better right? Hadn't he dropped his nickels and dimes in the collection basket every Sunday and Holyday of Obligation from the time he was a tot until—?

The Blessed Virgin and Father Crumlish and the parishioners of St. Brigid's were never going to miss a few measly dimes. Besides, he was only "borrowing" until something turned up. And some day, wait and see, he'd walk down the center aisle of the church, dressed fit to kill, proud as a peacock, and put a $100 bill in the basket for the whole church to see just as easy as you please!

A small smile brushed against Blue's thin lips, struggled to reach the dull sunken eyes, gave up in despair, and disappeared. Blue dozed a little.

He might more appropriately have been called Gray. For there was a bleak grayness about him that bore the stamp of fog and dust, of the gray pinched mask of death and destruction. His withered bones seemed to be shoved indifferently into threadbare coat and trousers; and from a disjointed blob of cap a few sad straggles of hair hung listlessly about his destroyed face. Time had long ceased to mean anything to Blue—and he to Time.

All that mattered now was the warm, lovely, loving liquid and the occasional bite of biscuit to wash it down. And thanks to St. Brigid's parishioners, thanks to his knowledge of Father Crumlish's unfailing nightly routine, Blue didn't have to worry about where the next bottle was coming from. The job was easy. And afterward he could doze in peace in the last pew of the church until it came time to mingle with the faithful, as they arrived for six o'clock morning mass, and then easily slip unnoticed out the door.

Now, kneeling in the confines of the Confessional, Blue jerked his head up from his wasted chest and stiffened. Sudden silence roared in his ears. For some unseen reason Father Crumlish had broken off in the middle of the third bar of *Tralee*.

Then, in the deathly pale quiet, the priest's voice rang out.

"Who's there?"

Sweet Jesus! thought Blue. Did I snore?

"Answer me!" More insistent now. "Who's there?"

Blue, his hand on the Confessional doorknob, had all but risen when the answer came.

"It's me, Father . . . Johnny Sheehan."

Sinking back to his knees, Blue could hear every word in the choir loft, clear as a bell, resounding in the shuttered, hollow church.

"What's on your mind, Johnny?"

Blue caught the small note of irritation in the priest's voice and knew it was because Father Crumlish treasured his few unguarded moments with *The Rose of Tralee*.

"I—I want to go to Confession, Father."

A long pause and then Blue could almost hear the sigh of resignation to Duty and to God's Will.

"Then come along, lad."

Now how do you like that for all the lousy luck, Blue thought, exasperated. Some young punk can't sleep in his nice warm beddy-bye until he confesses—

Confesses!

Blue felt the ice in his veins jam up against his heart. Father Crumlish would most certainly bring the repentant sinner to *this* Confessional since it was next to the side-door entrance. Even now Blue could hear the oncoming footsteps. Suppose he opens *my* door instead of the other one? Dear God, please let him open the first door!

Trembling, Blue all but collapsed with relief as he heard the other door open and close, heard the settling of knees on the bench, and lastly, the faint whisper of cloth as Father Crumlish entered the priests' enclosure that separated himself from Blue on one side and from Johnny Sheehan on the other by thin screened windows of wood.

Now Blue heard the far window slide back and knew that Johnny Sheehan was bowing his head to the screen, fixing his eyes on the crucifix clasped in the Confessor's hands.

"Bless me, Father, for I have sinned . . ."

The voice pulled taut, strained, and snapped.

"Don't be afraid to tell God, son. You know about the Seal of Confession—anything you tell here you confess to God and it remains sealed with Him forever."

Confess you stole a bunch of sugar beets and get it over with, Blue thought angrily. He was getting terribly tired and the pain in his knees was almost more than he could bear.

"I . . . she . . ."

She! Well, what do you know? Blue blinked his watery eyes in a small show of surprise. So the young buck's got a girl in trouble. Serves him right. Stick to the warmer embrace of the bottle, my lad. It'll keep you out of mischief.

"I heard your first confession when you were seven, Johnny. How old are you now? Sixteen?"

"Y-yes, Father."

"This girl. What about her?"

"I—I killed her!"

In the rigid silence Blue heard the boy's body sag against the wooden partition and was conscious of a sharp intake of breath from the priest. Blue was as alert now as he ever was these soft, slow days and nights, but he knew that sometimes he just thought he heard words when actually he'd only dreamed them. Yet . . . Blue eased one hurting kneecap and leaned closer to the dividing wood.

Father Crumlish shifted his weight in his enclosure. "Killed?"

Only retching sobs.

"Tell me, Johnny." Father Crumlish's voice was ever so gentle now.

Then the words came in a torrent.

"She laughed at me . . . said I wasn't a man . . . and I couldn't stand it, Father. When Vera May laughed . . ."

"Vera May!" the priest broke in. "Vera May Barton?"

Even in the shifting mists and fog of his tired memory, Blue recognized that name. Who didn't these past few weeks? Who didn't know that every cop in the city was hunting Vera May Barton's murderer? Why, even some of Blue's best pals had been questioned. Always ready to hang a rap on some poor innocent.

Blue rarely read newspapers, but he listened to lots of talk. And most of the talk in the wine-shrouded gloom of his haunts these past weeks had been about the slaying of 16-year-old Vera May Barton, a choir singer at St. Brigid's. Someone had shown Blue her picture on the front page of a newspaper. A beautiful girl, blonde and soft and smiling. But someone, someone with frantic, desperate hands, had strangled the blonde softness and choked off the smile.

Blue was suddenly conscious once more of the jagged voice.

"She wasn't really like they say, Father. Vera May wasn't really good! She just wanted you to think so. But sometimes, when I'd deliver my newspapers in the morning, sometimes she'd come to the door with hardly any clothes . . . And when I'd ask her to go to a show or something, she'd only laugh and say I wasn't a man . . ."

"Go on," Father Crumlish said softly.

"I—she told me she was staying after choir practice that night to collect the hymnals—"

The priest sighed. "I blame myself for that. For letting her stay in the church alone—even for those few moments—while I went over to the rectory."

"And then—then when she left," the halting words went on, "I followed her out in the alley . . ."

Blue's pals had told him about that—how one of St. Brigid's early morning mass parishioners found Vera May lying like a broken figurine in the dim alley leading from the church to the rectory. She wasn't carrying a purse, the newspapers said. And she hadn't been molested. But her strangler, tearing at her throat, had broken the thin chain of the St. Christopher's medal around her neck. It had her initials on the back but the medal had never been found.

"What did you do with the medal, Johnny?" Father Crumlish asked quietly.

"I—I was afraid to keep it, Father." The agonized voice broke again. "The river . . ."

The weight of the night pressed heavily on Blue and he sighed deeply. But the sigh was lost in the low murmuring of the priest to the boy—too low for Blue to catch the words—and perhaps, against all his instincts, he dozed. Then there was a sudden stirring in the adjoining cubicles. Blue knelt rigid and breathless while the doors opened, and without turning his head toward the faint candlelight shimmering through the cracks in the door of his enclosure, he knew that Father Crumlish had opened the side entrance and released Johnny Sheehan to the gaunt and starless dark.

Slowly the priest moved toward the first pew before the center altar. And now Blue risked glancing through the sliver of light in his door. Father Crumlish knelt, face buried in his hands . . .

A wisp of thought drifted into the wine-eroded soil of Blue's mind. Was the priest weeping?

But Blue was too engrossed in his own discomfort, too aware of the aching, ever-increasing, burning dryness of his breath and bones. If only the priest would go and leave Blue to his business and his sleep!

After a long time he heard the footsteps move toward the side door. Now it closed. Now the key turned in the lock . . .

Now!

Blue stumbled from the Confessional and collapsed in the nearest pew. Stretched full length, he let his weary body and mind sag in relief. Perhaps he slept; he only knew that he returned, as if from a long journey. Sitting upright, he brought out the tools of his trade from somewhere within the tired wrappings that held him together.

First the chewing gum—two sticks, purchased tonight.

Blue munched them slowly, carefully bringing them to the proper consistency. Then, rising, he fingered a small length of wire, and leaving the pew, shuffled toward the offering box beneath the Blessed Virgin's troubled feet.

Taking the moist gum from his mouth, Blue attached it to the wire and inserted it carefully into the slot of the box. A gentle twist and he extracted the wire. Clinging to the gummed end were two coins, a nickel and a dime.

Blue went through this procedure again and again until he had collected the price of a bottle. Then he lowered himself into the nearest pew and rested a bit. He began to think of what had happened in the Confessional. But it had been so long since Blue had made himself concentrate on anything but his constant, thirsting need that it took a while for the rusted wheels to move, for the pretty colored lights to cease their small whirlings and form a single brightness illuminating the makings of his mind.

Finally he gave up. The burning dryness had gripped him again and he began to yearn for the long night to be over so that he could spend, in the best way he knew, the money he held right in his hand this minute.

Two bottles! I should have two bottles for all the trouble I've been through tonight, Blue thought. They owe it to me for making me kneel there so long and robbing me of my sleep. Yes, they owe it to me! And so thinking, he took out the gum once more from some secret fold, and bringing it to his mouth, chewed it again into pliable moistness.

The first try at the offering box brought him only a dime, but the second try—God was good—another dime, a nickel, and a dollar bill!

Too exhausted to drag himself to his customary last-pew bed, Blue stretched out once more on the nearest wood plank and slept.

Some time later, the unrelenting dryness wakened him. This "in-between" period was the only time Blue ever approached sobriety. And in the sobering, everything seemed terribly, painfully clear. He began to relive the events of the night, hearing the voices again with frightening clarity. Father Crumlish's and then the kid's . . .

Blue's own voice screamed in his ears.

"Out! I've got to get out of here! Nobody knows but me . . . nobody knows about the murder but me. I've got to tell . . . But first I'll have to have a little sip. I need a little sip. And then I'll tell . . ."

In a flurry of cloth and dust Blue rushed to the side door. He had never before tried to let himself out this way and had no idea if the door was locked. But the knob gave easily, and in an instant he had closed the door behind him and leaning heavily against it, was breathing the night's whispering wind.

It had been a long time since Blue had been out alone in the deep dark and suddenly, with the night's dreadful knowledge inside him, it was overpowering. Shadows rushed at him, clawed at his face and fingers, and crushed him so bindingly that he could scarcely breathe.

In an agony to get away, he plunged into the blackness and began to run.

And in his urgency Blue never heard the shout behind him, the pounding feet on the pavement. He never heard the cry to halt or risk a bullet. He only knew that he was flying, faster and faster, yet not fast enough, soaring higher and higher, until a surprisingly small, jagged thrust of sidewalk clawed at him and brought him to his knees. The bullet from his pursuer, meant to pierce his worn and weary legs, pierced his back.

Suddenly it was calm and quiet and there was no longer any need for speed. He lay on his side, crumpled and useless, like a discarded bundle of rags. A wave, a wine-red wave, swept over him and Blue let himself rock and toss for a moment in its comforting warmth. Then he opened his eyes and, dimly, in the fast-gathering darkness, recognized Father Crumlish bending over him.

"Poor devil," Blue heard the priest say. "But don't blame yourself, Officer. The fellow probably just didn't know that you'd be suspicious of his running away like that. Particularly around here—now—after the Barton girl. The poor devil probably just didn't know."

Didn't know? Blue didn't know? He knew, all right! And he had to tell.

"Father!"

Quickly the priest bent his ear to Blue's quivering lips.

"I . . . was in the Confessional too."

"The Confessional?"

The wave rushed to envelop him again. Before he could speak the urgent words he heard the officer's voice.

"He came out of the church door, Father. I saw him."

"I don't see how that's possible," the priest said bewilderedly.

Blue forced the breath from his aching lungs.

"I heard . . . the kid confess . . . I have to tell . . ."

"Wait!" Father Crumlish said sharply, cutting Blue off. "You have nothing to tell. Maybe you heard. But you don't know about that boy. The poor confused lad's come to me to confess to every robbery and murder in this parish for years. You have nothing to tell, do you hear me?"

"Nothing?"

Blue almost laughed a little. For the pain was gone now and he felt as if—as if he were walking down St. Brigid's center aisle, dressed fit to kill, proud as a peacock, and putting a $100 bill in the collection basket for the whole church to see just as easy as you please.

"There's something . . ."

His voice was strong and clear as he brought his fumbling fingers from within the moldy rags and stretched out his hand to the priest.

"I was 'borrowing' from the Blessed Virgin, Father. Just enough for a bottle, though. I need it, Father. All the time. Bad! . . . She caught me at it. And she was running to tell you. But if she did, where in the world would I ever get another bottle, Father? Where? . . . So I had to stop her!"

Fighting the final warm, wine-red wave that was washing over him, Blue thrust into Father Crumlish's hand a St. Christopher's medal dangling from a broken chain and initialed V.M.B.

"I've been saving it, Father. In a pinch, I thought it might be worth a bottle . . ."

RUMPOLE AND THE MAN OF GOD

John Mortimer

As I take up my pen during a brief and unfortunate lull in Crime (taking their cue from the car-workers, the villains of this city appear to have downed tools, causing a regrettable series of layoffs, redundancies, and slow-time workings down the Old Bailey), I wonder which of my most recent Trials to chronicle.

Sitting in Chambers on a quiet Sunday morning (I never write these memories at home for fear that She Who Must Be Obeyed, my wife Hilda, should glance over my shoulder and take exception to the manner in which I have felt it right, in the strict interests of truth and accuracy, to describe domestic life *à côté de* Chez Rumpole); seated, as I say, in my Chambers I thought of going to the archives and consulting the mementoes of some of my more notorious victories.

However, when I opened the cupboard it was bare, and I remembered that it was during my defense of a South London clergyman on a shoplifting rap that I had felt bound to expunge all traces of my past and destroy my souvenirs. It is the curse, as well as the fascination of the law, that lawyers get to know more than is good for them about their fellow human beings, and this truth was driven home to me during the time that I was engaged in the affair that I have called "Rumpole and the Man of God."

When I was called to the Bar, too long ago now for me to remember with any degree of comfort, I may have had high-flown ideas of a general practice of a more or less lush variety, divorcing duchesses, defending stars of stage and screen from imputations of unchastity, getting shipping companies out of scrapes. But I soon found that it's crime which not only pays moderately well, but which is also by far the greatest fun. Give me a murder on a spring morning with a decent run and a tolerably sympathetic jury, and Rumpole's happiness is complete.

Like most decent advocates, I have no great taste for the law; but I flatter myself I can cross-examine a copper on his notebook, or charm the Uxbridge Magistrates off their Bench, or have the old darling sitting number four in the jury-box sighing with pity for an embezzler with two wives and six starving children. I am also, and I say it with absolutely no desire to boast, about the best man in the Temple on the subject of bloodstains. There is really nothing you can tell Rumpole about blood, particularly when it's out of the body and onto the clothing in the forensic laboratory.

The old Head of my Chambers, C. H. Wystan, now deceased (also known reluctantly to me as "Daddy," being the father of Hilda Wystan, whom I married after an absent-minded proposal at an Inns of Court Ball. Hilda now rules the Rumpole household and rejoices in the dread title of She Who Must Be Obeyed), old C. H. Wystan simply couldn't stand bloodstains. He even felt queasy looking at the photographs, so I started by helping him out with his criminal work and soon won my spurs round the London Sessions, Bow Street, and the Old Bailey.

By the time I was called on to defend this particular cleric, I was so well known in the Ludgate Circus Palais de Justice that many people, to my certain knowledge, called Horace Rumpole an Old Bailey Hack. I am now famous for chain-smoking small cigars, and for the resulting avalanche of ash which falls down the waistcoat and smothers the watch chain, for my habit of frequently quoting from the *Oxford Book of English Verse*, and for my fearlessness in front of the more savage type of Circuit Judge (I fix the old darlings with my glittering eye and whisper "Down Fido" when they grow overexcited).

Picture me then in my late sixties, well nourished on a diet consisting largely of pub lunches, steak-and-kidney pud, and the cooking claret from Pommeroy's Wine Bar in Fleet Street, which keeps me astonishingly regular. My reputation stands very high in the remand wing of Brixton nick, where many of my regular clients, fraudsmen, café-blowers, breakers-in, and carriers of offensive weapons smile with everlasting hope when their solicitors breathe the magic words, "We're taking in Horace Rumpole."

I remember walking through the Temple Gardens to my Chambers one late-September morning, with the pale sun on the roses and the first golden leaves floating down on the young solicitors' clerks and their girl friends, and I was in a moderately expansive mood. Morning was at seven, or rather around 9:45, the hillside was undoubtedly dew-pearled, God was in his heaven, and with a little luck there was a small crime or two going on somewhere in the world. As soon as I got into the clerk's department of my Chambers at Number 3 Equity Court, Erskine-Brown said, "Rumpole. I saw a priest going into your room."

Our clerk's room was as busy as Paddington Station with our young and energetic clerk Henry sending barristers rushing off to distant destinations. Erskine-Brown, in striped shirt, double-breasted waistcoat, and what I believe are known as "Chelsea Boots," was propped up against the mantelpiece reading the particulars of some building claim Henry had just given him.

"That's your Con, Mr. Rumpole," said Henry, explaining the curious manifestation of a Holy Man.

"Your con*version?* Have you seen the light, Rumpole? Is Number 3 Equity Court your Road to Damascus?"

I cannot care for Erskine-Brown, especially when he makes jokes. I chose to ignore this and go to the mantelpiece to collect my brief, where I found old Uncle Tom (T. C. Rowley), the oldest member of our Chambers, who looks in because almost anything is preferable to life with his married sister in Croydon.

"Oh dear," said Uncle Tom. "A vicar in trouble. I suppose it's the choirboys again. I always think the Church runs a terrible risk having choirboys. They'd be far safer with a lot of middle-aged lady sopranos."

I had slid the pink tape off the brief and was getting the gist of the clerical slipup when Miss Trant, the bright young Portia of Equity Court (if Portias now have rimmed specs and speak with a Roedean accent), said that she didn't think vicars were exactly my line of country.

"Of course they're my line of country," I told her with delight. "Anyone accused of nicking half a dozen shirts is my line of country." I had gone through the brief instructions by this time. It seems that the cleric in question was called by the somewhat Arthurian name of the Reverend Mordred Skinner. He had gone to the summer sales in Oxford Street (a scene of carnage and rapine in which no amount of gold would have persuaded Rumpole to participate), been let off the leash in the gents' haberdashery, and later apprehended in the Hall of Food with a pile of moderately garish shirtings for which he hadn't paid.

Having spent a tough ten minutes digesting the facts of this far from complex matter (well, it showed no signs of becoming a State trial or House of Lords material), I set off in the general direction of my room, but on the way I was met by my old friend George Frobisher, exuding an almost audible smell of "bay rum" or some similar unguent.

I am not myself against a little *Eau de Cologne* on the handkerchief, but the idea of any sort of cosmetic on my friend George was like finding a Bishop "*en travestie*," or saucy seaside postcards on sale in the vestry. George is an old friend and a dear good fellow, a gentle soul who stands up in Court with all the confidence of a sacrificial virgin waiting for the sunrise over Stonehenge, but a dab hand at *The Times* crossword and a companionable fellow for a drink after Court in Pommeroy's Wine Bar off Fleet Street. I was surprised to see he appeared to have a new suit on, a silvery tie, and a silk bandana peeping from his top pocket.

"You haven't forgotten about tonight, have you?" George asked anxiously.

"We're going off for a bottle of Chateau Fleet Street in Pommeroy's?"

"No . . . I'm bringing a friend to dinner. With you and Hilda."

I had to confess that this social engagement had slipped my mind. In any event it seemed unlikely that anyone would wish to spend an evening with She Who Must Be Obeyed unless they were tied to her by bonds of matrimony, but it seemed that George had invited himself some weeks before and that he was keenly looking forward to the occasion.

"No Pommeroy's then?" I felt cheated of the conviviality.

"No, but . . . We might bring a bottle with us! I have a little news. And I'd like you and Hilda to be the first to know." He stopped then, enigmatically, and I gave a pointed sniff at the perfume-laden haze about him.

"George, you haven't taken to brilliantine by any chance?"

"We'll be there for seven-thirty." George smiled in a sheepish sort of fashion and went off whistling something that someone might have mistaken for the "Tennessee Waltz" if he happened to be tone deaf. I passed on to keep my rendezvous with the Reverend Mordred Skinner.

*   *   *

The Man of God came with a sister, Miss Evelyn
Skinner, a brisk woman in sensible shoes who had
foolishly let him out of her sight in the haberdashery,
and Mr. Morse, a grey-haired solicitor who did a lot
of work for the Church Commissioners and whose
idea of a thrilling trial was a gentle dispute about how
many candles you can put over the High Altar on the
third Sunday in Lent. My client himself was a pale,
timid individual who looked, with watery eyes and a
pinkish tingle to his nostrils, as if he had caught a
severe cold during his childhood and had never quite
got over it. He also seemed puzzled by the mysteries
of the Universe, the greatest of which was the arrival
of six shirts in the shopping-bag he was carrying
through the Hall of Food. I suggested that the whole
thing might be explained by absent-mindedness.

"Those sales," I said, "would induce panic in the
hardiest housewife."

"Would they?" Mordred stared at me. His eyes behind steel-rimmed glasses seemed strangely amused.
"I must say I found the scene lively and quite
entertaining."

"No doubt you took the shirts to the cash desk,
meaning to pay for them."

"There were two assistants behind the counter. Two
young ladies, to take money from customers," he said
discouragingly. "I mean there was no need for me to
take the shirts to any cash desk at all, Mr. Rumpole."

I looked at the Reverend Mordred Skinner and relit
the dying cheroot with some irritation. I am used to
grateful clients, cooperative clients, clients who are
willing to pull their weight and put their backs to the
wheel in the great cause of Victory for Rumpole. The
many murderers I have known, for instance, have all
been touchingly eager to help, and although one draws
the line at simulated madness or futile and misleading
alibis, at least such efforts show that the customer has
a will to win. The cleric in my armchair seemed, by

contrast, determined to put every possible obstacle in my way.

"I don't suppose you realized that," I told him firmly. "You're hardly an *habitué* of the sales, are you? I expect you wandered off looking for a cash desk, and then your mind became filled with next week's sermon, or whose turn it was to do the flowers in the chancel, and the whole mundane business of shopping simply slipped your memory."

"It is true," the Reverend Mordred admitted, "that I was thinking a great deal, at the time, of the Problem of Evil."

"Oh really?"

With the best will in the world I didn't see how the Problem of Evil was going to help the defense.

"What puzzles the ordinary fellow is," he frowned in bewilderment, "if God is all-wise and perfectly good—why on earth did he put evil in the world?"

"May I suggest an answer?" I wanted to gain the poor cleric's confidence by showing that I had no objection to a spot of theology. "So that an ordinary fellow like me can get plenty of briefs round the Old Bailey and London Sessions."

Mordred considered the matter carefully and then expressed his doubts.

"No . . . No, I can't think *that*'s what He had in mind."

"It may seem a very trivial little case to you Mr. Rumpole . . ." Evelyn Skinner dragged us back from pure thought, "But it's life and death to Mordred." At which I stood and gave them all a bit of the Rumpole mind.

"A man's reputation is never trivial," I told them. "I must beg you both to take it extremely seriously. Mr. Skinner, may I ask you to address your mind to one vital question? Given the fact that there were six shirts in the shopping-basket you were carrying, how the hell did they get there?"

Mordred looked hopeless and said, "I can't tell you. I've prayed about it."

"You think they might have leapt off the counter, by the power of prayer? I mean, something like the loaves and the fishes?"

"Mr. Rumpole." Mordred smiled at me. "Yours would seem to be an extremely literal faith."

I thought that was a little rich coming from a man of such painful simplicity, so I lit another small cigar, and found myself gazing into the hostile and somewhat fishy eyes of the sister.

"Are you suggesting, Mr. Rumpole, that my brother is guilty?"

"Of course not," I assured her. "Your brother's innocent. And he'll be so until twelve commonsensical old darlings picked at random off Newington Causeway find him otherwise."

"I rather thought—a quick hearing before the Magistrates. With the least possible publicity." Mr. Morse showed his sad lack of experience in crime.

"A quick hearing before the Magistrates is as good as pleading guilty."

"You think you might win this case, with a jury?" I thought there was a faint flicker of interest in Mordred's pink-rimmed eyes.

"Juries are like Almighty God, Mr. Skinner. Totally unpredictable."

So the conference wound to an end without divulging any particular answer to the charge, and I asked Mordred to apply through the usual channels for some sort of defense when he was next at prayer. He rewarded this suggestion with a wintry smile and my visitors left me just as She Who Must Be Obeyed came through on the blower to remind me that George was coming to dinner and bringing a friend, and would I buy two pounds of cooking apples at the tube station, and would I also remember not to loiter in Pommeroy's Wine Bar taking any sort of pleasure.

As I put the phone down, I noticed that Miss Evelyn Skinner had filtered back into my room, apparently desiring a word with Rumpole alone. She started in a tone of pity.

"I don't think you quite understand my brother . . ."

"Oh. Miss Skinner. Yes, well . . . I never felt totally at home with vicars." I felt some sort of apology was in order.

"He's like a child in many ways."

"The Peter Pan of the Pulpit?"

"In a way. I'm two years older than Mordred. I've always had to look after him. He wouldn't have got anywhere without me, Mr. Rumpole, simply nowhere, if I hadn't been there to deal with the Parish Council, and say the right things to the Bishop. Mordred just never thinks about himself, or what he's doing half the time."

"You should have kept a better eye on him, in the sales."

"Of course I should! I should have been watching him like a hawk every minute. I blame myself entirely."

She stood there, busily blaming herself, and then her brother could be heard calling her plaintively from the passage.

"Coming, dear. I'm coming at once," Evelyn said briskly, and was gone. I stood looking after her, smoking a small cigar and remembering Hilaire Belloc's sound advice to helpless children:

"Always keep tight hold of nurse,
For fear of finding something worse."

George Frobisher brought a friend to dinner, and, as I had rather suspected when I got a whiff of George's perfume in the passage, the friend was a lady, or, as I think Hilda would have preferred to call her, a woman. Now I must make it absolutely clear that this type of conduct was totally out of character in my friend George. He had an absolutely clean record so far as women were concerned. Oh, I imagine he had a mother, and I have heard him occasionally mutter about sisters; but George had been a bachelor as long as I had known him, returning from our convivial claret in Pommeroy's to the Royal Borough

Hotel, Kensington, where he had a small room, reasonable *en pension* terms, and colored television after dinner in the residents' lounge, seated in front of which device George would read his briefs, occasionally taking a furtive glance at some long-running serial of Hospital Life.

Judge of my surprise, therefore, when George turned up to dinner at Casa Rumpole with a very feminine, albeit middle-aged, lady indeed. Mrs. Ida Tempest, as George introduced her, came with some species of furry animal wreathed about her neck, whose eyes regarded me with a glassy stare, as I prepared to help Mrs. Tempest partially disrobe.

The lady's own eyes were far from glassy, being twinkling and roguish in their expression. Mrs. Tempest had reddish hair (rather the color of falsely glowing artificial coals on an electric fire) piled on her head, what I believe is known as a "Cupid's Bow" mouth in the trade, and the sort of complexion which makes you think that if you caught its owner a brisk slap you would choke in the resulting cloud of white powder. Her skirt seemed too tight and her heels too high for total comfort; but it could not be denied that Mrs. Ida Tempest was a cheerful and even a pleasant-looking person. George gazed at her throughout the evening with mingled admiration and pride.

It soon became apparent that in addition to his lady friend, George had brought a plastic bag from some off-license containing a bottle of non-vintage Moët. Such things are more often than not the harbinger of alarming news, and sure enough as soon as the pud was on the table George handed me the bottle, to cope with an announcement that he and Mrs. Ida Tempest were engaged to be married, clearly taking the view that this news should be a matter for congratulation.

"We wanted you to be the first to know," George said proudly.

Hilda smiled in a way that can only be described as "brave" and further comment was postponed by the explosion of the warm Moët. I filled everyone's glasses and Mrs. Tempest reached with enthusiasm for the booze.

"Oh, I do love bubbly," she said. "I love the way it goes all tickly up the nose, don't you, Hilda?"

"We hardly get it often enough to notice." She Who Must Be Obeyed was in no celebratory mood that evening. I had noticed, during the feast, that she clearly was not hitting it off with Mrs. Tempest. I therefore felt it incumbent on me to address the Court.

"Well then. If we're all filled up, I suppose it falls to me. Accustomed as I am to public speaking . . ." I began the speech.

"Usually on behalf of the criminal classes!" Hilda grumbled.

"Yes. Well . . . I think I know what is expected on these occasions."

"You mean you're like the film star's fifth husband? You know what's expected of you, but you don't know how to make it new." It appeared from her giggles and George's proud smile that Mrs. Tempest had made a joke. Hilda was not amused.

"Well then!" I came to the peroration. "Here's to the happy couple."

"Here's to us, George!" George and Mrs. Tempest clinked glasses and twinkled at each other. We all took a mouthful of warmish gas. After which Hilda courteously pushed the food in George's fiancee's direction.

"Would you care for a little more Charlotte Russe, Mrs. Tempest?"

"Oh, Ida. Please call me Ida. Well, just a teeny-weeny scraping. I don't want to lose my sylphlike figure, do I, Georgie? Otherwise you might not fancy me any more."

"There's no danger of that." The appalling thing was that George was looking roguish also.

"Of you not fancying me? Oh, I know . . ." La Tempest simpered.

"Of losing your figure, my dear. She's slim as a bluebell. Isn't she slim as a bluebell, Rumpole?" George turned to me for corroboration. I answered cautiously.

"I suppose that depends rather on the size of the bluebell."

"Oh, Horace! You are terrible! Why've you been keeping this terrible man from me, George?" Mrs. Tempest seemed delighted with my enigmatic reply.

"I hope we're all going to see a lot of each other after we're married." George smiled round the table, and got a small tightening of the lips from Hilda.

"Oh, yes, George. I'm sure that'll be very nice."

The tide had gone down in Mrs. Tempest's glass, and after I had topped it up she held it to the light and said admiringly, "Lovely glasses. So tasteful. Just look at that, George. Isn't that a lovely tasteful glass?"

"They're rejects actually," Hilda told her. "From the Army and Navy Stores."

"What whim of providence was it that led you across the path of my old friend George Frobisher?" I felt I had to keep the conversation going.

"Mrs. Tempest, that is Ida, came as a guest to the Royal Borough Hotel." George started to talk shyly of romance.

"You noticed me, didn't you, dear?" Mrs. Tempest was clearly cast in the position of prompter.

"I must admit I did."

"And I noticed him noticing me. You know how it is with men, don't you, Hilda?"

"Sometimes I wonder if Rumpole notices me at all." Hilda struck, I thought, an unnecessarily gloomy note.

"Of course I notice you," I assured her. "I come home in the evenings—and there you are. I notice you all the time."

"As a matter of fact, we first spoke in the Manageress's Office," George continued with the narration, "where we had both gone to register a complaint on the question of the bath water."

"There's not enough hot to fill the valleys, I told her, let alone cover the hills!" Mrs. Tempest explained gleefully to Hilda, who felt, apparently, that no such explanation was necessary.

"George agreed with me. Didn't you, George?"

"Shall I say, we formed an alliance?"

"Oh, we hit it off at once. We've so many interests in common."

"Really." I looked at Mrs. Tempest in some amazement. Apart from the basic business of keeping alive I couldn't imagine what interests she had in common with my old friend George Frobisher. She gave me a surprising answer.

"Ballroom dancing."

"Mrs. Tempest," said George proudly, "that is Ida, has cups for it."

"George! You're a secret ballroom dancer?" I wanted Further and Better Particulars of this Offense.

"We're going for lessons together, at Miss McKay's *École de Dance* in Rutland Gate."

I confess I found the prospect shocking, and I said as much to George. "Is your life going to be devoted entirely to pleasure?"

"Does *Horace* tango at all, Hilda?" Mrs. Tempest asked a foolish question.

"He's never been known to." Hilda sniffed slightly and I tried to make the reply lightly ironic.

"I'm afraid crime is cutting seriously down on my time for the tango."

"Such a pity, dear." Mrs. Tempest was looking at me with genuine concern. "You don't know what you're missing."

At which point Hilda rose firmly and asked George's intended if she wanted to powder her nose, which innocent question provoked a burst of giggles.

"You mean, do I want to spend a penny?"

"It is customary," said Hilda with some *hauteur*, "at this stage, to leave the gentlemen."

"Oh, you mean you want a hand with the washing-up . . ." Mrs. Tempest followed Hilda out, delivering her parting line to me. "Not too many naughty stories now, Horace. I don't want you leading my Georgie astray." At which I swear she winked.

When we were left alone with a bottle of the Old Tawney, George was still gazing foolishly after the vanishing Ida. "Charming," he said, "isn't she charming?"

Now at this point I became distinctly uneasy. I had been looking at La Belle Tempest with a feeling of déjà vu. I felt sure that I had met her before, and not in some previous existence. And, of course, I was painfully aware of the fact that the vast majority of my social contacts are made in cells, courtrooms, and other places of not too good repute. I therefore answered cautiously. "Your Mrs. Tempest . . . seems to have a certain amount of vivacity."

"She's a very able businesswoman, too."

"Is she now?"

"She used to run an hotel with her first husband. Highly successful business apparently. Somewhere in Kent . . ."

I frowned. The word "hotel" rang a distant but distinctly audible bell.

"So I thought, when we're married, of course, she might take up a small hotel again, in the West Country perhaps."

"And what about you, George? Would you give up your work at the Bar and devote all your time to the veleta?" I rather wanted to point out to him the difficulties of the situation.

"Well. I don't want to boast, but I thought I might go for a Circuit Judgeship." George said this shyly, as though disclosing another astonishing sexual conquest. "In fact I *have* applied. In some rural area . . ."

"*You* a judge, George? A *judge*? Well, come to think of it, it might suit you. You were never much good in Court, were you, old darling?" George looked slightly puzzled at this, but I blundered on. "It wasn't Ramsgate, by any chance? Where your *inamorata* kept a small hotel?"

"Why do you ask?" George was lapping up the port in a sort of golden reverie.

"Don't do it, George!" I said, loudly enough, I hoped, to blast him out of his complacency.

"Don't be a judge?"

"Don't get married! Look, George. Your Honor. If your Lordship pleases. Have a little consideration, my dear boy." I tried to appeal to his better nature. "I mean . . . where would you be leaving me?"

"Very much as you are now, I should imagine."

"Those peaceful moments of the day. Those hours we spend with a bottle of Chateau Fleet Street from five-thirty on in Pommeroy's Wine Bar. That wonderful oasis of peace that lies between the battle of the Bailey and the horrors of Home Life. You mean they'll be denied me from now on? You mean you'll be bolting like a rabbit down the Temple Underground back to Mrs. Tempest and leaving me without a companion?"

George looked at me, thoughtfully and then gave judgment with, I thought, a certain lack of feeling.

"I am, of course, extremely fond of you, Rumpole. But you're not exactly . . . Well, not someone who one can share *all* one's interests with."

"I'm not a dab hand at the two-step?"

I'm afraid I sounded bitter.

"I didn't *say* that, Rumpole."

"Don't do it, George! Marriage is like pleading guilty, for an indefinite sentence. Without parole." I poured more port.

"You're exaggerating!"

"I'm not, George. I swear by Almighty God. I'm not." I gave him the facts. "Do you know what happens on Saturday mornings? When free men are lying in bed, or wandering contentedly towards a glass of breakfast Chablis and a slow read of the Obituaries? You'll both set out with a list, and your lady wife will

spend your hard-earned money on things you have no
desire to own, like Vim, and saucepan scourers, and
J-cloths . . . and Mansion polish! And on your way
home, you'll be asked to carry the shopping-basket
. . . I beg of you, don't do it!"

This plea to the jury might have had some effect,
but the door then opened to admit La Belle Tempest,
George's eyes glazed over, and he clearly became deaf
to reason. And then Hilda entered and gave me a
brisk order to bring in the coffee tray.

"She Who Must Be Obeyed!" I whispered to
George on my way out. "You see what I mean?" I
might as well have saved my breath. He wasn't
listening.

Saturday morning saw self and She at the checkout
point in the local Tesco's, with the substantial fee for
the Portsmouth Rape Trial being frittered away on
such frivolous luxuries as sliced bread, Vim, cleaning
materials, and so on, and as the cash register clicked
merrily up Hilda passed judgment on George's fiancee.

"Of course she won't do for George."

I had an uneasy suspicion that she might be correct,
but I asked for further and better particulars.

"You think not? Why exactly?"

"Noticing our glasses! It's such bad form noticing
people's things. I thought she was going to ask how
much they cost."

Which, so far as She was concerned, seemed to ade-
quately sum up the case of Mrs. Ida Tempest. At
which point, having loaded up and checked that the
saucepan scourers were all present and correct, Hilda
handed me the shopping-basket, which seemed to be
filled with lead weights, and strode off unimpeded to
the bus stop with Rumpole groaning in her wake.

"What we do with all that Vim I can never understand." I questioned our whole way of life. "Do we
eat Vim?"

"You'd miss it, Rumpole, if it wasn't there."

*　　*　　*

On the following Monday I went down to Dockside Magistrates Court to defend young Jim Timson on a charge of taking and driving away a Ford Cortina. I have acted for various members of the clan Timson, a noted breed of South London villain, for many years. They know the law, and their courtroom behavior, I mean the way they stand to attention and call the magistrate "Sir," is impeccable. I went into battle fiercely that afternoon, and it was a famous victory. We got the summons dismissed with costs against the police. I hoped I'd achieve the same happy result in the notable trial of the Reverend Mordred Skinner, but I very much doubted it.

As soon as I was back in Chambers I opened a cupboard, sneezed in the resulting cloud of dust, and burrowed in the archives. I resisted the temptation to linger among my memories and pushed aside the Penge Bungalow photographs, the revolver that was used in the killing at the East Grimple Rep, and old Charles Monti's will written on a blown ostrich egg. I only glanced at the drawing an elderly R. A. did, to while away his trial for soliciting in the Super Loo at Euston Station, of the Recorder of London. I lingered briefly on my book of old press cuttings from the *News of the World* (that fine Legal Text Book in the Criminal Jurisdiction), and merely glanced at the analysis of bloodstains from the old Brick Lane Billiard Hall Murder when I was locked in single-handed combat with a former Lord Chief Justice of England and secured an acquittal, and came at last on what I was seeking.

The blue folder of photographs was nestling under an old wig tin and an outdated work on forensic medicine.

As I dug out my treasure and carried it to the light on my desk, I muttered a few lines of old William Wordsworth's, the Sheep of the Lake District—

> "Perhaps the plaintive numbers flow
> For old, unhappy, far-off things,
> And battles long ago."

On the cover of the photographs I had stuck a yellowing cutting from the *Ramsgate Times*. "Couple Charged in Local Arson Case" I read again. "The Unexplained Destruction of the Saracen's Head Hotel!" I opened the folder. There was a picture of a building on the sea front, and a number of people standing round. I took the strong glass off my desk to examine the figures in the photograph and saw the younger, but still roguishly smiling face of Mrs. Ida Tempest, my friend George's intended . . .

Having tucked the photographs back in the archive, I went straight to Pommeroy's Wine Bar, nothing unusual about that, I rarely go anywhere else at six o'clock, after the day's work is done; but George wasn't in Chambers and I hoped he might drop in there for a strengthener before a night of dalliance with his *inamorata* in the Royal Borough Hotel. However, when I got to Pommeroy's the only recognizable figure, apart from a few mournful-looking journalists and the opera critic in residence, was our Portia, Miss Phillida Trant, drinking a lonely Cinzano Bianco with ice and lemon. She told me that she hadn't seen George and said, rather enigmatically, that she was waiting for a person called Claude, who, on further inquiry, turned out to be none other than our elegant expert on the Civil side, my learned antagonist Erskine-Brown.

"Good God, is he Claude? Makes me feel quite fond of him. Why ever are you waiting for him? Do you want to pick his brains on the law of mortgages?"

"We *are* by way of being engaged," Miss Trant said somewhat sharply.

The infection seemed to be spreading in our Chambers, like gippy tummy. I looked at Miss Trant and asked, simply for information, "You're sure you know enough about him?"

"I'm afraid I do." She sounded resigned.

"I mean, you'd naturally want to *know* everything, wouldn't you—about anyone you're going to commit matrimony with?" I wanted her confirmation.

"Go on, surprise me!" Miss Trant, I had the feeling, was not being entirely serious. "He married a middle-aged Persian contortionist when he was up at Keble? I'd love to know that—and it'd make him *far* more exciting."

At which point the beloved Claude actually made his appearance in a bowler and overcoat with a velvet collar and announced he had some treat in store for Miss Trant, such as Verdi's *Requiem* in the Festival Hall, whilst she looked at him as though disappointed at the un-murkiness of the Erskine-Brown past. Then I saw George at the counter making a small purchase from Jack Pommeroy and I bore down on him. I had no doubt, at that stage, that my simple duty to my old friend was immediate disclosure. However, when I reached George I found that he was investing in a bottle far removed from our usual Chateau Fleet Street.

"1967. Pichon-Longueville? Celebrating, George?"

"In a way. We have a glass or two in the room now. Can't get anything decent in the restaurant." George was storing the nectar away in his briefcase with the air of a practised boulevardier.

"George. Look. My dear fellow. Look . . . will you have a drink?"

"It's really much more comfortable up in the room," George babbled on regardless. "And we listen to the BBC Overseas Service, old Victor Sylvester records requested from Nigeria. They only seem to care for ballroom dancing in the Third World nowadays." My old friend was moving away from me, although I did all I could to stop him.

"Please, George. It'll only take a minute. Something . . . you really ought to know."

"Sorry to desert you, Rumpole. It would never do to keep Ida waiting." He was gone, as Jack Pommeroy with his purple face and the rosebud in his buttonhole asked what was my pleasure.

"Red plonk," I told him. "Chateau Fleet Street. A large glass. I've got nothing to celebrate."

After that I found it increasingly difficult to break the news to George, although I knew I had to do so.

The Reverend Mordred Skinner was duly sent for trial at the Inner London Sessions, Newington Causeway in the South East corner of London. Wherever civilization ends, it is, I have always felt, somewhere just north of the Inner London Sessions. It is a strange thing but I always look forward with a certain eagerness to an appearance at the Old Bailey. I walk down Newgate Street, as often as not, with a spring in my stride and there it is, in all its glory, a stately law court, decreed by the City Fathers, an Edwardian palace with a modern extension to deal with the increase in human fallibility. Terrible things go on down the Bailey, horrifying things. Why is it I never go through its revolving door without a thrill of pleasure, a slight tremble of excitement? Why does it seem a much jollier place than my flat in Gloucester Road under the strict rule of She Who Must Be Obeyed?

Such pleasurable sensations, I must confess, are never connected with my visits to the Inner London Sessions. While a hint of spring sunshine often touches the figure of Justice on the dome of the Bailey it always seems to be a wet Monday in November at Inner London. The Sessions House is stuck in a sort of urban desert down the Old Kent Road, with nowhere to go for a decent bit of steak-and-kidney pud during the lunch hour. It is a sad sort of Court, with all the cheeky Cockney sparrows turned into silent figures waiting for the burglary to come on in Court 2, and the juries there look as if they relied on the work to eke out their social-security.

I met the Reverend gentleman after I had donned the formal dress (yellowing wig bought second-hand from an ex-Attorney General of Tonga in 1932, somewhat frayed gown, collar like a blunt extension). He seemed unconcerned and was even smiling a little, although his sister Evelyn looked like one about to attend a burning at the stake; Mr. Morse looked thoroughly uncomfortable and as if he'd like to get back to a nice discussion of the Almshouse charity in Chipping Sodbury.

I tried to instil a suitable sense of the solemnity of the occasion in my clerical customer by telling him that God, with that wonderful talent for practical joking which has shown itself throughout recorded history, had dealt us His Honor Judge Bullingham.

"Is he very dreadful?" Mr. Skinner asked almost hopefully.

"Why he was ever made a judge is one of the unsolved mysteries of the universe." I was determined not to sound reassuring. "I can only suppose that his unreasoning prejudice against all black persons, defense lawyers, and probation officers comes from some deep psychological cause. Perhaps his mother, if such a person can be imagined, was once assaulted by a black probation officer who was on his way to give evidence for the defense."

"I wonder how he feels about parsons." My client seemed not at all put out.

"God knows. I rather doubt if he's ever met one. The Bull's leisure taste runs to strong drink and all-in wrestling. Come along, we might as well enter the *corrida*."

A couple of hours later, His Honor Judge Bullingham, with his thick neck and complexion of a beetroot past its first youth, was calmly exploring his inner ear with his little finger and tolerantly allowing me to cross-examine a large gentleman named Pratt, resident flatfoot at the Oxford Street Bazaar.

"Mr. Pratt? How long have you been a detective in this particular store?"

"Ten years, sir."

"And before that?"

"I was with the Metropolitan Police."

"Why did you leave?"

"Pay and conditions, sir, were hardly satisfactory."

"Oh, really? You found it more profitable to keep
your beady eye on the ladies' lingerie counter than do
battle in the streets with serious crime?"

"Are you suggesting that this isn't a serious crime,
Mr. Rumpole?" The learned judge, who pots villains
with all the subtlety of his namesake animal charging
a gate, growled this question at me with his face going
a darker purple than ever, and his jowls trembling.

"For many people, my Lord," I turned to the jury
and gave them the message, "six shirts might be a
mere triviality. For the Reverend Mordred Skinner,
they represent the possibility of total ruin, disgrace,
and disaster. In this case my client's whole life hangs
in the balance." I turned a flattering gaze on the
twelve honest citizens who had been chosen to pro-
nounce on the sanctity or otherwise of the Reverend
Mordred. "That is why we must cling to our most
cherished institution, trial by jury. It is not the value
of the property stolen, it is the priceless matter of a
man's good reputation."

"Mister Rumpole." The Bull lifted his head as if
for the charge. "You should know your business by
now. This is not the time for making speeches. You
will have an opportunity at the end of the case."

"And as your Honor will have an opportunity *after*
me to make a speech, I thought it as well to make
clear who the judges of *fact* in this matter are." I
continued to look at the jury with an expression of
flattering devotion.

"Yes. Very well. Let's get on with it." The Bull
retreated momentarily. I rubbed in the victory.

"Certainly. That is what I was attempting to do." I
turned to the witness. "Mr. Pratt. When you were in
the gents' haberdashery . . ."

"Yes, sir?"

"You didn't see my client remove the shirts from
the counter and make off with them?"

"No, sir."

"If he had, no doubt he would have told us about

it," Bullingham could not resist growling. I gave him a little bow.

"Your Honor is always so quick to notice points in favor of the defense." I went back to work on the store detective. "So why did you follow my client?"

"The Supervisor noticed a pile of shirts missing. She said there was a Reverend been turning them over, your Honor."

This titbit delighted the Bull and he snatched at it greedily. "He might not have told us that if you hadn't asked the wrong question, Mr. Rumpole."

"No question is wrong if it reveals the truth," I informed the jury and then turned back to Pratt. I had an idea, an uncomfortable feeling that I might just have guessed the truth of this peculiar case. "So you don't know if he was carrying the basket when he left the shirt department?"

"No."

"Was he carrying it when you first spotted him, on the moving staircase?"

"I only saw his head and shoulders . . ."

The pieces were fitting together. I would have to face my client with my growing notion of a defense as soon as possible. "So you first saw him with the basket in the Hall of Food?"

"That's right, sir."

At which point Bullingham stirred dangerously and raised the curtain of his top lip on some large yellowing teeth. He was about to make a joke. "Are you suggesting, Mr. Rumpole, that a basket full of shirts mysteriously materialized in your client's hand in the Tinned Meat Department?"

At which the jury laughed obsequiously. Rumpole silenced them in a voice of enormous gravity.

"Might I remind your Honor of what he said. This is a serious case."

"As you cross-examined, Mr. Rumpole, I was beginning to wonder." Bullingham was still grinning.

"The art of cross-examination, your Honour, is a little like walking a tightrope."

"Oh, is it?"

"One gets on so much better if one isn't continually interrupted."

At which Bullingham relapsed into a sullen silence and I got on with the work in hand.

"It would have been quite impossible for Mr. Skinner to have paid at the shirt counter, wouldn't it?"

"No, sir. There were two assistants behind the counter."

"Young ladies?"

"Yes, sir."

"When you saw them, what were they doing?"

"I . . . I can't exactly recall."

"Well then, let me jog your memory." Here I made an informed guess at what any two young lady assistants would be doing at the height of business during the summer sales. "Were they not huddled together in an act of total recall of last night in the disco or Palais de Hop? Were they not blind and deaf to the cries of shirt-buying clerics? Were they not utterly oblivious to the life around them?"

The jury was looking at me and smiling, and some of the ladies nodded understandingly. I could feel that the old darlings knew all about young lady non-assistants in Oxford Street.

"Well, Mr. Pratt. Isn't that exactly what they were doing?"

"It may have been, your Honor."

"So is it surprising that my client took his purchase and went off in search of some more attentive assistance?"

"But I followed him downstairs, to the Hall of Food."

"Have you any reason to suppose he wouldn't have paid for his shirts there, given the slightest opportunity?"

"I saw no sign of his attempting to do so."

"Just as you saw no sign of the salesladies attempting to take his money?"

"No but . . ."

"It's a risky business entering your store, isn't it, Pratt?" I put it to him. "You can't get served and no one speaks to you except to tell you that you're under arrest."

I sat down to some smiles from the jury and a glance from the Bull. An eager young man named Ken Rydal was prosecuting. I had run up against this Rydal, a ginger-haired, spectacled wonder who might once have been a senior scout, and won the Duke of Edinburgh award for being left out on the mountainside for a week. "Ken" felt a strong sense of team spirit and loyalty to the Metropolitan Police, and he was keen as mustard to add the Reverend Mordred Skinner to the notches on his woggle.

"Did you see Mr. Skinner make any attempt to pay for his shirts in the Hall of Food?" Ken asked Pratt.

I read a note from my client that had finally arrived by way of the usher.

"No. No, I didn't," said Pratt.

Ken was smiling, about to make a little scoutlike funny. "He didn't ask for them to be wrapped up with a pound of ham, for instance?"

"No, sir." Pratt laughed and looked round the Court—to see that no one was laughing. And the Bull was glaring at Ken.

"This is not a music hall, Mr. Rydal. As Mr. Rumpole has reminded us, this is an extremely serious case. The whole of the Reverend gentleman's future is at stake." The judge glanced at the clock, as if daring it not to be time for lunch. The clock cooperated, and the Bull rose, muttering, "Ten past two, members of the jury."

I crumpled my client's note with some disgust and threw it on the floor as I stood to bow to the Bull. The Reverend Mordred had just told me he wasn't prepared to give evidence in his own defense. I would have to get him on his own and twist his arm a little.

"I simply couldn't take the oath."

"What's the matter with you? Have you no religion?"

The cleric smiled politely and said, less as a question than a statement of fact, "You don't like me very much, do you?"

We were sitting in one of the brighter hostelries in Newington Causeway. The bleak and sour-smelling saloon bar was sparsely populated by two ailing cleaning-ladies drinking stout, another senior citizen who was smoking the dog ends he kept in an old Oxo tin and exercising his talents as a Cougher for England, and a large drunk in a woolly bobble-hat who kept banging in and out the Gents with an expression of increasing euphoria. I had entrusted to Mr. Morse the solicitor the tricky task of taking Miss Evelyn Skinner to lunch in the public canteen at the Sessions House. I imagined he'd get the full blast of her anxiety over the grey, unidentifiable meat and two veg. Meanwhile I had whisked the Reverend out to the pub where he sat with the intolerably matey expression vicars always assume in licensed premises.

"I felt you might tell me the truth. You of all people. Having your collar on back to front must mean something."

"Truth is often dangerous. It must be approached cautiously, don't you think?" My client bit nervously into a singularly unattractive sausage. I tried to approach the matter cautiously.

"I've noticed with women," I told him, "with my wife, for instance, when we go out on our dreaded Saturday morning shopping expeditions, that She Who Must Be Obeyed is in charge of the shopping-basket. She makes the big decisions. How much Vim goes in it and so forth. When the shopping's bought, I get the job of carrying the damn thing home."

"Simple faith is far more important than the constant scramble after unimportant facts." Mordred was back on the old theology. "I believe that's what the lives of the Saints tell us."

Enough of this Cathedral gossip. We were due back in Court in half an hour and I let him have it between the eyes. "Well, my simple faith tells me that your sister had the basket in the shirt department."

"Does it?" He blinked most of the time, but not then.

"When Pratt saw you in the Hall of Food you were carrying the shopping-basket, which she'd handed you on the escalator."

"Perhaps."

"Because she'd taken the shirts and put them in the bag when you were too busy composing your sermon on the Problem of Evil to notice." I lit a small cigar at that point, and Mordred took a sip of sour bitter. He was still smiling as he started to talk, almost shyly at first, then with increasing confidence.

"She was a pretty child. It's difficult to believe it now. She was attracted to bright things, boiled sweets, red apples, jewelry in Woolworth's. As she grew older it became worse. She would take things she couldn't possibly need . . . Spectacles, bead handbags, cigarette cases—although she never smoked. She was like a magpie. I thought she'd improved. I try to watch her as much as I can, although you're right, on that day I was involved with my sermon. As a matter of fact, I had no need of such shirts. I may be old-fashioned but I always wear a dog collar. Always."

"Even on rambles with the Lads' Brigade?"

"All the same," my client said firmly, "I believe she did it out of love."

Well, now we had a defense: although he didn't seem to be totally aware of it.

"Those are the facts?"

"They seem to be of no interest to anyone—except my immediate family. But that's what I'm bound to say, if I take my oath on the Bible."

"But you were prepared to lie to me," I reminded him. He smiled again, that small, maddening smile.

"Mr. Rumpole. I have the greatest respect for your skill as an advocate, but I have never been in danger of mistaking you for Almighty God."

"Tell the truth *now*. She'll only get a fine. Nothing!"

He seemed to consider the possibility, then he shook his head.

"To her it would be everything. She couldn't bear it."

"What about you? You'd give up your whole life?"

"It seems the least I can do for her." He was smiling again, hanging that patient little grin out like an advertisement for his humility and his deep sense of spiritual superiority to a worldly Old Bailey Hack.

I ground out my small cigar in the overflowing ashtray and almost shouted. "Good God! I don't know how I keep my temper."

"I do sympathize. He found His ideas irritated people dreadfully. Particularly lawyers." He was almost laughing now. "But you do understand? I am quite unable to give evidence on oath to the jury."

As every criminal lawyer knows, it's very difficult to get a client off unless he's prepared to take the trouble of going into the witness-box, to face up to the prosecution, and to demonstrate his innocence or at least his credentials as a fairly likeable character who might buy you a pint after work and whom you would not really want to see festering in the nick. After all, fair's fair—the jury have just seen the prosecution witnesses put through it, so why should the prisoner at the Bar sit in solemn silence in the dock? I knew that if the Reverend told his story, with suitable modesty and regret, I could get him off and Evelyn would merely get a well earned talking-to. When he refused to give evidence I could almost hear the rustle of unfrocking in the distance.

Short of having my client dragged to the Bible by a sturdy usher, when he would no doubt stand mute of malice, there was nothing I could do other than address the jury in the unlikely hope of persuading them that there was no reliable evidence on which they could possibly convict the silent vicar. I was warming to my work as Bullingham sat inert, breathing hoarsely, apparently about to erupt.

"Members of the jury," I told them. "There is a Golden Thread that runs throughout British justice. The prosecution must prove its case. The defense has to prove nothing."

"*Mr.* Rumpole . . ." A sound came from the judge like the first rumble they once heard from Mount Vesuvius.

I soldiered on. "The Reverend Mordred Skinner need not trouble to move four yards from that dock to the witness-box unless the prosecution has produced evidence that he *intended* to steal—and not to pay in another department."

"Mr. *Rumpole.*" The earth tremor grew louder. I raised my voice a semitone.

"Never let it be said that a man is forced to prove his innocence! Our fathers have defied kings for that principle, members of the jury. They forced King John to sign Magna Carta and sent King Charles to the scaffold and it has been handed down even to the Inner London Sessions, Newington Causeway."

"If you'd let me get a word in edgeways . . ."

"And now it is in your trust!"

I'm not, as this narrative may have made clear, a religious man; but what happened next made me realize how the Israelites felt when the waters divided, and understand the incredulous reaction of the disciples when an uninteresting glass of water flushed darkly and smelt of the grape. I can recall the exact words of the indubitable miracle. Bullingham said, "Mr. Rumpole. I entirely agree with everything you say. And," he added, glowering threateningly at the Scout for the prosecution, "I shall direct the jury accordingly."

The natural malice of the Bull had been quelled by his instinctive respect for the law. He found there was no case to answer.

I met my liberated client in the Gents, a place where his sister was unable to follow him. As we stood side by side at the porcelain I congratulated him.

"I was quite reconciled to losing. I don't think my

sister would have stood by me somehow. The disgrace, you see. I think," he looked almost wistful, "I think I should have been alone."

"You'd have been unfrocked."

"It might have been extremely restful. Not to have to pretend to any sort of sanctity. Not to pretend to be different. To be exactly the same as everybody else."

I looked at him standing there in the London Sessions loo, his mac over his arm, his thin neck half-strangled by a dog collar. He longed for the relaxed life of an ordinary sinner, but he had no right to it.

"Don't long for a life of crime, old darling," I told him. "You've obviously got no talent for it."

Upstairs we met Evelyn and Mr. Morse. The sister gave me a flicker of something which might have been a smile of gratitude.

"It was a miracle," I told her.

"Really? I thought the judge was exceedingly fair. Come along, Mordred. He's somewhere else, you know, Mr. Rumpole. He can't even realize it's all over." She attacked her brother again. "Better put your mac on, dear. It's raining outside."

"Yes, Evelyn. Yes. I'll put it on." He did so, obediently.

"You must come to tea in the Rectory, Mr. Rumpole." I had a final chilly smile from Evelyn.

"Alas, dear lady. The pressure of work. These days I have so little time for pleasure."

"Say goodbye to Mr. Rumpole, Mordred."

The cleric shook my hand, and gave me a confidential aside. "Goodbye, Mr. Rumpole. You see it was entirely a family matter. There was no need for anyone to know anything about it."

And so he went, in his sister's charge, back to the isolation of the Rectory.

> "Will no one tell me what she sings?
> Perhaps the plaintive numbers flow
> For old, unhappy, far-off things
> And murders long ago."

Had I, against all the odds, learned something from the Reverend? Was I now more conscious of the value of secrecy, of not dropping bombs of information which might cause ruin and havoc on the family front? It seems unlikely, but I do not know why else I was busily destroying the archive, pushing the photographs into the unused fireplace in my Chambers and applying a match, and dropping the durable articles, including the ostrich egg, into the wastepaper basket. As the flames licked across the paper and set Mrs. Tempest the arsonist curling into ashy oblivion the door opened to admit Miss Trant.

"Rumpole! What on earth are you doing?"

I turned from the smoking relics.

"You keep things, Miss Trant? Mementoes? Locks of hair? Old letters, tied up in ribbon? 'Memories,' " I started to sing tunelessly, " 'were made of this.' "

"Not really."

"Good."

"I've got my first brief. From when I prosecuted you in Dock Street." This was the occasion when I tricked Miss Trant into boring the wretched Beak with a huge pile of law, and so defeated her. It was not an incident of which I am particularly proud.

"Destroy it. Forget the past, eh? Miss Trant. Look to the future!"

"All right. Aren't you coming up to Guthrie Featherstone's room? We're laying on a few drinks for George."

"George? Yes, of course. He'll have a lot to celebrate."

Guthrie Featherstone, Q.C., M.P., the suave and elegant Conservative-Labour M.P. for somewhere or another who, when he is not passing the "Gas Mains Enabling Bill" or losing politely at golf to various of Her Majesty's judges, condescends to exercise his duties as Head of Chambers (a post to which I was due to succeed by order of seniority of barristers in practice, when I was pipped at the post by young Guthrie taking silk. Well, I didn't want it anyway); Guthrie

Featherstone occupied the best room in Chambers (first floor, high windows, overlooking Temple Gardens) and he was engaged in making a speech to our assembled members. In a corner of the room I saw our clerk Henry and Dianne the typist in charge of a table decorated by several bottles of Jack Pommeroy's cooking champagne. I made straight for the booze, and at first Featherstone's speech seemed but a background noise, like Radio Four.

"It's well known among lawyers that the finest advocates never make the best judges. The glory of the advocate is to be opinionated, brash, fearless, partisan, hectoring, rude, cunning, and unfair."

"Well done, Rumpole!" This, of course, was Erskine-Brown.

"Thank you very much, Claude." I raised my glass to him.

"The ideal judge, however," Featherstone babbled on, "is detached, courteous, patient, painstaking, and above all, quiet. These qualities are to be found personified in the latest addition to our Bench of Circuit Judges."

" 'Circus' Judges, Rumpole calls them," Uncle Tom said loudly, to no one in particular.

"Ladies and gentlemen," the Q.C., M.P. concluded, "please raise your glasses to His Honor Judge George Frobisher."

Everyone was smiling and drinking. So the news had broken. George was a Circuit Judge. No doubt the crowds were dancing in Fleet Street. I moved to my old friend to add my word of congratulation.

"Your health George. Coupled with the name of Mrs. Ida Tempest?"

"No, Rumpole. No." George shook his head—I thought sadly.

"What do you mean, 'No'? Mrs. Tempest should be here. To share in your triumph. Celebrating back at the Royal Borough Hotel, is she? She'll have the Moët on ice by the time you get back."

"Mrs. Tempest left the Royal Borough last week,

Rumpole. I have no means of knowing where to find her."

At which point we were rudely interrupted by Guthrie Featherstone calling on George to make a speech. Other members joined in and Henry filled up George's glass in preparation for the great oration.

"I'm totally unprepared to *say* anything on this occasion," George said, taking a bit of paper from his pocket to general laughter. Poor old George could never do anything off the cuff.

"Ladies and gentlemen," George started. "I have long felt the need to retire from the hurly-burly of practice at the Bar."

"Comes as news to me that George Frobisher had a practice at the Bar," Uncle Tom said to no one much in a deafening whisper.

"To escape from the benevolent despotism of Henry, now our senior clerk." George twinkled.

"Can you do a Careless Driving at Croydon tomorrow, your Honor?" Henry called out in the cheeky manner he had adopted since he was an office boy.

Laughter.

"No, Henry, I can't. So I have long considered applying for a Circuit Judgeship in a Rural Area . . ."

"Where are you going to, George? Glorious Devon?" Featherstone interrupted.

"I think they're starting me off in Luton. And I hope, very soon, I'll have the pleasure of you all appearing before me!"

"Where did George say they were sending him?" Uncle Tom asked.

"I think he said Luton, Uncle Tom," I told him.

"Luton, glorious Luton!" Henry sometimes goes too far, for a clerk. I was glad to see that Dianne ssshed him firmly.

"Naturally, as a judge, as one, however humble, of Her Majesty's judges, certain standards will be expected of me," George went on, I thought in a tone of some regret.

"No more carousing in Pommeroy's with Horace Rumpole!" Uncle Tom was still barracking.

"And I mean to try, to do my best, to live up to those standards. That's really all I have to say. Thank you. Thank you all very much."

There was tumultuous applause, increased in volume by the cooking champagne, and George joined me in a corner of the room. Uncle Tom was induced to make his speech, traditional and always the same on all Chambers' occasions, and George and I talked quietly together. "George. I'm sorry. About Mrs. Tempest . . ."

"It was your fault, Rumpole." George looked at me with an air of severe rebuke.

"My fault!" I stood amazed. "But I said nothing. Not a word. You know me, George. Discretion is Rumpole's middle name. I was silent. As the tomb."

"When I brought her to dinner with you and Hilda. She recognized you at once."

"She didn't show it!"

"She's a remarkable woman."

"I was junior Counsel, for her former husband. I'm sure he led her on. She made an excellent impression. In the witness-box." I tried to sound comforting.

"She made an excellent impression on me, Rumpole. She thought you'd be bound to tell me."

"She thought that?"

"So she decided to tell me first."

I stood looking at George, feeling unreasonably guilty. Somewhere in the distance Uncle Tom was going through the usual form of words.

"As the oldest member of Chambers, I can remember this set before C. H. Wystan, Rumpole's revered father-in-law, took over. It was in old Barnaby Hawks' time and the young men were myself, Everett Longbarrow, and old Willoughby Grime, who became Lord Chief Justice of Basutoland . . . He went on Circuit, I understand, wearing a battered opera hat and dispensed rough justice . . ."

The other barristers joined in the well known chorus "Under a Bong Tree."

"As I remember, Ida Tempest got three years."

"Yes," said George.

"Her former husband got seven." I was trying to cheer him up. "I don't believe Ida actually applied the match."

"All the same, it was a risk I didn't feel able to take."

You didn't notice the smell of burning, George? Any night in the Royal Borough Hotel . . .?"

"Of course not! But the Lord secretary had just told me of my appointment. It doesn't do for a judge's wife to have done three years, even with full remission."

I looked at George. Was the sacrifice, I wondered, really necessary? "Did you *have* to be a judge, George?"

"I thought of that, of course. But I had the appointment. You know, at my age, Rumpole, it's difficult to learn any new sort of trade."

"We had no work in those days," Uncle Tom continued his trip down memory lane. "We had no briefs of any kind. We spent our days practicing chip shots, trying to get an old golf ball into the wastepaper basket with . . ."

"A mashie niblick!" the other barristers sang.

"Well, that was as good a training as any for life at the Bar," Uncle Tom told them.

I filled George's glass. "Drink up, George. There may be other ladies . . . turning up at the Royal Borough Hotel."

"I very much doubt it. Every night when I sit at the table for one, I shall think—if only I'd never taken her to dinner at Rumpole's! Then I might never have known, don't you see? We could have been perfectly happy together."

"Of course, C. H. Wystan never ever took silk. But now we have a Q.C., M.P. and dear old George Frobisher, a Circus, beg his pardon, a Circuit Judge!" Uncle Tom was raising his glass to George. His hand was trembling and he was spilling a good deal on his cuff.

"Sometimes I feel it will be difficult to forgive you, Rumpole," George said, very quietly.

"But I do recall when dear old Willoughby Grime was appointed to Basutoland, we celebrated the matter in song."

"George, what did I do?" I protested. "I didn't say anything." But it wasn't true. My mere existence had been enough to deny George his happiness. At which point the other barristers raised their glasses to George and started to sing "For He's a Jolly Good Fellow." I left them, and went out into the silence of the Temple, where I could still hear them singing . . .

Next Saturday morning I was acting the part of the native bearer with the Vim basket, following She Who Must Be Obeyed on our ritual shopping expedition.

"They've never made George Frobisher a judge!" My wife seemed to feel it an occasion for ridicule and contempt.

"In my view an excellent appointment. I shall expect to have a good record of acquittals. In the Luton Crown Court."

"When are they going to make you a judge, Rumpole?"

"Don't ask silly questions . . . I'd start every Sentence with, 'There but for the Grace of God goes Horace Rumpole.' "

"I can imagine what *she's* feeling like." Hilda sniffed.

"She . . .?"

"The cat-that-swallowed-the-cream! Her Honor Mrs. Judge. Mrs. Ida Tempest'll think she's quite the thing, I'll be bound."

"No. She's gone."

"Gone, Rumpole? What did George say about that?"

"Cried, and the world cried too, 'Our's the Treasure.'

Suddenly, as rare things will, she vanished."

We climbed on a bus, heavily laden, back to Casa Rumpole.

"George is well out of it, if he wants my opinion."

"I don't think he does."

"What?"

"Want your opinion."

Later, in our kitchen, as she stored the Vim away under the sink and I prepared our Saturday morning G and T, a thought occurred to me. "Do you know? I'm not sure I should've taken up as a lawyer."

"Whatever do you mean?"

"Perhaps I should have taken up as a vicar."

"Rumpole. Have you been getting at the gin already?"

"Faith not facts, is what we need, do you think?"

Hilda was busy unpacking the saucepan scourers. Perhaps she didn't quite get my drift. "George Frobisher has always been a bad influence, keeping you out drinking," she said. "Let's hope I'll be seeing more of you now he's been made a judge."

"I'd never have got to know all these *facts* about people if I hadn't set up as a lawyer."

"Of course you should have been a lawyer, Rumpole!"

"Why exactly?"

"If you hadn't set up as a lawyer, if you hadn't gone into Daddy's Chambers, you'd never have met me, Rumpole!"

I looked at her, suddenly seeing great vistas of what my life might have been. "That's true," I said. "Dammit, that's very true."

"Put the Gumption away for me, will you, Rumpole?"

She Who Must Be Obeyed. Of course I did.

Thou Shalt Subscribe To

Ellery Queen's Mystery Magazine offers exciting new stories by the top writers in the mystery field. Enjoy issue after issue of spine-tingling suspense stories, humorous detectiverse, and insightful reviews of current mystery novels.

Alfred Hitchcock's Mystery Magazine features detective stories, suspense filled tales of espionage and more. In the Hitchcock tradition, top authors keep readers guessing...right up until the final, tension filled page.
